A DETECTIVE MCDANIEL THRILLER

HOLD BACK THE NIGHT

AXEL BLACKWELL

Hold Back The Night
2019 by Axel Blackwell

WWW.AXELBLACKWELL.COM

Printed in the United States of America

ISBN 978-1-70-725567-2

First Edition
10 9 8 7 6 5 4 3 2 1

The cradle rocks above an abyss. Our existence is but a brief crack of light between two eternities of darkness.

– Vladimir Nabokov

CHAPTER 1

THE CHILD DIDN'T have a name. It was easier that way. She'd had a name once, before the nightmare, and if she ever awoke, perhaps she would have her name again. But this terror had outlasted all other dreams, had endured even longer than her waking life. She often feared she would die in this nightmare and be buried beneath the cellar floor with the nameless children who had come before. She had nearly resigned herself to that fate.

But tonight, as she lay on the floor, kicking against the manacle that chained her ankle to the wall, she thought maybe she might wake after all.

The funny, scary little man who visited her every night sometimes pretended she was his child and called her "Kiki" and brought her gifts and fed her cakes and candy. Other times he wore a ski mask and climbed on top of her, hurting her the way these men had always hurt her, and stuffing her face into a pillow until her lungs burned and she lost consciousness.

Tonight it had been sweets and gifts – white frosting over pink cake with pink sprinkles, a plastic tiara with fake jewels. He had talked in his odd, lilting language which she could barely understand and had sipped tea and held her hand and brushed her hair.

Then, his phone rang.

He answered with no lilt in his voice, and soon he was yelling into the phone. His face reddened and his eyes changed to the eyes she would see through the holes in the knitted mask on the nights he showed his true self. Moments later, he stormed out the door and slammed it behind him.

He took his overcoat with him. The keys were in the left pocket. She knew which one fit the manacle around her ankle and which one fit the door. Of these two things, she was keenly aware, even if the rest of her existence was a blur. He had taken the coat, but the umbrella he forgot. He'd propped it in the corner when he arrived, and it leaned there still.

The chain was about twelve feet long, running from the manacle around her ankle to a large eyebolt sunk into the concrete wall. It allowed her access to most of this small, brightly-painted room, as well as to the tiny closet that housed a toilet and sink. The far wall lay just out of her reach. No matter how she stretched or kicked, the chain just would not give the extra two inches she needed to grab the umbrella. And she needed that umbrella.

The manacle dug into the top of her foot as she pulled. If it bloodied her sock, the man would be angry. But somehow, he was less terrifying when he was angry. And though she didn't dare think the thought, some part of her hoped that he would never see her bloody sock – or the child who wore it – again.

Tired of the twisting and straining and stretching, she let her head fall to the carpet. Something poked into her scalp.

The tiara. It was silver-painted plastic, with pink plastic gems, useless for prying at the chain.

But perhaps not useless now.

The child touched it with trembling fingers, then snatched it from her head and reached out with it. It just barely slipped around the umbrella's metal tip. She tugged, gently. The tip had sunk into the carpet, and the tiara's soft plastic semicircle opened, at first unable to budge the sturdy umbrella. The child jiggled the tiara, twisted, tugged, moving the tip bit by bit. Finally, it pulled free of the carpet and came to her.

She wrapped her fingers around the shiny metal tip, feeling the umbrella's weight. It was heavy and well-made, almost as long as she was tall, with a metal shaft and a thick wooden handle. She knew little about the world beyond walls and cages and chains, but she knew what a lock was and she knew how a screw worked. The eyebolt was a screw, twist it the right way long enough and it would fall free from the wall.

Tiny flecks of concrete dusted the carpet under the eyebolt. Perhaps her kicking had loosened it just a bit. She hoped so, hoped it would be enough.

She stabbed the umbrella's shiny tip through the eye of the bolt and pulled to one side, gently at first, then with increasing pressure. The umbrella bowed under her strain. Then the bolt gave, twisted, grating against its concrete fitting.

The child pulled the handle all the way to the floor, reset it on the other side of the bolt, then cranked it all the way to the floor again. After the fifth full turn, it was loose enough to twist with just her fingers. A few seconds later, the bolt fell free from the wall.

The child sat and stared at the bolt in her hand, disbelieving. In this nightmare, the end was never really the end, and what was next was always worse. But this was something new. What did it mean? Where would it lead?

The man would be angry. She knew that for sure. Blood had, indeed, stained her sock, quite a lot of it; some had soaked into the carpet, and some had stained the hem of the frilly white dress he made her wear. That, too, would make him angry.

Suddenly, she *wanted* to make him angry.

The quiet fantasy she would not admit, the one about not ever seeing the man again, now seemed just a little less absurd. There was still the door and its locks, but she had never felt trapped by the door. It was the chain that held her. The door never had stopped her from escaping because she had never reached it. Having freed herself from the wall, she felt blithe optimism about the door. But that didn't last long.

She managed, with much effort, to work the umbrella's tip into the gap between the door and the jam, but her prying accomplished nothing. Eventually, she snapped the tip off the shaft, leaving it embedded in the gap.

She broke off one of the metal spokes and pushed it into the keyhole of each lock, twisting it this way and that until she rubbed her fingers raw. She kicked the door. She swung the chain at it, again and again. She wrapped the chain around the knob and yanked. Nothing budged the door.

She screamed at it. She threw one of the plastic chairs at it. The table was small but heavy. She tried to throw it at the door, but by then, she was exhausted. The table hit the floor in front of the door and rolled to the side. One of its legs punched a hole in the wall beside the door.

The child stared, panting, astonished. The wall by her bed, the one that the eyebolt had been sunk into, was concrete. She'd assumed all the walls were concrete, but this was something different. This was something soft.

She grabbed up the now-tattered umbrella and smashed it against the soft barrier, just above the hole left by the table. The wall crumbled like chalk and paper. She peered through, into the darkness of the dirt-floored cellar.

The other girls who had been his princess prisoners in this room were buried under that floor. He had told her this on the nights he wore the mask.

Somewhere beyond the cellar was the outside world. She didn't know what waited for her there, but maybe it would be better than this. She quickly broke out all the chalky wallboard between two wooden beams, then squeezed through them into the dark.

Light spilled out of the hole she had made, highlighting the contours of the black floor. The others lay beneath those mounds.

How long had they been there? Would they be jealous she had escaped the fate that had taken them?

Maybe. But she would try not to step on them and they would not try to stop her.

The child used the words she knew to make a promise. If she somehow found her way out of this place, she would tell about the children buried here. She would tell anyone who would listen.

The buried children made no answer to her promise. Perhaps they did not understand her words.

She gathered her chain to her belly, its every clink and rattle jarring her frayed nerves. Feeling her way along the wall, avoiding the mounds, she passed a corner where the chalky-paper wall met concrete.

She inched down the concrete wall until she found stairs. The stairway ascended to a pair of wooden doors that lay flat across the ceiling. She pushed up on these. They gave a little, then a chain above rattled softly and the doors stopped.

The gap, where the top stair met the two doors, was very thin, but the child was very thin as well. She crammed herself into the space, like she had crammed the umbrella in to the door jam. The stairs scraped one cheek while the doors dug into the other. She dropped the chain, using all her strength to force her head through the opening, straining with her back and legs to push the doors wider.

Wood splintered. Splinters dug into her skin.

Her shoulders and arms cleared the opening. She reached out, grasping the concrete lip of the stairwell, and pulled herself forward, wriggling like an earthworm. Her hips slid free. Her legs followed. The doors fell back into their jambs, closing on her chain.

A sudden terror gripped her – one of those buried below had grabbed the chain and would pull her back down into the darkness. She seized it, hauling it to herself. The links pinged and clanked, echoing through the black below. Too loud. Much too loud. But she couldn't stop herself.

Her world had shrunk to that chain and whatever might be trying to catch it just beyond the closed cellar door. When the last bit of chain finally pulled free, relief hit her like a physical blow. She fell to the ground on her butt, wide-eyed and panting.

But relief was short-lived. The child found herself in a thick forest in the dead of night. Hard pellets of water pelted her from above. She knew what rain was, had a vague memory of it from before the nightmare began, but then the rain had been warm.

What fell now was icy. It soaked through her flimsy dress before she even had a chance to stand, plastering the thin white cotton to her body like a second skin. If there had been warm rain before the nightmare, did the cold, dark rain now signal the nightmare's end? And if so, what manner of waking would it be?

She did not know and chose not to care. What she did know was that it had to end. Above, a pinkish-gray glow reflected off low clouds, but not a hint of that light penetrated the deep woods. The house was nothing more than a moldering heap, nearly indistinguishable from the surrounding shadows. She turned her back to it and walked into the woods, carrying her chain in a ball at her belly.

Her socks offered little protection against thorny vines and sharp sticks that littered the ground, and no protection at all against the knee-deep puddles of near-freezing water. Within minutes, shivering wracked her small body. She felt no elation or joy at being free from the man. The nightmare still had her. She plodded onward, tripping often, cutting her palms and arms as well as her feet and legs.

The night dragged on. At one point, the ground fell away in a short drop followed by a swampy pool. Eventually, a slightly brighter darkness colored one side of the sky and she adjusted her course towards it. She now felt as if she had been wandering in the forest even longer than she had been chained in the basement. The trees began to move around her, and things behind the trees followed her. The children from beneath the cellar floor? Tracking her progress, ensuring she made good on her promise?

Extreme weariness overtook her, and she noticed the shivering had stopped, but she walked on. The nightmare *had* to end. By the time she discovered the dirt pathway, her weariness was gone, replaced by a sense of detachment. Things still moved through the trees alongside her, but now she felt more like one of those things than like herself.

The path was easy to walk, leading across a footbridge and depositing her in a wide open, grassy field. To one side, brightly colored and oddly twisted pipes sprang up in fanciful configurations from a bed of wood chips. The child had never seen anything like it. She stood and looked at the colorful pipes. Later, she realized she was still looking at them. Maybe an hour had passed.

Maybe a day. The rain ran over her, soaking through her skin, running through every part of her, cold and relentless.

Her eyes were drawn to a pair of lights, moving quickly, zipping through the night on a road at the far side of the field. It was there and gone again before she really even understood what it had been. A streetlight hovered over the road, illuminating a glass booth. No rain fell inside the booth, and the wooden bench within looked like the most comfortable bed she had ever lain upon.

When she started toward it, she found her limbs had frozen. She could barely walk. The distance to the booth seemed impossibly long, seemed to grow longer with each step she took. She watched her foot move up, slide forward, plunk down through the wet grass. Her socks were black with mud. Her dress, too, was now filthy and shredded. The man would be furious. She smiled. It felt a little like waking up.

Then she was inside the booth, lying on the bench, not remembering how this had come about. She was no longer cold. A comfortable, almost euphoric peace settled over her. The cuts on her feet and the scrapes on her legs ached, but in a dull and uninteresting way. She was very tired now; the rise and fall of her chest seemed like a waste of effort. The dream was coming to an end.

Before she slept, she remembered her promise.

She did not know how many others had been buried in the basement, nor did she know how to count, but she remembered the contours of the dirt floor, the low, oblong mounds. She peeled a muddy sock from her foot, and with it she drew the lines on the dusty glass wall of the booth.

Then she remembered a symbol, the only symbol she had ever learned. She carefully drew it next to the lines. When it was done, the child curled up on the bench and closed her eyes for the last time. The nightmare finally ended.

CHAPTER 2

"IT'S A BAD one, Darren," Officer Beverly Conklin said, her voice low and slightly distorted over the phone lines.

"It's Griggs' rotation," Darren said, also whispering. "I'm not even out of bed yet."

"I can't just dump this off on Griggs. You know how he is, and he's headed to Cabo San Lucas on Tuesday. Might as well give the perp a get-out-of-jail-free card."

Darren groaned. He wanted to rub his eyes, but the hand not holding the phone was pinned under his wife and he didn't want to disturb her, his half-awake brain still clinging to the fantasy that he might have a chance of sleeping in this morning.

"What have you got?" he asked, knowing he'd regret the question.

"It's a little girl, Darren. Can't be more than ten. She was found at the bus stop by Stewart Park," Officer Conklin said. A noise followed this, but Darren couldn't tell if it was Beverly swallowing hard or just static on the line. "She has a chain around her ankle."

He groaned again, this time in resignation. His bed was far too comfortable and much too warm. He could not lay there while processing the information Officer Conklin had just provided. "Okay, Bev," he said, "Gimme about twenty."

"Thank you, Darren," she said, and this time the tremble in her voice could not be mistaken for static.

Darren let his arm fall away from his ear, the cellphone sinking into the thick down comforter. His wife, Katheryn, rolled over, sliding her hand across his bare chest and nuzzling her face into the hollow under his chin. "Don't leave me for that woman," she mumbled, her lips brushing the skin at his throat.

He ran his arm up her back and neck, then buried it in her hair. "Why are you so cruel to me?" he asked, kissing her forehead.

"You want me to make coffee…?" her voice trailed off. He couldn't tell whether she had actually awakened or was talking in her sleep.

"You stay right where you are. Keep it warm for me, okay?" he said, petting her head. "I'll come back to you as soon as I can."

"Mmm-hmm," she mumbled, nodding against him, then made a plaintive sound as he began the clumsy process of untangling his limbs from hers.

He was into and back out of the shower before the water had fully warmed. He had grabbed his go-clothes from the closet, dark slacks and a darker suit coat over a white shirt. He pulled these on, completely covering the scars and the tattoo.

The clothes could have belonged to a bank executive or a preacher. The man wearing them looked like neither. Detective Darren McDaniel, in his mid-forties, had a physique any twenty-year-old would envy. But the lines on his face and the stillness in his eyes conveyed a depth of experience typically seen in a man twice his age.

He considered those eyes now in the mirror, taking a breath, steeling himself for what was to come. The crime scene would be an injury to his psyche, in this case, a more painful injury than most others had been. The pursuit would be therapeutic, and the eventual capture would heal the wound. But wounds like these always left scars. He took another breath, smelling the shampoo he had just used and the fragrances of his wife's various soaps.

Darren understood scars on a deep and intimate level. There were degrees of pain in this world, and horror, that few people had experienced as intensely as he had. Yet his life now bordered on idyllic. Someone, a young girl apparently, had recently experienced that pain and horror but had not survived, had not had the chance to reclaim her life. It was now up to him to discover what had happened to her, how it had happened, and who had done it. One more scar, at this point, would be of little consequence.

After a final deep breath, Darren clipped his H&K .40 and his detective's badge to his belt and headed for the stairs. On the main floor, he smelled fresh coffee. All the lights were out, and no one else was up. Something beeped in the kitchen. He remembered the new coffee-pod-thing Katheryn told him about. She had an app on her phone that allowed her to brew a single cup remotely. Apparently, she had done just that while he was in the shower.

Darren grinned with one corner of his mouth. That his wife owned a palm-sized super-computer which she used to brew a single coffee, without actually waking up, seemed both utterly absurd and somehow inevitable. He took the coffee, drew a heart on a Post-It note which he stuck to the brew station, and headed for the door to the garage.

Another noise drew his attention, a thin whistly sound coming from the living room. He ducked his head around the corner and was again bemused. The living room was the perfect picture of elegant order, with tastefully selected furnishings and décor – Katheryn's doing. But the effect was either ruined or accentuated by the debris pile in the corner of the sectional couch, what his nineteen-year-old daughter, Robyn, liked to call her study nest.

It was a semi-circle of blankets, stuffed critters, books, pillows, papers, a popcorn bowl, energy drink cans, a computer, slippers, bathrobe. Robyn, herself, sprawled in the center of the heap, snoring softly. A physics book lay propped against a large teddy bear, inches from her nose.

Beyond her, a streetlight rippled through the sheets of rain flowing down the picture window. It suddenly seemed very warm, here in his home, an impossible perfection of order and security, a precarious paradise. The heat of the coffee seeped through the mug into his palm. He indulged memory, the smell of Katheryn's hair, the feel of her hand on his chest, her warmth. Then he stepped into the garage, putting those thoughts out of his mind, replacing them with intention and focus. This pristine security came at a price. He intended to pay it in full.

· · · · · · · · · · · · · · · · · · · ·

ONCE IN HIS car, McDaniel texted his partner, Brent Vanderwyk, but did not receive an immediate reply. Next, he called Beverly Conklin back. Four years ago, in his last year before making detective, McDaniel had been a Field Training Officer. Conklin was one of his better trainees.

She filled him in on the details as he drove. The initial call had come in at 4:13 a.m. A barista had walked to the bus stop from a near-by apartment complex, discovered the body and called for a paramedic. The call center dispatched police as well, based on the barista's explanation of what she had found. Officer Conklin had been the first to arrive.

"So, she was alive when the barista found her?" McDaniel asked.

"The paramedics say probably no," Conklin told him. "They didn't attempt any resuscitation, said rigor had started in the girl's jaw by the time they arrived."

"And you held onto the barista?"

"Well, I didn't have to, the medics have her. She took her coat off, laid it over the body. The paramedics are treating her for shock and mild hypothermia."

"Shit."

"Yeah," Conklin said, "the medics removed the coat when they started their eval, so I bagged it. They determined she was already gone before disturbing the scene too much, and we locked it down pretty quick after we arrived. There shouldn't be any additional contamination."

"You see anyone unusual hanging around?"

"Well, the lightshow has attracted a couple gawkers. No one I could say for sure was out of place, though."

"Right," McDaniel said. "I'm just around the corner. See you in a sec."

CHAPTER 3

ETECTIVE McDANIEL ARRIVED on scene at 5:27 a.m. Patrol cars blocked the road on either side of the scene. The officers assigned to those cars had the unenviable duty of standing in the freezing drizzle, redirecting grumpy early-morning commuters. The officer who checked his credentials before letting him pass greeted him with a "good morning, sir," that sounded suspiciously like, *it's about time you showed up.*

Conklin had not been exaggerating when she said "lightshow." In addition to the patrol cars blocking access to the scene, four ambulances, a fire truck, and three more patrol cars clustered around the glass bus stop shelter. All had their lights going. White and red and blue strobes flashed, freezing individual raindrops in mid-fall. The lights flared across the rain-soaked roadway and sidewalk.

Officer Conklin met him as he stepped out of his car. "Thank you for coming," she said. "Griggs is on his way, but I'm sure he won't fight you for it."

"He'll pretend to be pissed, but we'll all know better," McDaniel said, shrugging into an overcoat and popping his umbrella. "Show me what we've got."

Conklin led him to the booth. The girl lay on the bench, curled up as if napping. She had black hair cut short in a bob. Her features were Eastern, Chinese maybe. Her age was hard to guess, could be eight, could be twelve. The frilly white dress she wore was tattered and soaked through with muddy water, revealing the girl's birdlike bone structure. She couldn't have weighed more than forty-five pounds.

Scratches and minor cuts marred her extremities, but there were no signs of injury sufficient to cause death. One foot was bare, the tiny toes pale and wrinkled. The other foot, the one still wearing a muddy sock, also wore a steel manacle. It appeared to be made from a galvanized clamp intended for use as part of a chain-link fence. A brass padlock secured it closed. A bolt connected the clamp to a length of mid-grade steel chain.

Her discarded sock lay on the floor below her head. On the wall, just above it, some sort of message was scrawled in mud – six vertical lines followed by an oriental character of some kind.

"Any idea what that means?" he asked Conklin.

She shook her head. "Officer Nguyed said it wasn't Vietnamese, thinks it might be Korean, but doesn't know for sure."

"Right, okay, we'll figure it out. Do we have an ETA for the forensics guys or the M.E.'s office?"

"On their way."

"And you've got a log going?" McDaniel asked.

"Right here." A wiry, red-haired officer waved a water-proof notebook.

"Everyone who shows up gets noted in that log," McDaniel said. "No exceptions."

"I know how a crime scene log works," the officer said.

McDaniel nodded, then turned back to Conklin. "We need to clean this up a bit. Get rid of all the EMTs except the two that touched the body. We need a couple units for traffic control, a couple to set up a perimeter. Anyone who doesn't have a job needs to clear out. Can you get that done for me?"

"Yeah, no problem." Then she nodded toward the roadblock, "Heads up."

Detective Griggs' rust-and-beige 1980's Impala had just pulled to a stop beside the scene control officer. Griggs was the senior homicide detective on Bellingham's force, and this was his case. Depending on his mood, and blood-alcohol level, the situation could turn ugly. McDaniel had a few things he needed to nail down before locking horns with the senior detective.

"Where is the barista?" McDaniel asked.

"First ambulance. She's with the two EMTs you want to talk to."

"Thanks, Bev," McDaniel said, then headed for the ambulance, keeping a wary eye on Griggs.

CHAPTER 4

THE BARISTA WAS slender with high cheekbones and huge eyes, a face that likely won her tips to rival McDaniel's salary. But not today. Her mascara streamed in lines from beneath her eyes to the delicate curve of her chin. An oxygen mask hung around her neck, hissing softly. She sat on the back edge of the aid car, wrapped in a blanket, feet dangling. The two EMTs appeared smitten, administering more aid than she needed.

"Gentlemen, I'm Detective McDaniel," he said. "I will need to speak to each of you in a minute, but first I'd like to have a word with this young woman."

The two EMTs stood. Their eyes looked almost as haunted as the barista's. McDaniel reevaluated them, then, understanding that their doting on the barista was not a function of her damsel-in-distress beauty but due to their own shock and need for distraction from the scene they had encountered.

"Yeah, sure thing," the older of the two said. "We'll just, uh, wait up front, I guess."

The younger followed him, fishing a cigarette out of his breast pocket as he went.

"Ma'am, My name's Detective McDaniel…"

"Yeah, I heard," she said in a vacant tone without looking up. "Why the fuck has this shit always gotta happen to me?"

"I guess I'm not the guy who can answer that for you," McDaniel said. "I do need to get just a bit of information from you, then I can call a friend or a family member to come pick you up."

"I already called my sister. What do you want to know?"

"Let's start with your name."

"Leslie High," she said. "That's High with four letters, not two. That girl cop who showed up first already wrote my name down in her little book, and my phone number, too, so don't ask 'cause I don't give it out to guys I just met."

"Alright, Leslie, I don't need your phone number. I do need you to cooperate. This won't take long."

"I am cooperating," she said, finally looking up at him with a withering glare. "It's just…what the fuck, man? I mean, what the actual fuck?" She shuddered violently under the blanket. "Can I get a cigarette? Please? And a Xanax?"

"Can't let you smoke with that oxygen mask on. My partner might have something for you, though. Can you hang tight for one minute?"

"Like I got a choice," she said, looking back down at her feet.

Griggs was stalking toward the booth, lower jaw jutted. McDaniel intercepted him. "Hey, Griggs, can I get a quick word?"

"McDaniel, what are you doing, huh?" the older man asked. His short gray hair bristled. The harsh light of emergency flashers accentuated the deeply carved lines of his face. "Poaching my case?" He surreptitiously flicked his umbrella, spraying McDaniel with rain.

McDaniel pretended not to notice. "You can have it, man, if you want, but you've got vacation coming up, like day after tomorrow, right? I figured I'd go ahead and run with it since I was already in the area."

Griggs studied him for a moment. Then, his red-rimmed, rheumy eyes shifted, looking over McDaniel's shoulder to where the dead girl lay. "That's awful white of you. You thinking this is going to be high profile? Get your name in the papers and all that?"

"You know that's not what I'm about. This is less than a mile from my house, where my family sleeps…"

"McDingle, cut the horse shit. I know why you're here. Your nugget, Conklin, saw this poor dead girl, guessed it would be my case, and assumed that, because I'm old, I wouldn't pursue it with the same vigor as her dashing FTO would. That about sum it up?"

"Not because you're old," McDaniel said. "Because your close rate is for shit. Other than that, I'd say you've got it pretty close."

Griggs made a thin whistling noise through his teeth. "Well, at least now we're being honest. You wanna be the hero, be my guest."

"But?" McDaniel asked.

"But nothing. Go. Find the clues. Solve the case. Save the world," Griggs said, a broad grin spreading across his face. "There are plenty of vicious, evil fucks to go around. You catch this one.

I'll catch the next one. And by the time we put those two away, fourteen more will have sprung up."

"You got your flask on you?" McDaniel asked.

"That's the spirit!" Griggs rumbled a phlegmy sounding chuckle. "Though, if you remembered half of what I taught ya, you'd be carrying your own."

"The woman who found the body is a little spun up," McDaniel said.

"Of course, she is," Griggs said, pulling the silver flask from inside his jacket. "Here, keep it, I've got another. Don't say I never gave you nothing."

McDaniel took the flask.

"And just to show there are no hard feelings," Griggs continued, "let me give you another little nudge along the path. Your dead girl left you a message. Those six lines are hash marks, numbers. Maybe how many miles she walked, how many days she's been missing, how many blow jobs she gave, who knows? But that last symbol is a name, probably her name. It's the *Hangul* alphabet, used in Korea and a few Chinese provinces. The name is Seong. It means 'Victory.'"

CHAPTER 5

McDaniel returned to the rear of the ambulance. Leslie High still huddled there under her blanket, shuddering. Her oxygen mask was gone, replaced by one of the EMT's cigarettes. She eyed McDaniel over its glowing tip as if challenging him to say something about it.

He smiled and took a seat beside her. "I was never a smoker," he said, inhaling deeply, "but my father was, would smoke outside when we were working together. Second-hand smoke is one of my favorite aromas, always reminds me of home."

"That's precious," she said, exhaling in his general direction.

He offered her the flask, keeping it low. "My partner was out of Xanax."

Her dour, vacant façade cracked just a little as she took it. "I bet he was," she said with the ghost of a chuckle. She tipped the flask back, downing a healthy slug of whiskey as if it were water. She took a long, deep breath, then another swallow from the flask.

"Leslie," McDaniel said, "I need to say thank you for calling this in, for staying with her until we arrived. That took some fortitude on your part. I admire that."

Leslie handed the flask back to him, rocking gently. "I told you I'd answer your questions. You don't gotta butter me up."

"Leslie, look at me."

She turned her head slowly, until her eyes met his.

"Staying with the girl, giving her your coat, that's courage, compassion, self-sacrifice. Just a few more people like you in this world and I'd be out of a job." He looked into her eyes a moment longer to make sure he had her undivided attention, then said, "Thank you."

Her mouth worked, as if trying to decide what to say, then she swiped at a tear and looked away. "What else was I gonna do?" she asked, sniffling.

The early morning around them had calmed a bit. Conklin had done as McDaniel had asked, clearing all unnecessary units from the area. The only lights still flashing were the two patrol cars blocking either end of this stretch of road. The ambulance and other cars had shut their emergency lights off. McDaniel's partner, Detective Vanderwyk, had finally arrived and was being brought up to speed by one of the uniforms. Yellow crime scene tape fluttered in the restless morning air. And the rain fell.

"Can you tell me about it?" McDaniel asked. "From the beginning?"

"Sure," she said. "I came down to the bus stop this morning, just like always."

"Came down from where?"

"I live in the apartments just a block that way." She pointed back over her shoulder. "I was on my way to work – the Woods Coffee by where the Costco used to be. I came down to the bus stop just like I do every morning."

"And what time was that?"

"Quarter after four."

"Did you see anyone hanging around or driving by slowly?"

"No. There wasn't anyone out, not that time of morning. Never is. The bus didn't even come by. I think you people got here first and blocked it."

"Tell me what you saw when you approached the bus stop. Take it slow. Tell me anything that stood out."

"I thought it was a hoax, I mean, at first," Leslie said, her voice trembling. "I thought it was, like, a left-over Halloween prop. And it really creeped me out, you know, with the chain and the markings on the wall. I sent a picture to my friend, Erin. She's all into the creepy shit." She met his eyes briefly, maybe checking for judgment, then glanced away.

"I didn't want to go in there because it freaked me out, but then it got cold standing out here in the rain, and I got, like, pissed, you know? Some little brat put a Halloween dummy in my bus stop so now I have to stand out in the rain?" She sniffled, and took a long pull on her cigarette.

"Hell no, I said, and I went in and that's when I realized that it – that she was real. And I thought oh my God, because I was so cold and this little girl is just wearing a little dress. She must be freezing, so I put my coat over her and tried to talk to her, but she wouldn't wake up."

Leslie sobbed and wiped at her face again. She sniffed, looking around the back of the ambulance for a tissue.

McDaniel pulled a sterile gauze pad from one of the many drawers and handed it to her.

"Did you touch her, or move her at all?"

"I…I guess I knew she was…wasn't going to wake up. I put my hand on her shoulder, you know, to give her a little shake, and…" She sobbed again and shuddered. She dabbed at her eyes with the gauze pad. "She was just so *cold*." Leslie looked at her palm, then rubbed it against the other. "I put my coat over her, I didn't know what else to do. Then I called the ambulance."

"You did fine, Leslie. You did good," McDaniel said. "Have you ever seen this girl before? Do you recognize her?"

Leslie shook her head.

"Is there anything else you might have seen or heard, maybe as you were approaching the bus stop before you reached the booth?"

She stared ahead for a long moment. McDaniel couldn't tell if she was thinking or just shutting down. Eventually, she said, "I don't think so."

Detective Vanderwyk and a uniformed officer approached, but stopped about ten feet from the ambulance, waiting on a signal from McDaniel that he was finished with the interview. He waved them forward, then said to Leslie, "If you do think of anything else, I want you to call me right away. Can you do that?"

Leslie nodded.

McDaniel handed her a card with his contact info. "I think your sister is here to pick you up," he said, eyeing the uniform for confirmation.

The officer nodded. "She's waiting just outside the perimeter."

"Okay, officer, would you please ask her to drive up here?" He didn't want Leslie to have to walk past the body again. If her sister chose to look as she drove by, that was on her. The officer nodded and walked off in that direction.

"So, she'll be right here," he said. "I just need to ask you a couple favors, then you'll be done with all this, okay?"

"Mmm-hmm."

"First, I need you to send me that photo you took, the one you sent to your friend…Erin, I think you said, then I need you to delete it off your phone."

"Can you do that?" she asked, pulling the phone out from somewhere beneath the blanket. "I don't want to ever see it again."

"If you like. Punch in your security code. I'll do the rest." She handed the iPhone to him and he went to work. "Your friend is going to need to delete her copy as well. It's important to preserve as much scene integrity as possible. That includes controlling what information is made public. Would you contact Erin, or would you rather I do that?"

"You do it," Leslie said, looking more and more distant as the moments passed. "Her number's in there under Erin…with an 'E' not two 'A's."

McDaniel texted the number to his phone, then handed the device back to her. A car pulled up beside the ambulance, driven by an older version of the barista. "One last thing, Leslie, I am sending a community crisis officer to meet with you later this morning. She will help you process your experience and work through some of what you are feeling. Don't blow her off, okay?"

"Okay," she said, nodding. "My big sister is here. Can I go home now?"

McDaniel stood and offered her his hand. She took it and stood, trancelike. He walked her to her sister's car, opened the door and helped her in. He repeated the information about the crisis officer to the sister, handed her one of his cards, then sent them away.

CHAPTER 6

BRENT VANDERWYK WAS a towering, red-faced man who was almost always smiling. His white-blond hair would curl up into a mane if it hadn't been cropped so close to his scalp. He had been a cop several years longer than McDaniel, but had decided to become a detective only a year ago, thinking a change of pace might do him good after his third marriage collapsed. He approached McDaniel now, as an officer let the two women out of the barricaded area. "Fuck, Darren," he muttered, not smiling.

"Right?" McDaniel said. "You think I should have let Griggs take it?"

"No, you did right. I'm just thinking maybe I should have decided to be a plumber. I've got a real bad feeling about this one."

"Plumber?"

"Can't imagine the worst day plumbing being worse than this," Vanderwyk said.

"Yeah," McDaniel said. "Whatever we turn up, it's going to be ugly."

Vanderwyk grumbled under his breath. It sounded like agreement. Then he said, "So, she walked here from somewhere, right? She wasn't dumped."

"That's what I'm thinking," McDaniel said. "If it was a dump, I don't think they would have left the chain on her. See, it's still attached to that bolt? Also, her feet and legs are all cut up…" He paused. "And her position on the bench, I guess someone could have staged that, but it looks like she just curled up and went to sleep. We'll know more after we hear from the M.E. but I think she walked through some pretty rough terrain, then died right there on that bench."

"That chain," Vanderwyk said. "Somebody is missing a little girl. I'm betting whoever it is isn't going to file a report."

A flash drew their attention back to the booth. Then another. One of the forensics team had begun taking photos. These pictures would be the scenes McDaniel would take to bed with him each night and wake up with each morning until this case was closed. He felt his gut tighten at the thought and exchanged a knowing look with his partner.

Vanderwyk said, "You interviewed the paramedics?"

"They're up next. You want to take that? I've got a call to make."

"Gotta check in with the wife already?"

"No, our first-on-scene sent a photo to her friend…"

"What?" Vanderwyk nearly shouted. "She's a ghoulie?"

"No, it was a misunderstanding, but her friend might be. I'll explain in a minute. Let me see if I can do some damage control. Get a statement from those boys and cut them loose. Then we'll compare notes and come up with a plan."

"Ten-four," Vanderwyk said and walked to the front of the ambulance.

The phone went to voicemail the first two times McDaniel tried to call her. On the third attempt, Erin Castillo answered with an inarticulate mumble.

"Ma'am, this is Detective McDaniel with the Bellingham Police Department," he said.

"Whadda you want? It's like…not even…what time isssit?"

"Ma'am, this will only take a second."

"Who is this? I just got asleep…like, not even…what?"

"Ma'am, my name is Detective McDaniel. I need you to focus. This is very important."

"Um, okay, officer," she said, slurring but a bit more coherent. "I'm listening."

"You received a message from your friend, Leslie High, at around 4:15 this morning. It contained a photo of--"

"Oh, yeah, that creepy doll at the bus stop…wait, is Leslie okay? Did something happen to her?"

"No, ma'am, Leslie is fine, but I need you to delete that picture. This is very important. You have your phone in your hand right now, right?"

"Um," she considered this for a moment then guessed, "yeah?"

"So, I need you to delete that picture, off your camera roll, photo cache, and anywhere else it might be stored."

"Right now?"

"Yes, ma'am," he said, "and then let me know that you have done so."

"Um, okay, hold on." McDaniel heard shuffling and rustling, then she was back. "Okay, it's gone. But, man, what's the deal? Why do I gotta delete Leslie's photo?"

"The scene is part of an ongoing investigation. Thank you for being so cooperative. I apologize for having to wake you."

"Yeah, man, I'm pretty cooperative when I'm high," she giggled as if sharing a naughty secret, then said, "but it's legal now so you can't touch me. That wasn't a doll, was it? You wouldn't be calling if it was just a doll."

"I really can't comment on that, Miss Castillo."

"Ooh, that tells me everything I need to know," she said, giggling again. "I guess since I'm being all cooperative, I should probably tell you that the picture auto-posted to my sites, you know, as soon as she sent it to me. I can take it down, but it's already got some likes and shares."

McDaniel felt his heart sink. "Please delete it from anywhere you posted it. And please do not discuss it with anyone. Can you tell me where exactly the photo posted?"

"Um…just my Instagram. Oh, and I have a Creepy Doll blog. I think it posted there, too. My fans love that stuff. Maybe Facebook? I…wait, no, Facebook isn't on my auto-post list. I don't think. Gimme… two… seconds…" McDaniel heard clicking in the background, "and… boom, done. No more creepy-doll-that's-not-a-doll photos on any of my accounts. Maybe you'll remember this next time y'all try to bust me. Can I go back to sleep now?"

"Yes, Miss Castillo. Thank you."

She let out an exasperated sigh and clicked off.

Vanderwyk returned from his interview with the paramedics. "Nothing of value up there," he said. "They showed up, the girl was already in early stages of rigor, so they made necessary notifications and turned their attention to the barista. She was hypothermic, and possibly heading into shock," he explained. "They removed the coat she had placed over the body, and moved the girl's head a few degrees, but otherwise claim the scene is just about how they found it."

"Okay," McDaniel said. "We have the barista's photo of the body before anyone touched it – she thought the whole thing was a prank – but we can compare that to the photos from our forensics team, see if anything got moved or disappeared."

The flash continued to pop around the booth every ten seconds or so. The rain continued to fall. At the barricade, an officer was checking in the medical examiner's team. Overhead, clouds hurried past, as if they had somewhere important to be. Or perhaps they just didn't want to be here. McDaniel could relate.

"You eat this morning?" he asked Vanderwyk.

"No, you wanna grab breakfast and have a powwow?"

"That's what I'm thinking. Give these guys a chance to go over the scene and give us a chance to develop a plan. Sun will be up by the time we're back," McDaniel surveyed the empty park in the drizzly darkness and the thick woods that lay beyond. "I have a feeling you and I are going to be doing a lot of walking today."

CHAPTER 7

CAL'S DINER WAS about four-hundred square feet of stainless steel and Formica crammed into the back of an office complex between a dry cleaner and a customs brokerage. It wouldn't usually be the detectives' first choice (or *anybody's* first choice, for that matter) but it was close, and quick. The general lack of customers made it private, which also helped.

McDaniel opened his laptop on the table and logged onto the office complex's Wi-Fi. He ordered bacon, eggs, and toast without looking at the menu or the waitress. Vanderwyk had slid in beside him, on the same side of the table in order to see the laptop screen. He spent more time examining the waitress than the menu.

As his partner ordered, McDaniel pulled up Google Maps and typed the address of the bus stop. He began playing with the map, zooming in and out to familiarize himself with the area. Their food arrived within minutes, which should have concerned McDaniel, but his mind was elsewhere.

"That park is about two acres," Vanderwyk said between bites. He had ordered a pan-san, which consisted of four eggs, four bacon strips and about four potatoes-worth of hash browns sand-wiched between a pair of pancakes smothered in syrup, and had devoured half of it by the time McDaniel had buttered his toast. "Most of that area is wooded. It's got a nice wide foot-path running from one end to the other."

"We don't know if she came from the park, though," McDaniel said. "Could have come through the woods across the street, from the south side."

The park was a narrow strip of lawn between a curve of road and an undeveloped swath of woodland. The bus stop was at one end, a play area at the other. Large apartment complexes lay to the east and west of the park, woods to the north and south. Beyond the green belt to the south, a housing development sprawled. From the Google satellite view, it looked like a maze. The woods to the north crossed out of the city limits, spreading deep into the county. Dirt roads wound through the trees, but only a few homes dotted the green canopy.

"Hmm…" Vanderwyk mused. "For that matter, she could have come from either apartment complex. But my bet is she came through the woods behind the park."

"Okay, tell me why?"

"We agree that she was probably in the woods at some point?"

McDaniel nodded. "The condition of her clothing, the cuts on her feet and legs support that."

"If you are a lost child, and there is a forest, your number one goal is to get out of the forest. If she started out in the development to the south, or at either apartment complex, she would have had to go *into* the woods." He pointed at McDaniel with a syrup-soggy chunk of pancake on the end of his fork. "Opposite of natural instinct. I'm thinking she must have started in the woods and worked her way out."

"What if someone chased her into the woods?"

"Really?" Vanderwyk gave him an incredulous look. "She's tiny. She's dragging a chain around with her that probably weighs more than she does. And she has no shoes. Anyone who chased her would have caught her."

"So, she hid in the woods, right after she escaped from whoever chained her," McDaniel suggested. "Then she got turned around, lost her way, and ended up walking out the other side."

"Man, you are really pushing for the south side."

"No, I'm just testing your theory." McDaniel said. He took a sip of coffee, then added, "I think I agree that the north is the better bet. That's where you and I will start. But we will also need to canvas the apartments and talk to anyone who regularly uses that bus stop. See if anyone recognizes the girl."

"This one right here," Vanderwyk said, tapping the larger of the two complexes on the map, "has an extensive video surveillance system. I've worked a couple burglaries there. It won't show the actual bus stop, but I think the camera they have on their front entrance covers the street and sidewalks. We should be able to see her if she walked in from this side. Also, any other traffic from last night."

McDaniel nodded and was about to respond when his phone buzzed. He had asked the forensics team to notify him when they had finished processing the scene. The text said, *just wrapping up.* A second text came through as he was reading the first, *M.E. will be ready to load by the time you get back.*

McDaniel signaled the waitress to bring their check, then turned his attention back to Vanderwyk. "I think the brass will give us priority on this, shouldn't have any trouble getting a crew of uniforms to canvas the apartments and get a copy of the video. Also, need to assign an officer to plow through missing persons reports, see if any match our victim."

Vanderwyk heaved a sigh. His face tightened and he stared through the window at the soggy gray sky. McDaniel knew that his partner was actually seeing the crime scene, considering its details. Eventually, Vanderwyk said, "What do you make of that symbol she drew?"

"Griggs said the boxy thing after the six lines, is a name, Seong, written in Korean letters."

"Griggs! What does he know?" Vanderwyk said, chuckling.

"You'd be surprised. He was a good cop once," McDaniel said. "We'll definitely check that with a Korean translator, but I think we'll find it to be true."

"Okay, assuming it is a name, whose name is it? Hers or her killer's?"

"Could be either. Could be her mother's name for that matter."

"Her mom, wow," Vanderwyk said, his smile fading. "That's tough."

"Yeah," McDaniel said, looking down at what remained of his breakfast. "Yeah, it's tough."

The waitress appeared with their bill and offered to refill their coffees. McDaniel asked for his to go. "Actually," he said, "can you bring me six to-go coffees? In a carrier?"

"Kinda cold out there today, is it?" the waitress asked.

McDaniel gazed through the rain-washed windows at the watery gray dawn. When he turned back to the waitress, something in his eyes caused her smile to falter. "Yeah," he said, "colder than you know."

CHAPTER 8

McDANIEL OFFERED COFFEES to the officers manning the barricades at either end of the crime scene. Three of them accepted, but the red-haired officer with the logbook told him to fuck off.

"You know that guy?" McDaniel asked as he and Vanderwyk headed toward the bus stop. "He's had a bug up his butt all morning."

"That's Murphy," Vanderwyk said. "He's Irish."

"What's that supposed to mean?"

"It means he can't help it," Vanderwyk said. "They named it Ire-land because it is a land full of angry people."

"McDaniel's Irish," McDaniel said.

"Hmmm..." Vanderwyk mused.

"Well at least he's not Dutch."

"I am not Dutch," Vanderwyk nearly growled.

"I'm here for you if you ever decide to come out," McDaniel said, with a sly grin.

Vanderwyk glowered at him. The ribbing was a subconscious diversion. As they walked through the drizzle and mist from the barricade back to the bus stop, the medical examiner's van stood between them and the booth, blocking their view of the little girl's body. In just a moment, the horror of the crime would consume their focus, would likely do so for several days. The two knew this, and they knew that humor, even of a coarse variety, was a necessary shield against the weight of that burden.

As they arrived at the M.E.'s van, McDaniel was surprised to see Conklin still on scene. It was now just after seven o'clock and her overnight shift ended at six.

"Hey, Bev, what are you still doing here?" McDaniel asked her.

She gave him a sad smile. "I got permission to do a couple hours of overtime. I kinda felt like I should stay, at least until they took her away."

McDaniel put a hand on her shoulder and squeezed. "You want some coffee?"

She took one of the cups and thanked him. The other two coffees he gave to the crime scene techs, a couple of twenty-somethings who were known around the office as Sam and Frodo. Sam's name actually was Sam, but his partner, a six-foot-tall woman of Kenyan ancestry, came into the world with the name Faraja Odilo. Under the circumstances, her nickname was obvious, and Frodo had a lot of fun with it.

The two had collected every bit of litter from the scene, including cigarette butts and a few wads of chewing gum. They had created a diagram, documenting the location where each bit of debris had been collected and had taken over 400 photos in and around the booth. This was straw-grasping at its finest. McDaniel knew it and he figured they did, too. The person responsible for this girl's death had probably never been here. It was unlikely that any useful evidence would turn up, other than the girl's body itself, but if there was something to find, they were sure as hell going to find it.

Their best hope was that the autopsy would reveal details about this girl, how she died and who had put that chain on her. The Medical Examiner had sent one of his medico-legal techs, a guy named Trevor Shield, to do the on-site examination and collect the body. He now informed Vanderwyk that his examination was complete and they were cleared to examine the body and move it as needed.

The detectives gloved up and entered the booth with Trevor. The girl seemed paler now than she had been when they first saw her. This slight change revealed a detail McDaniel had missed initially. An unnatural pink patch bloomed on her cheek. A pink sheen covered the blueish pallor of her lips.

"She's wearing makeup," Vanderwyk said, stooping for a closer look.

"Yes," Trevor said. "And there's this." He lifted her tiny hand and uncurled the fingers. Each nail had been painted with pink glitter polish.

"Huh," Vanderwyk said, scratching his wooly scalp.

McDaniel lifted the back collar of her dress, revealing the tag. He made a note of the manufacturer and item number. There was a scar on her neck, several more on her arms. There were cuts and scratches from last night's travels.

He said, "She has old injuries, and the injuries she sustained last night, but no other recent wounds, nothing half-healed or scabbed over."

"Right," Trevor said, "I noticed that, too. Also, there is no obvious cause of death, but look at this." He placed his hands on either side of her face and gently rotated it, exposing the cheek that had been laying against the bench. Bright, almost cherry-red blotches mottled the side of her face.

"The lividity is all wrong," Vanderwyk said. "It should be darker purple."

"I've seen that before," McDaniel said. "Poisoning, right? I've seen cherry-red lividity on a couple different people who died of carbon monoxide poisoning."

"That could account for it," Trevor said, "but there is a more plausible explanation. The blood chemistry consistent with carbon monoxide poisoning is similar to that which accompanies hypothermia. With this girl's extremely low BMI and the conditions to which she was exposed," he indicated her wet and tattered dress, "I am expecting hypothermia is going to be your cause of death. Of course, nothing official until the doc takes a look, but…" he trailed off, nodding his head.

"So that's going to screw up time of death calculations?" Van-derwyk asked.

Trevor blew through his lips, making a *pfft* sound. "Again, her Body Mass Index, the low temps out here…" He shook his head. "Our standard calculations for heat loss are out the window. Her core body temp is so low, if you used the standard charts, her time of death would be yesterday morning sometime."

"Hypothermia fits our early theory, I think," McDaniel said, "that she escaped from somewhere, wandered through the woods and found her way here. She was conscious long enough to make those markings on the wall, then succumbed to the elements. Sound plausible, Trev?"

"Like I said, nothing is official until the doctor has a look, but I don't see anything here to contradict that theory," Trevor said. "Two other items of note, she has slight bruising between her eyes, here, near the top of her nose. Notice the greenish color?"

It was very faint, but when he focused his light on the area, the bruising appeared.

"An older bruise," McDaniel said.

"Correct. The doc will have more for you on that, but it would have happened several days ago. In addition to the bruising, she has several large wood splinters embedded in the back of her dress, here," Trevor rolled the body toward them slightly to show the splinters. "We will send these to the techs as soon as we have completed the autopsy. As you can see, some of these splinters have flecks of paint and appear to have come from pieces of dimensional lumber. That may give you a clue to where she had been held."

"What can you tell us about the chain?" Vanderwyk asked.

"It's a chain," Trevor said, then shrugged. "We work with the body. Scene techs will process the chain once we remove it." He thought for a moment then added, "There may be a trace amount of concrete on the bolt. If so, they may be able to analyze it and come up with something, but that's a long shot. There may have been fingerprints on it, but I doubt they survived being dragged through the woods and rain. But like I said, techies will process it and let you know."

"Alright," McDaniel said. "Anything else you can tell us?"

"I have been updating Doc Haverstock as to the situation out here," Trevor said. "He has a table waiting for her. The sooner I get her there, the sooner he will have answers for you."

"Okay," McDaniel nodded, "let's get her on her way, then."

CHAPTER 9

B Y SEVEN-THIRTY, THE M.E. van was headed to St. Joseph's Hospital. The roadblocks were also gone. The clouds hung low and ugly, drizzling a half-hearted rain. The two detectives and Officer Conklin waited for the other officers who were on their way to canvas the apartments and housing development. Despite the rain and cold, they did not seek shelter inside the covered bus stop booth.

"You know Officer Conklin?" McDaniel asked Vanderwyk.

"Sure, I know Bev," he said smiling at her. "We worked together a few times before I made detective. She shows potential and aptitude. I think she might even have been a great cop if she had had adequate training."

"Hey!" she said, "Darren was a great FTO."

"Of course, you'd say that. He's standing right here," Vanderwyk said. "But, you notice they haven't asked him to train anybody else after you."

"When she makes detective, I'll let *you* train her," McDaniel said. "See if you can do any better."

"You put in for detective?" Vanderwyk asked.

"Not yet," she said, "I need a few more years on the beat before I'm ready for that."

"Well, why don't you tag along? We'll show you how it's done," Vanderwyk said. "We're about to go for a stroll in the woods."

"Sure, I'll tag."

Two patrol cars arrived and a pair of officers stepped out of each. Two more officers were on their way. McDaniel explained how he wanted them to conduct the knock-and-talks. Vanderwyk assigned one of the officers to secure the video footage from the east complex. He would be by later to watch the tape and see if there was anything to see. Then, McDaniel, Vanderwyk, and Conklin set off across the narrow strip of lawn toward the woods.

The foot-path entered the woods at one end of the park, meandered between the trees and across a foot-bridge over a creek, then exited the woods at the other end. They started their search at the play area near the east trail-head, but found nothing.

Inside the tree line the atmosphere changed. The weak light that had slowly crept into the morning was all but lost under the evergreen canopy. The trees blocked the wind and the ambient sounds of the city waking up. Under other circumstances, it may have been a relaxing, peaceful walk. Today, it felt isolating and claustrophobic, like walking into the mouth of an abandoned mine shaft. McDaniel felt an uneasiness he would not have admitted to anyone, and he found himself hoping that their victim hadn't had to walk this path alone last night.

As they pushed beyond the first few trees, into the hovering mist and shadow, Vanderwyk cleared his throat then said, "How about some wild hare scenarios?" The tightness in his voice told McDaniel he wasn't alone in his unease. "If our working theory is wrong, what else might have happened?"

McDaniel pulled a compact flashlight from his coat pocket and shone it at the ground. Coarse wood chips had been laid over the path, protecting walkers from the mud that surely would have overtaken it otherwise. It made for a soft and quiet walking surface but left absolutely no trace of anyone who had passed here before.

"Well," he said, "let's see…What if someone found her, or knew that she was chained up in their neighbor's basement, right? But this someone has legal issues of their own, a warrant, unpaid child support, you know, whatever, so they… I don't know, they can't unlock the manacle so they just pull the chain out of the wall. But, they can't bring her to the cops, so they drop her off here, expecting someone else to find her and bring her to us."

Vanderwyk said, "If you're going to dump her somewhere, why not just drop her off at the hospital?"

"Why not pay your child support so you don't find yourself in this position to begin with?" Conklin asked.

The detectives looked at her, eyebrows raised.

"Okay, okay, I guess that is a bit far-fetched," she said. "The reason this hypothetical didn't drop her at the hospital, or anywhere else where she might have been found sooner, is the same reason he didn't go to the cops. Hospital has security cameras everywhere. Out here, nothing is on tape, no witnesses, but your subject could have believed someone would find her sooner than five o'clock this morning."

"Alright officer," McDaniel said, "you don't like my wild hare, come up with something better."

"Um…CO poisoning. The medico said that was a possibility. Where would she get a lethal dose of carbon monoxide?"

"Usually, we see that when people try to heat their homes with propane heaters that weren't meant to be used indoors. Often non-English speaking people or folks from third-world countries who haven't had experience with those types of devices," McDaniel said.

"So maybe she is from an undocumented immigrant family," Conklin said. "The girl died from a faulty heater and they put her body here rather than report it because they were afraid of deportation."

"Doesn't explain the chain or her cut-up feet," Vanderwyk said.

"What if the cuts on her feet were post-mortem? If she had, let's say, died from a faulty heater, right, like at a sweat-shop, that's why she was chained…" Conklin spoke slowly, piecing it together as she went. "So, she's dead and whoever had her, dragged her through the woods to here, and her feet got all cut up while she was being dragged?"

"But why drag her *here*?" McDaniel wondered.

They had reached the bridge, which was only wide enough for one to cross at a time. The underlayment of wood chips had given up no hint of who had passed this way. Beyond the bridge, the path deteriorated somewhat. The layer of chips was thinner and puddles of still water dotted the path here and there.

"She was in the trunk," Conklin suggested as she started across. "She escaped, her captor chased and caught her and put her in the trunk of his old POS car. It has an exhaust leak. When he gets her back to his dungeon, she's dead, so he dumps her..."

"At a bus stop, where she is sure to be found within hours?" McDaniel asked. "No. She's tiny. He could have buried her, stuffed her in a dumpster, left her in the woods. I just don't see any way that her captor dumped her body here. Just doesn't work for me."

"Maybe he wanted her to be found," Vanderwyk said. "Maybe she isn't the one who made those marks on the wall. Maybe her killer did that. If it was a forced labor situation, maybe this was supposed to be a warning to other families who are also being exploited..."

"Hey," Conklin said in an urgent whisper, "right there." She held the beam of her Maglite on a depression in the path, a patch of squishy mud not covered by wood chips.

McDaniel and Vanderwyk crouched down for a closer look. The mud was just slightly firmer than chocolate pudding and about a half an inch deep. The depression Conklin had seen was unmistakably a child's socked footprint. The heel and five toe indentations were obvious. The woven pattern of the sock fabric was not as obvious, but discernible in places.

"That's got to be her, right?" Conklin whispered.

"I'd put money on it," Vanderwyk said, his voice low.

McDaniel took a deep breath and rubbed his hand over his chin, staring along the path and deeper into the woods, eyes narrowing. After a moment, he said, "Let's find some more." He stood and played his light across the path, focusing on the muddy patches.

"Conklin," he said, "radio one of those units working the apartments. Ask him to run crime scene tape across both ends of this trail. I don't want anyone in here until we can document this."

"Yeah, sure thing," she said, excitement covering the sadness that had permeated her voice ever since she had called him this morning. "Should we get the crime scene techs back out here?"

"No, I don't want to pull Sam and Frodo off the material we sent them this morning..." he said, then stopped to think for a second.

"You and Bev work your way up the path looking for additional prints," Vanderwyk said. "I've got an evidence kit in my trunk and a camera. I'll stay with this print until that unit from the apartment detail arrives with the tape. He can guard the print until I get my gear and collect it."

"Works for me," McDaniel said. "Bev?"

"Yeah," she said with a predatory smile, "I'm in."

CHAPTER 10

OVER THE NEXT fifty yards, they found two more distinct prints and a third depression that may or may not have been a footprint. The farther they walked the path, the more it deteriorated into mud, but they found no additional prints. Eventually, they came to a mud patch that spread across the entire path.

"She couldn't have crossed that without leaving a mark," McDaniel said. "So, either she entered the woods from the playground area, walked all the way back here, then turned around and went back out…or she walked to this spot from somewhere deeper in the woods."

"All the prints we found show her walking out of the woods," Conklin said.

"Right…I'm thinking she had to have come from somewhere out there," McDaniel said, nodding toward the dark stand of trees spreading several hundred acres to the north and east. "We'll make our way back to the last track and look for the place where she broke out of the woods onto the path."

It didn't take them long to find it, once they knew what they were looking for. The dirt berm at the path's edge was flattened. Broken twigs and a gnarly strand of blackberry vine had been pulled out of the woods onto the path. Between large ferns, about two feet into the forest, water had filled a hole that was the right size and shape to be another foot-print.

McDaniel and Conklin peered into the trees. Cedars and maples twisted together with dense underbrush, forming a forbidding wall of vegetation. The ground, carpeted in moss and leaves, rose and fell with undulating irregularity.

"Can you track her through that?" Conklin asked.

"I don't know," McDaniel said. "It looks pretty rough. I doubt she could have traveled far through that. But, if we start stomping around in the woods and lose her trail, we might never pick it back up again."

"What about a K-9 unit?" she asked.

"Hmm, we've got some of the best tracking dogs in the state. Usually, they figure out where someone went, but I guess they could probably follow her trail to find out where she started. I'll put a call in to the Dog House and see if they can help us out." McDaniel hit the speed dial and explained their situation to a Bellingham City dispatcher. She assured him she would have a response for him soon.

His phone buzzed moments later. K-9 Officer Joe Gilbert explained that they had two tracking dogs but that both were on loan to the Whatcom County Sheriff. The dogs were currently deployed in a search and rescue operation, looking for a lost hiker on Mount Baker.

"If we locate him before nightfall, I'll bring my dog over and see what we can do," Gilbert said. "Just, whatever you do, don't disturb the trail or Rosco won't be able to pick up her scent."

"Yeah, no, we didn't enter the woods at all, have it all taped off for you," McDaniel assured him. "Any chance you could send one dog now, since you have a second to stay on task there?"

"No go, McDaniel. Your vic is dead. Mine is presumably still alive," Gilbert said. "I'd like to help you, but no way would that fly, especially with all his family scrutinizing our every move. I promise to call you the second I'm free."

"Alright, Joe," McDaniel said. "Thanks, I'll wait for your call."

Vanderwyk returned with his camera and kit. McDaniel took several pictures of each footprint, with and without a little ruler for scale, then marked each of the three prints with yellow flags. Vanderwyk then drew a detailed diagram in his notebook showing the location and orientation of each print as well as the opening in the brush line where the girl had broken out of the woods onto the path.

"So now what?" Conklin asked as they finished.

"We'll wait for Gilbert to call back. We can check city and county records to see if there are any structures out there within walking distance," Vanderwyk said.

"Let me give Spooner a call," McDaniel said. "He and Rourke can run down county records. While we're waiting on them, let's go see how the knock and talks are going, maybe get a peek at the video footage from last night."

CHAPTER 11

THE LAST BUS had stopped at the scene at 11:45 the prior night. Vanderwyk got the number from Whatcom Transit Authority and called the driver at home. He was just sitting down to breakfast when Vanderwyk called. After a moment or two to consider, the driver confirmed that there was certainly not a dead girl at the bus stop at any time during his shift. He also stated that he dropped off one rider at that stop, a guy in a puffy white coat with a hood. He remembered this because he dropped that same guy at that same stop every night.

The manager of the Spring Haven apartment complex invited the detectives into his office and showed them his digital video surveillance system. McDaniel selected the camera labeled Entry Driveway, then cued the footage to start at 11:45. The view showed the main drive coming into the complex as well as the road and the sidewalk beyond. At 11:47, the WTA bus slid across the monitor. A moment or two later, the man in the puffy coat appeared. He crossed the road and entered the complex. From that time until 4:30 the next morning, when Leslie High found the body, seven cars and two pickup trucks drove past the complex. The little girl did not appear in any of the footage.

Vanderwyk made a note describing each vehicle, the time it passed, and the direction of travel in his notebook. He then copied the footage onto a thumb drive.

"We'll need to send an officer up here tonight, see if we can get a name and a statement from puffy coat," McDaniel said. "If nothing else, we nail down the time frame."

"What we really need to be doing is plunging into that forest," Conklin said. "We know that's where she came from. These folks didn't see her. She was never here."

"Gotta wait for the dog," McDaniel said. "Besides, you never know what you don't know until you find out. Canvasing the complex might turn up some leads we weren't expecting."

But, three hours later, no such leads had emerged. They had knocked on every door in each complex and talked to everyone who answered. No one had seen the girl. No one had seen any unusual activity at Stewart Park. At a little after noon, McDaniel released the officers detailed to his investigation, then invited Conklin and Vanderwyk to lunch.

The two detectives rode in McDaniel's car, leaving Vanderwyk's at the scene. Conklin followed in her cruiser. Two miles south of Stewart Park, in the borderland between old-town Bellingham and its more modern sprawl, he pulled to the curb in front of Good Girl, Bad Girl Café and Tattoo.

Vanderwyk groaned. "Really?"

"Don't even start," McDaniel said. "You know you love it."

Good Girl, Bad Girl, or GGBG as the college kids called it, was a narrow, deep space crammed between two larger retail establishments – a vinyl record store on the right and a specialty tea and health food co-op on the left. The café took up the first floor, with a coffee bar, pastry case, and micro-grill for hot sandwiches along one side. Booths, and a few tables, filled the remaining space. At the back, a staircase led to the tattoo parlor on the second floor. As the breakfast and lunch business died down, the tattoo business would pick up.

GGBG had been around as long as McDaniel could remember. It was run by twin sisters, Noreen and Karri, who could have been twenty-five or forty-five, depending on whether the guess was based on appearance or attitude. Both claimed to be fully inked from the neck down. McDaniel had no idea if this claim were true, or any interest in finding out, but he knew they made delicious sandwiches.

He also knew, from personal experience, that tattooing was a long and painful process for the recipient. Folks getting inked tended to talk, a lot, as they had nothing else to take their mind off that buzzing needle. He had invested significant time developing a relationship with the GGBG sisters, and that relationship had provided him with case-solving information on more than one occasion.

He didn't expect them to be able to provide any insight on his current case, but he thought it a good opportunity to introduce the sisters to Conklin. It was also fun watching Vanderwyk walk the tightrope between being fascinated by the painted twins and pretending not to be uncomfortable around them. And he wanted a sandwich.

The three took the booth at the back corner, huddling around McDaniel's laptop and Vanderwyk's pile of notes. A James Blunt song played softly over the café's speakers, but up above, something heavier rumbled through the tattoo parlor. McDaniel thought it might be This Corrosion, by Sisters of Mercy.

He had signaled to Karri as they walked in and, a few minutes later, she delivered three sandwiches – fresh baked ciabatta bread with a layer of grilled vegetables, then smothered in enough meat and sauce to guard against any accidental health benefit from the veggies. She came back with Cokes and individual chip bags, but otherwise left them alone.

Vanderwyk dived into his sandwich, making a concerted effort not to follow Karri with his eyes as she walked away, hips and long black hair swaying. Conklin settled back in her chair, taking in the whole place before getting to her lunch. McDaniel was just about to take his first bite when his cell rang.

"This is McDaniel."

"It's Osen," McDaniel's lieutenant said through his nose on the other end of the phone.

McDaniel could tell by the stress level in Osen's voice that red patches had already formed on the man's cheeks, and his combover was probably sagging under a load of sweat.

"What can I do for you, sir?"

"Well, you can start by explaining to me why I have reporters requesting a statement about a serial killer operating in my city?"

McDaniel was glad he hadn't taken a bite. If he had he would have choked on it. Conklin and Vanderwyk both looked at him. He regained his composure and said, "We're not far enough into this thing to even start speculating about a serial killer. Are you sure the reporter was asking about this case?"

"She said she had information that the 'Creepy Doll Killer' had dumped a body at the bus stop on McCormack Parkway."

"The creepy what?"

"Creepy Doll Killer. Apparently, they're calling him CDK. It's all over social media. I've had two reporters and an official from the college call me about this already," Osen said. "What, exactly, have you gotten into up there?"

McDaniel gave the lieutenant a quick rundown of the case so far, including the photo that had been posted and shared before Leslie High had contacted police. "It sounds like someone is trying to drive traffic to their website, trying to exploit this thing. We don't have any evidence to suggest this is the work of a serial killer."

"That's what I've been putting out." Osen gave an exasperated sigh, then said, "We do not want the media running this, right?"

"Right," McDaniel said.

"Make sure to tell me about any new developments before I see it posted to my niece's Twitter feed," Osen said and hung up.

Vanderwyk and Conklin looked at him over their sandwiches. McDaniel shook his head. "We are now hunting the 'Creepy Doll Killer.' That's CDK, for short."

"The media has it already?" Vanderwyk asked.

"They have something, but they don't know what," McDaniel said. "We need to figure it out before their speculations get too wild."

Vanderwyk nodded and swallowed a bite. "Her trail in the woods, I think that's where we need to focus. We'll need to decide what to do about that. It's going to start getting dark just after four o'clock. If we wait much longer, we won't be able to do anything until tomorrow morning."

McDaniel grumbled under his breath. "Yeah, let me call Gilbert again. If we can't get a dog, we're going to have to try to track her ourselves."

He punched the number. Officer Gilbert answered on the third ring.

"No dice, bro," Gilbert said before McDaniel had said anything. "We haven't found this dude. Even if we found him now, it would be too late by the time I got packed up and back down the hill."

"What about first thing in the morning?"

"Even worse," Gilbert said, sounding truly apologetic. "Too much time will have passed, especially in this rain. We don't like to start a track on sign that's more than two to three hours old. You're already at about twelve hours. That's tough. Add another fifteen or twenty hours and it's a straight no-go. Wish I had better news for you."

"Hey, thanks for trying, Joe. Good luck out there."

"Yeah, man, you too."

McDaniel put the phone down and looked at the other two. "No dog."

"Figures," Vanderwyk said, then took an enormous bite out of his sandwich. "Mmmm…wow, this is really good!" he said around the mouthful.

"This is his favorite restaurant, but I've got to twist his arm to get him in here," McDaniel told Conklin. "He's afraid someone will tell his mom he was at a tattoo parlor."

"If you knew my mom, you'd understand," Vanderwyk said.

"So, what made you break down today?" Conklin asked.

"Moment of weakness," Vanderwyk said, licking his fingers. "One that I am likely to repeat. You ever been in here before?"

"No, but I've had my eye on the place," Conklin said. "Trying to decide if I want another tat."

"Ugh," Vanderwyk said. "Why would you want to put a mark on your body you can't ever get off?"

"It's about commitment, Brent," Conklin said, patting his hand. "You wouldn't understand."

"Oooh, that's cold," McDaniel said.

"What about you, Darren? You ever get ink done here?" Conklin asked.

"Nah, just come here for the sandwiches…"

"Now, wait a minute!" Vanderwyk cut him off. He gave Conklin a sly look. "If you are going to be a detective, Conklin, you need to learn to ask the right questions. He hasn't had ink done *here*. But that's not to say he hasn't had it done somewhere else."

"So, Darren," she said, "let's hear it. You have a heart on your arm that says '*mom*'?"

"No," he said. "I got an octopus."

"Ha, ha! 'An octopus,' he says," Vanderwyk laughed. "You wanna show her your octopus?"

"No, Brent, I am not going to show her my octopus…"

"I'm not sure I want to see it…" Conklin said.

"You don't," McDaniel assured her.

"Then give her the whole story, not just 'it's an octopus,'" Vanderwyk said.

McDaniel looked at Vanderwyk, then at Conklin. She looked like she was wired on caffeine, but likely to crash at any moment. He figured she was sneaking up on twenty hours without sleep. Vanderwyk was in better shape, but a few minutes away from the case would do them all some good.

"Fine, Brent, but you are buying pie when we're done with lunch."

"Oh, none for me," Conklin said.

"And after lunch," McDaniel said to Conklin, "you are off the case. Go home and get some sleep before you fall over."

"Come on," she said, "that's not cool."

"You can barely keep your eyes open as it is," McDaniel said. "And this isn't a debate. I will give you a full update when I see you tomorrow morning. And I promise to request you for any details related to this case. So, I need you to be rested up and ready to go."

"Fine," she said, slouching back into the booth's comfy cushions. "So, what's the big deal about your octopus?"

"Well," McDaniel said, "it covers about a quarter of my body, the whole right side."

"Really?" she said, sitting back up.

"Yeah, when I was a kid, like fifteen, I was in… Well, there was this, uh, fire. I got burned pretty bad. A barrel melted and exploded. It splattered me with melted plastic. You can see a couple small scars here." He pointed to dots on his neck and behind his ear that looked like cigarette burns. "Most of the scars are bigger than that, like dime and quarter size. But they are all nearly perfect circles."

"That's terrible," Conklin said. "That must have really hurt."

"Burned like hell. I spent a while in the hospital. But that's a different story," McDaniel said. "As soon as I turned 18, I started working on covering the scars. It took about three years to complete. The burns were all round holes in my skin. Someone told me it looked like I had been attacked by an octopus, so I had the tattoo artist draw up an octopus. The tentacles twist so the suction cups line up with my burn scars. He's got tentacles going down this leg, and others going up to my shoulder, front and back. His head is my whole right ass cheek."

"Ugliest octopus I ever seen," Vanderwyk put in.

"I bet," Conklin laughed. "You ever regret getting a tattoo? Once you got older?"

"Shit, I regretted it before it was even finished," McDaniel said. "But, I don't regret it now. It proves I was alive, that that person existed, you know. It's part of who I am."

"An octopus is part of who you are?" Vanderwyk chuckled. "That explains a lot."

"Yeah, and you've got your mom to remind you who you are," McDaniel said.

"Ooh-kay, if this is going to devolve into 'your mama' jokes, I guess I don't mind getting kicked off the case," Conklin said. "That is a cool story about the octopus, though."

"Hey, sit tight, you're not off the case until we have some pie," McDaniel said, and waved at Noreen.

As she approached, his phone rang.

"McDaniel," he answered.

"Detective, this is Doctor Haverstock. Are you available to look over the autopsy results?"

"You're done already?" McDaniel asked.

"Don't sound so surprised, detective," Haverstock said. "This isn't Chicago or L.A. We get fewer than a dozen homicides a year, and there is a lot of interest in this one…As there should be."

"How do you mean?" McDaniel asked.

"There are details about this girl I find very distressing. I think you will want this information before you go much further with your investigation."

"Sure, we were just wrapping up out here. I can be there in about ten," McDaniel said. "But can you give me an overview?"

The doctor sighed, then said, "I believe this girl to be the victim of human trafficking."

CHAPTER 12

McDaniel and Vanderwyk stepped off the elevator on the bottom floor of Saint Joseph's Hospital. These halls were quiet and empty, the way the above-ground floors might be at three in the morning. An orderly eyed them over a cart of linens but said nothing. At the end of the hall stood a door with a small square of safety glass as a window, and a simple plaque stating, "Morgue."

Beyond the door, the air carried a heavy chemical smell which covered the subtler odor of death. Dr. Haverstock waited for them, a grim, gray man with a deeply-lined face. Beside him, on the exam table, lay the girl, her tiny frame draped in a white sheet atop the stainless-steel.

"Doctor," McDaniel said.

"Detectives," the doctor nodded to them, the corners of his jaw jutting. It seemed to take an effort for him to say more than that. He thumped a file folder against his palm several times before beginning. Finally, he said, "This, this is a travesty. I have done my work here thoroughly to ensure that you have everything you need to close this case. You must find these people and stop them. I don't want to have to do another examination like this one. Ever."

"Tell us what you have, Doc," Vanderwyk said, with a gravity he rarely displayed. "Darren and I feel the same way."

The doctor looked back and forth between the two of them, then opened his file. "Cause of death, I am ruling as hypothermia. Time of death is almost impossible to nail down due to the fact that she has very little body fat and is generally underdeveloped. The cold temperatures affect onset of lividity and rigor. My best guess is that she died two to four hours before her body was discovered, between midnight and two a.m., though even that is questionable.

"I am placing her age at about twelve years based on her dental development. She appears much younger due to lack of appropriate nutrition. She was likely starved intentionally to maintain a prepubescent appearance." The doctor looked up from his notes, pinning McDaniel with his eyes. "Younger girls bring a higher price in certain markets."

McDaniel felt his teeth grind together. He nodded, then jotted something in his notepad, mainly to break Haverstock's stare. The lunch he had eaten wasn't settling, and he was glad they had been called away before ordering pie.

The doctor swallowed, then continued. "There is no evidence of dental work. The gums have receded, another sign of malnutrition, but, paradoxically, I found traces of candy lodged in her teeth, some sort of gummy or jellybean. I also discovered some newer cavities. These tend to indicate a high sugar diet in recent months.

"She sustained multiple superficial punctures, contusions, and lacerations within a few hours prior to death. These are all consistent with walking barefoot through a forest at night. It looks as if she nearly tore her foot off, trying to pull free from the shackle. But all of these most recent injuries appear to be as a direct result of her escape attempt, rather than having been inflicted on her by another person.

"She does show signs of significant physical abuse, but most of that is older. She has several broken bones that have healed in place, that is, without any medical aid. Most of these are finger or foot bones, though her left arm was broken twice. She also has a minor skull fracture that healed on its own. In short, this girl suffered multiple serious injuries but there is no evidence that she received medical care for any of them.

"Of note, however, these injuries are more than a year old. In fact, other than this," he pointed to a discolored patch between her eyes, "there is no evidence of physical abuse in the last twelve months. This suggests a change in environment. She was moved from a place where physical abuse was common to a place where it was less common.

"She was, however, sexually abused, as recently as three days ago. The evidence suggests that she experienced extensive and sustained sexual violence. There is no way to know for sure when it started, but it has been going on, I would guess, for years."

Vanderwyk said. "The discoloration between her eyes, what can you tell us about that?"

Dr. Haverstock pursed his lips. His brow wrinkled, pulling his wild gray eyebrows together in the center. He sighed, then said, "At some point in the last three to eight days, something damaged the bridge of her nose…without causing any additional bruising elsewhere on her face. I have seen this before in homicide-by-smothering cases. It suggests something soft, like a pillow, was pressed and held firmly over her face. However, in this case, it did not cause death. The coloration of the bruise shows that this happened a few days prior to death.

"I won't have a full report ready for you until tomorrow, but based on my preliminary findings, I feel very strongly that this girl was a victim of human trafficking. If that is the case…when I said I don't want to do another exam like this, I wasn't speaking hypothetically."

McDaniel said, "If she was part of a trafficking ring, there are more victims…."

"Who may still be alive," Vanderwyk said. Then, "The lines she drew on the bus stop wall. You think that means there are six other girls?"

"Good lord," Haverstock muttered.

"We need to find out," McDaniel said. "Fast."

The doctor handed him the file of preliminary notes. "There's additional information in there, and I'll have more for you in the morning. Call me on my personal cell, anytime, really, *any* time if you have questions about any of it."

CHAPTER 13

"WE'RE GOING TO have to try tracking her through the woods," McDaniel said as they drove back to the bus stop from the hospital.

"I was afraid you might say that," Vanderwyk said.

"I just don't know how much farther we can push this until we figure out where she came from."

Vanderwyk nodded, then asked, "What do you think about having our sketch artist draw up a picture to put on the news tonight? Ask for anyone who may have seen her to call in?"

"I don't think we want to go public with this just yet. I don't want her captor to know she's gone, if he doesn't already. The minute he realizes she has escaped, our job becomes a lot more difficult, and dangerous," McDaniel said. "But, that is a good idea about the sketch. We should get it prepared for when we are ready to go to the press."

McDaniel's cell rang and he answered it. "McDaniel."

"Detective, this is Frodo, um, Faraja Odilo, from the lab."

"Frodo, what have you got for me?" he asked.

"Detective," she said, "the clamp that was around the little girl's leg – Dr. Haverstock said there may have been multiple victims. So, I thought that maybe there would be blood from multiple victims on the clamp - If it had been used on other girls. So, I prepared and tested blood samples that I collected from that clamp. What I discovered in the preliminary tests was that there were two different blood types on the clamp."

"Two different girls?" McDaniel asked.

"No, not just that," Frodo continued. "I thought I had made a mistake, so I rechecked. But I, again, got two different blood types. So, then I took the clamp apart and made samples from the older blood. Inside the clamp, where the metal pressed against metal, some old blood was trapped in there. And when I made samples, I found three types of blood."

"You're saying there could be two more victims?"

"No, detective," Frodo continued, "I am saying there are *at least* two more victims. I only tested type, so far. The DNA tests take much longer – weeks. There may be multiple victims with the same blood type. But there cannot be just one victim with three blood types."

"Okay, Frodo, excellent work, thank you."

"Now Sam wants to tell you the thing that he found," Frodo said. "I am passing the phone to him."

"Hello? Detective McDaniel?" Sam sounded even younger over the phone than he looked in person.

"Yes, Sam, this is McDaniel."

"Sir, hey, I was looking at those splinters, the big toothpick-looking things that were in the back of the dress?" The kid sounded as if his nervousness was surpassed only by his excitement. "Anyway, I discovered square-head wood-beetle holes in the splinters – and, well there's also the lead-based paint, of course – but it's the square-head wood-beetle holes that really tell us something."

"Wood-beetles?" McDaniel asked.

"Not just wood-beetles, square-heads. The round-heads are re-infesters, but the square-heads won't touch dead wood, not if they got a choice about it, anyway…"

"Cut to it, Sam," McDaniel said.

"Right, yeah, so here's the deal, the square-heads only lay eggs on live trees. And when it hatches, the little larvae live inside the wood, sometimes for as long as twenty years. Then they burrow out and become beetles. But, nowadays, all the trees that get turned into lumber, part of the process is kiln drying, so the larvae get cooked in the wood and never burrow out. So, the presence of square-head wood-beetle holes means that this lumber was never kiln dried."

"Where can you get lumber that hasn't been kiln dried?" McDaniel asked.

"Well, that's just the thing. You can't. Well, I mean, maybe if you owned a mill or something, but the lumber yards don't sell it that way. But more to the point, they haven't sold it for decades. I mean, this wood is crispy, it's so old. I'm still researching, trying to get you exact dates, but you are definitely looking for a pre-World War II structure. Probably something built in the twenties or earlier."

"Hmm, okay. Do me a favor, would you pass that info on to officers Rourke and Spooner? They are going through county records, looking for an address or physical location."

"Yeah, sure thing."

"And you said it was painted? What color?"

"Just white. I don't know if this tells you anything – it is an exterior grade paint, but it appears to have been applied to an interior surface."

"The exterior may or may not be painted white," McDaniel said.

"Exactly."

"Okay, Sam, Thanks. Remember…"

"To tell Fork and Spoon. Yeah, I got it. I've got them ringing on the other line as we… Hello? Officer F… Rourke?" Sam's voice faded as he moved from one phone's handset to the other. McDaniel's line went dead.

McDaniel pulled the phone away from his ear and gave it a quizzical look before dropping it back into his jacket pocket.

"What was that all about?" Vanderwyk asked.

"We have significant indication of at least two additional victims, and our first victim was kept in a pre-World War II structure that may or may not be painted white."

"What was the other ninety percent of that conversation about?"

"Square-heads."

"Is that another swipe at my heritage?"

"No," McDaniel said, "not unless your mother is a wood-boring beetle."

"I don't even know what that means."

"At least your kind are not re-infesters."

CHAPTER 14

VANDERWYK TURNED OFF Kellogg Road onto McCormack Parkway. Just as they rounded the corner past the Spring Haven Apartments, the news vans came into view. Four of them crowded around the bus stop. WTA workers had replaced the yellow crime-scene tape with red biohazard tape. It fluttered in the breeze and dripped rain. A four-foot orange diamond utility sign stood in front of the booth, proclaiming it closed. A laminated 8 ½ by 11 paper had been taped to the larger sign, telling would-be bus riders where they could find their rerouted bus.

"Oh, boy, it's the circus," Vanderwyk said with all the enthusiasm of a lobotomized sloth.

"I thought the clown craze had died down," McDaniel said.

"So, why did four truckloads of them have to show up at our crime scene?"

McDaniel gave him a grim smile. "The show must go on."

He drove past the news crews, far enough away that they would have to shout if they wanted him to hear them. Far enough away that he could pretend not to hear them if they did. He pulled to the curb next to the play area.

The detectives moved quickly to the trunk to equip themselves. They swapped out their dress shoes for rubber boots and their sport coats for heavy Bellingham Police jackets. Vanderwyk stuffed a backpack with first aid and evidence kits, as well as a small digital camera, a GPS, and flashlights.

"In-coming," McDaniel hissed. "Let's move."

"I'm up," Vanderwyk said, slinging the pack and slamming the trunk. The two made for the taped-off trail-head.

"Detective! Detective!" One of the reporters was sprinting across the field toward them. McDaniel hoped her heel would sink into the soggy earth and dump her on her ass.

No such luck.

She caught up with them just before they reached the trail-head and the two uniformed officers guarding it.

"Detective, Madison Castillo, cable news," she said, thrusting a microphone at Vanderwyk's face. "What can you tell us about the torture and murder of the young girl who was found here this morning?"

"Ma'am," Vanderwyk said, "if you can't find the number for our Public Information Officer, you're not much of an investigative journalist."

"Let it go, Vanderwyk," McDaniel whispered at him.

"How long has your office been investigating the Creepy Doll Killer?"

"The what?" Vanderwyk asked, the expression on his face and the tone of his voice conveyed such indignant contempt that McDaniel thought Ms. Castillo might wilt on the spot.

Again, no such luck, though she did take a step back and stammer a beat before launching her next question. "Is it true that the victim wrote the name of her killer on the wall with her own blood as she lay dying in a dingy, dimly-lit public transit booth?"

That stopped McDaniel in his tracks. Vanderwyk nudged his elbow, urging him toward the yellow tape, but McDaniel spun and faced Miss Castillo.

"'The Creepy Doll Killer?' You are basing your 'news' story on a photo you saw on Instagram this morning, aren't you?" McDaniel noted that this reporter was not accompanied by a camera man. Her microphone bore no network insignia. "'Cable news?' Which network?"

"I'm a freelance reporter…" Her voice was defiant, but the microphone sagged a bit.

"You mean you run a blog," McDaniel cut her off. "Castillo was the name of the woman who posted that picture. What, is she your sister? Cousin?"

"C'mon, man," Vanderwyk urged.

"So, you are admitting that there was a photograph?" Castillo asked, jabbing her microphone deep into McDaniel's personal space.

"How many new followers is this worth? Huh?" McDaniel asked. "You going to get a bunch of likes?"

"Descending like flies..." Vanderwyk said, tilting his chin at the field behind Castillo.

Over her shoulder, four more reporters and associated camera crews hustled across the field toward them. McDaniel clenched his teeth, glared at Castillo for a split-second, then turned and ducked under the tape. The two officers stepped between the detectives and the reporters. One was a black-haired bulldog of a man in his fifties who McDaniel knew well. The other was the Irish officer he had knocked heads with earlier that morning.

"Hey," McDaniel said, "you've been working since midnight shift last night. What're you still doing here?"

"Police work. You might try it some time," Officer Murphy said, then turned to Castillo, who was picking her way through the trees, trying to get around the yellow tape. His pepper spray was in his hand, aimed at her face before McDaniel even processed what he had said. "One more step, Lois, and I'll hose that pretty little smile right off your face."

"Move it," Vanderwyk said, pinching McDaniel's elbow and shoving him onto the trail. He was working hard to suppress a chuckle and sound gruff at the same time. "You don't want to be a witness, and we got work to do."

"'Police work,'" McDaniel muttered, grinning. He turned to the path, letting the back-and-forth clamor between the reporters and the uniforms fade behind them.

The woods swallowed the two detectives. It was only 2:30, but the sun was low, piercing the clouds in little spears of pink-orange light. At this northern longitude, within pissing distance of Canada, if the winds were right, the light would be gone completely within two hours.

McDaniel grabbed the GPS out of Vanderwyk's backpack and powered it up. Satellite reception would be spotty beneath the dense canopy, but if he could get a signal in a clearing or two, it would help guide others in. Worst case scenario, it would ensure he and Vanderwyk could find their way back out of the woods at the end of the day.

"You going to check in with the Lieutenant? Cell service might get weird out there," Vanderwyk said, nodding at the forbidding tangle of trees and underbrush.

The international border posed a difficult challenge for cellular networks. Weather, fluctuations in foliage density due to seasonal changes, solar flares, excessive selfie-postings, and numerous other factors affected the coverage provided by any given cell tower. In most areas, several towers shared the load, so as to provide uninterrupted service. However, to ensure that no customer made an international call without being charged international rates, the cell companies tried to balance coverage precisely *at* the border. They met with limited success in this endeavor. The typical result was cell coverage in the border regions that was excellent one hour and nonexistent the next.

"Right," McDaniel said, hitting speed dial. "Go ahead, I'll follow."

Vanderwyk stepped into the forest at the opening where the little girl had stepped out. He placed his foot a few inches to the right of her footprint. His boot sank into mud past the ankle. When he moved forward and pulled his foot out to take another step, black water seeped into the hole he left. McDaniel followed, struggling to keep his balance on the squishy ground while holding the phone to his ear.

The Lieutenant answered. "This is Osen."

"It's McDaniel."

"What have you got?"

"Sir, Doc Haverstock believes our victim may have escaped from a human trafficking organization. If that is the case, there are likely other victims at that same location. As soon as they realize she's missing, they'll go into high gear to cover their tracks. So, we need to find that location, fast."

"Holy…" Vanderwyk said. "She went under this tree. Look at that."

His voice covered whatever the lieutenant said next. An enormous felled maple lay crosswise in front of them, limbs splayed in all directions, it's trunk suspended about a foot above the earth by thick branches. The girl's passage under the tree was evident by disturbed maple leaves and fir needles.

"Say again, sir," McDaniel said into the phone as Vanderwyk hoisted himself up and over the massive tree trunk.

"What do you need from me?" Osen asked.

McDaniel tried walking around the felled tree, but blackberry brambles blocked his way on either side. "I have two officers going over property records, looking for structures out here. But this forested area crosses out of city limits. Most of it is in the county. We should probably request an agency assist from the Sheriff's Office."

"I'll make the call. Are you heading into the woods now?"

"Yes, sir. We may lose cell service, but we will be up on our handhelds, TAC channel. Hold on, I've got to get over this tree…" He hooked one arm around a thick branch and rolled himself up onto the tree trunk, then rolled off the other side, landing on both feet with something akin to grace. He put the phone back to his ear. "Can you get a couple uniforms in Tahoes and send them to our area? There is a maze of dirt roads out here. Get them in the area, with their eyes open. Stop and identify any vehicles, and be our backup if we find what we're looking for."

"You've already got eight officers guarding your site and running your errands. I have one unit I can send out there, for now. Find something and I'll send more," Osen said.

McDaniel pushed through low shrubs, trying to keep pace. Of the two, McDaniel was in better shape, but Vanderwyk's absurdly long legs gave him the advantage here. To the lieutenant, he said, "One other thing we need from you – see if you can get our Public Information Officer to run interference with the reporters. Make a statement or something. If the people who had this girl chained up haven't noticed her missing, we need to keep them in the dark as long as possible."

"You found a dead girl with a chain on her leg. How am I supposed to spin that?"

"Sir, I'm not the press guy, that's why the chief hired a PIO. I just need you to buy me a bit of time. Maybe say something about CPS looking into an abuse/neglect case…"

Vanderwyk tripped over a branch hidden in the underbrush. He fell to one knee, but caught himself, grabbing the trunk of a young alder.

"…or go with the Creepy Doll Serial Killer thing, I don't care, just obfuscate," McDaniel said, nearly losing his boot as he tried to pull his foot out of a mud hole. "You're a lieutenant, obfuscation should be second nature by now."

Osen was silent long enough for McDaniel to wonder if the call had dropped. Finally, he said, "Your traffickers are going to know she is missing sooner than later. You do your job, do it fast, and let me decide how to do mine."

"Yes, sir," McDaniel said and clicked off. When he looked up, he had no idea where he was. The groomed park path was somewhere behind them, but he could see no sign of it, nor could he hear road noise or the squabbling reporters.

"You doing okay up there?" he asked.

Vanderwyk had stopped a few yards ahead of McDaniel. Loops of blackberry vines formed a concertina-wire-like barrier to his left. To his right, leafless black stalks sprung out of the earth to a height of about five feet then drooped at the top.

"This is nuts, man," he said with his broad smile and a shake of his head. "You ever try tracking someone through a forest before?"

"Can't say that I have."

"I mean, I've been able to follow her this far, but I could just as easily lose her, you know, if the ground firms up or if the under-growth clears too much."

"We'll push it as far as we can. If we can't make it all the way back to her starting point, at least it'll give Rourke and Spooner a better idea where to focus their search," McDaniel said, thinking he should call the two uniforms for an update. "Can you tell where she went from here?"

Vanderwyk hesitated, stepping slowly forward, turning his head from side to side, then backing up again. "Here she is," he said, moving quickly to the right. Fallen stalks marked her passage. "These are stinging nettles. They're all dead now, but if it were summer, there's no way she would have walked through this."

McDaniel had a feeling she would have walked through just about anything, but didn't say so. The nettles would have been a formidable obstacle if they still had leaves. As it was, their brittle bones made following her back-trail easy work.

The nettles thinned as the ground rose. The spongy loam gave way to moss-covered gravel. Here and there, a patch of moss had been overturned, revealing the grit beneath. The detectives fol-lowed these marks to the top of the rise, then started down the other side.

By three-thirty, they had pushed more than a mile into the forest, following broken twigs, scuff marks and best guesses. Twice they had been sidetracked by deer trails, and twice more they *thought* they had been sidetracked by deer trails until patches of soft ground revealed human footprints. Once, her trail had been confirmed for them by a shred of the girl's dress snagged in a bramble thicket.

Her sign led them to a grove of birches growing in a shallow swamp. The smooth, white-barked trees stood like bone fingers thrust toward the sky. One lay half-submerged in the black water, its stump-end gnawed to a point by a beaver.

"You think she walked through that?" Vanderwyk asked, obviously not relishing the idea.

"Take a break," McDaniel said. "Get some water and regroup. I'm going to GPS this spot and make a couple calls."

"Good plan," Vanderwyk said, taking a seat on an old cedar log and unslinging his pack.

McDaniel put in a call to Spooner, relaying their coordinates and checking for any progress with property records. The cell reception threatened to fade out as they talked, forcing Spooner to repeat himself more than once. He informed McDaniel that they had run into a potential problem with the records.

"If a structure was condemned or otherwise deemed no longer inhabitable prior to the 1980 property valuations, the structure doesn't show up on the digitized records. We'll need to pull paper copies from county archives when they open on Monday."

"Look, we've covered almost a mile of difficult terrain, in a relatively straight line," McDaniel said. "I think she must have been guiding off the lights of the city. But I don't expect she could have made it too much farther. Focus your efforts close to our current location. Draw a line from our original coordinates to where we are now. Continue that line for, say…another half-mile. Focus on any properties, or even dirt roads, that touch that line."

"Okay, McDaniel, I got it," Spooner said. "Listen-- " but what he said next was gobbled up in static.

"I'm losing you, say again."

"Sean Hendry," Spooner yelled into his phone.

McDaniel grimaced, pulling the phone from his ear.

"Do you know him?" Spooner asked.

"Yeah, I know him, and don't yell. It's coming through clear now."

"Right, sorry. He's the unit roving in your area," Spooner said. "There are two sheriff's deputies out there with you, too. Jen something and Lindell. You know them?"

"We've met. Are they up on our TAC channel?"

"I can't hear you. Well, I heard the part about the channel. No, their system isn't programmed to link up with TAC. They reprogrammed their--" again, digitized warbles ate his words.

"Okay, listen, send them our coordinates," McDaniel realized he was yelling now, too, and tried to lower his voice. "Tell them to focus on the area I just described to you."

"I'm only…every other word…them…near you…"

The call dropped.

Vanderwyk raised his eyebrows at McDaniel. "Nothing?"

"Not yet," McDaniel said. "Hendry is out here with us, and a couple SO units." He surveyed their position. Beyond the shallow swamp, the ground rose in a steep hill topped with a stand of healthy fir trees. To either side, the swamp continued deep into the woods. "The SOs can't copy our handhelds for some reason. Give Hendry a shout on yours. See if he can raise them on his vehicle radio. I'm going up the ridge to try for better cell reception."

"You're calling your wife, aren't you?" Vanderwyk smiled. "Has she got your balls in her purse or did she let you bring them to work today?"

"You know what, Vanderwyk? I am not comfortable with your level of interest in my balls," McDaniel said, wading into the swamp.

Vanderwyk held up his hands. "Okay, man, you go do what you gotta do. I'll just sit here and work the case."

The black water never made it up over the tops of McDaniel's boots, but it came close a couple times. Deep, soft mud made up the bank on the far side. He spotted the girl's footprints entering the water a few paces to his left. He moved to them, then followed scuff marks up the steep bank to its top. He hoped to find the structure there, but saw only lush firs. Their dense boughs and the thick cloud cover created a premature night.

He checked his phone. It showed two bars of service, one more than he had had down by the swamp. Katheryn answered on the first ring. "Hey, honey," she said. "Are you doing okay?"

"I've been better," he said.

"You want to tell me about it?"

"No," he said, staring down at the boney birches in the black swamp. The last thing he wanted to do was burden her with the story of this young girl's desperate, tragic bid for freedom and her senseless death. "I just wanted to hear your voice, a bit of light in the darkness."

"You make me shine," she said, with total sincerity.

In the background, he heard Robyn yell, "You make me shine, too, Dad!" though she sounded less sincere than her mother.

"Did you catch that?" Katheryn asked, a smile in her voice.

"Yeah," McDaniel said. "Kiss her for me, will you?"

Below, Vanderwyk was looking up at him, questioning. McDaniel nodded and waved for him to come up.

"You won't be home tonight, will you?'

"It will be late…or early tomorrow. I'll try not to wake you."

"I hope you do," she said. Then, "Are you going to catch your bad guy?

"He's as good as booked."

"Is he dangerous?"

"Not to me."

"You be careful, anyway," she said.

Below, Vanderwyk was muttering and grumbling, sloshing through the dark muck. His radio squawked and chirped in his hand.

"I have to go, Kat," McDaniel said. "You keep shining. I'll be with you soon as I can."

"I love you," she said.

"I love you, too." He hung up.

The warmth and comfort of his home and his wife and his daughter filled him. The sharp contrast to his current view and the unfolding scenario – the chasm between the way things were and the way things were supposed to be – fueled his body and heightened his focus. Whatever else had happened to that little girl, she had walked through this swamp, with nothing on her feet but socks. What had she hoped to find? Her parents? Her home? Someone to help her?

What *had* she found? A cold bus bench and a bitter, lonely death.

And him.

He was her last hope for any part of her life to be the way it was supposed to be. All he could offer was justice. He hoped somehow it would ease her suffering or bring her peace. And, if they were fast enough, and clever enough, he might be able to offer help and light and hope to other children held by her captors.

This thought brought a new level of motivation. Not only would the other children be freed, but their rescue would make his victim's death meaningful – noble, even. Seong, *Victory,* He would tell that story over her coffin when she was laid to rest, he decided. Through her death, she could save the others. But only if he and Vanderwyk could get to them in time.

Vanderwyk had just reached this edge of the swamp. McDaniel saw him examining her footprints in the mud. His face was redder than usual and he seemed to be panting. "Did she go up that way?" he asked.

"Yeah, come on up," McDaniel called. He peered into the darkness beneath the fir boughs. His eyes narrowed and the corner of his lip curled. Somewhere nearby his quarry waited. He could almost smell it.

CHAPTER 15

THE GPS WAS useless under the thick canopy, and though the sun had not yet set, night had fallen here. The trees stood well apart from each other and there was almost no underbrush. A thick layer of fir needles carpeted the ground. The detectives left no footprints on this underlayment. The girl had left even fewer. Without any low shrubs for her to break or soggy ground for her to print, the detectives had nothing to go on but the hope that she had maintained her relatively straight course.

Hendry managed to link up with the SO units. He had explained to Vanderwyk that they had identified all the dirt roads within the search radius McDaniel had defined and had divided the roads between the three of them. He expected they would be able to cover the area before sunset at 4:35 that afternoon.

That time came and went. Darkness settled over the forest. Once, McDaniel heard a truck engine near their location, but it sounded more like a rough-and-rowdy diesel than a department-issued Tahoe.

Vanderwyk was grumbling about not bringing any food with them. He had taken the pack off to search for a granola bar he hoped might have been left over from the last time he went for a hike, but came up with only crumbs.

His radio squawked.

"Go for Papa-14," he said into the mic.

"Hey, the SO guy found something," Hendry's voice was clear and crisp. He must be close. "A recently graveled road, not on the map. It's not much, but we've been over everything out here twice. Nothing else looks out of place."

"Ask him about the diesel," McDaniel said.

"Hey, did you guys come across a big diesel truck?"

"Yeah," Hendry said. "We got all their info, but they're clear. Just a couple local kids out four-by-fouring."

"Okay, we've kinda hit a dead end here," Vanderwyk said.

McDaniel glowered at him. Vanderwyk was right, but McDaniel hadn't yet accepted that fact.

"Are you on your way to meet the SO?" Vanderwyk asked.

"Yeah, ten-four," Hendry said.

"Do me a favor, hit your horn every couple of minutes, we'll see if we can walk out to you."

"Yeah, no problem," Hendry said.

McDaniel said, "Tell those SO guys to hang back, watch that drive, don't let anyone out, but don't move in until we get there."

Vanderwyk relayed the message and Hendry acknowledged.

CHAPTER 16

T HE DETECTIVES HEARD Hendry's horn, distant at first, but by its third honk, it was close enough that they heard the crunch of gravel under the Tahoe's tires. Vanderwyk radioed Hendry to wait there. McDaniel tied a length of yellow tape around one of the firs to mark the spot. If this gravel road the sheriff's deputies had found turned out to be a dead-end, he wanted to be able to pick up the search for the girl's trail the following morning. He checked his GPS, but it showed no satellite reception under the thick canopy and was therefore unable to lock in the coordinates. Its compass, however, continued to function. McDaniel took a bearing, then he and Vanderwyk each counted paces as they walked out to Hendry's vehicle.

When they reached the road, the gap in the trees provided enough of a glimpse at the night sky for the GPS to get signal.

McDaniel read the coordinates to Vanderwyk who recorded them, along with the compass bearing and pace count, in his notebook. They then tied a second piece of yellow police tape around a tree trunk before heading for Hendry's Tahoe.

Hendry was an old codger. McDaniel figured he must have been past mandatory retirement age before a retirement age was mandated and had just been grandfathered in. He had excess seniority and a massive give-a-damn deficiency when it came to following orders. If he was out here on this detail it was because he wanted to be here. McDaniel took that as a good sign.

"One of you's going to have to ride in the cage," Hendry called out his window, "and I doubt Vanderwyk will fit back there."

The Tahoes were excellent vehicles in almost every regard. Their only major drawback was, once the security cage had been installed between the front and back seats, they offered less rear-seat legroom than a 1960's Volkswagen Beetle. McDaniel knew Vanderwyk wouldn't fit. He wasn't even sure if he could squeeze his own knees into the back. In the end, he ended up sitting sideways with his feet on the seat and his back to the door. The rear doors did not open from the inside, so Hendry left the window down to allow McDaniel to let himself out when they reached the SO units.

Once they were rolling, Hendry said, "I didn't want to put this out over the air, but there's a bit more to it than the sheriff's boys just happening to stumble across this drive."

"What do you mean?" Vanderwyk asked.

"They got a tip," Hendry said, sounding disgruntled. He probably would have been a bit miffed if the sheriff's units had found the site first on their own. The fact that they had what he considered an unfair advantage really chapped his hide. Then he added the kicker, "From Griggs."

"What?" McDaniel said through the wire mesh separating him from the front seat.

"Yeah, he claims he tried to call you on your cell but couldn't get through," Hendry said. "'Course, I don't carry one, being just a beat cop, and I guess Griggs figures he's too *something* to use a radio, so he called up one of the SO's boys."

"Where did Griggs get the tip?" Vanderwyk asked.

"Damned if I know," Hendry said. "I wasn't the one that got it, remember? Ask the SO guys."

They rounded a gentle curve and stopped. A pair of Sheriff's Department vehicles idled on the side of the dirt road. McDaniel reached out his window and opened his door. It took a bit of twisting and contorting to get his legs out and under him before the rest of his body left the vehicle. It reminded him of some of the more inventive poses he had seen his wife doing in her morning yoga sessions. By the time he made it out, the rest of the team had assembled in a semicircle around him.

"Jen Meyer," the Deputy introduced herself. "This is Deputy Lindell."

"Tell me about this tip you guys got," Vanderwyk said, as McDaniel unfolded himself and stood.

Deputy Meyer explained, "Your man, Griggs, told us he had a stack of files from an old investigation, something about squatters cooking meth in an abandoned house out here. Your Lieutenant Osen asked us to check all the homes in this wooded area, but according to Griggs, a bunch of the older buildings are no longer listed in the digitized files. He provided a list of properties that may have unlisted structures. We checked out all the locations he gave us, except we had a bit of trouble finding this one."

"We drove right past it three times before we saw what we were looking for," Deputy Lindell said. "Once we found it, we parked around the bend back here, so we'd be out of sight of the gate, but we haven't seen anyone in the area. Come on up and take a look." He waved them forward.

Another fifteen yards up the road, on the right side, Lindell pointed to the brush at the side of the road and said, "See?"

McDaniel did not see, not at first. It was full dark, but enough ambient light from the city reflected off the low cloud cover that a road or gravel drive should be easy to spot. All he could see here was a young fir tree on its side. He flicked on his pocket flashlight. Metal glinted through the fir's boughs.

He looked to Vanderwyk and raised his eyebrows. Together they approached the tree. The horizontal tree was attached to a steel I-beam that acted as a gate, blocking a graveled drive and shielding it from view. Unless one knew where to look, a person could easily drive right by it without seeing the gate.

"This is interesting," Vanderwyk said.

"So is this," McDaniel said, lifting the industrial-grade lock securing the gate closed.

"I've got bolt cutters in the back of my truck," Lindell said.

"Better to walk it if it's not too far," McDaniel said. "It's hard to sneak up on someone when you've got your headlights going." He killed his light and hopped over the gate. "Radio this in, Hendry. Let them know where we're at."

"Hold up," Vanderwyk said over Hendry's grumbling, "Check this out." He laid his copy of the map over the fence's metal bar. "This is an approximation of the last place we had her trail, based on our compass reading and pace count." He pointed to an X on the map, where they had tied the yellow tape. "And these are the three GPS readings you took. He pointed to three more Xs, the last being the birch swamp. He drew a line connecting the Xs. It pointed almost directly to their current location.

McDaniel consulted his GPS. It confirmed Vanderwyk's map work. "We are about one-point-two miles from our start point. All our previous points run nearly a straight line. There's only about a five-degree deviation to get us here."

"You think this is it?" Meyer asked.

"Let's go find out," McDaniel said.

CHAPTER 17

THE NEW GRAVEL ran about twenty-five yards, then stopped. The team had jogged up the drive, lights out. In the darkness, at the end of the drive, they saw nothing but tall firs on all sides.

"There's nothing here," somebody whispered.

After waiting a moment for their eyes to adjust, a darker mass seemed to emerge from the trees to their right, as if an empty hole stood there instead of tree trunks. Blackberry vines obscured the shape, camouflaging it, and one corner of the structure slouched low enough that its form was not readily recognizable.

McDaniel hissed through his teeth, catching the others' attention, then moved toward the dark heap of a house. It appeared as if it had been abandoned for several decades. Now that he knew what it was, McDaniel could pick out some of its features, even in the dark.

A small front porch sagged in its center, just below a dark rectangle that suggested a door. Broken windows glinted at either side of the porch. Above, the roofline gathered itself into a sad peak. To the right side, the chimney cut a thick, stubby silhouette against the night sky. To the left, a half-collapsed carport roof broke up the house's recognizably square lines. Alders and young firs grew so close to the house that their branches rested against its walls, cutting clean little arcs through the mold on the siding.

One thing McDaniel did not see was a doorknob. As he approached, he understood why. The dark rectangle he saw was not actually the front door. It was a door-sized sheet of plywood that had been screwed over the door. He was not yet ready to turn on his flashlight, so it was hard to tell for certain, but he thought the windows had been boarded up as well, from the inside. There was a flatness to the dark behind their broken panes that did not suggest depth.

"Over here," Vanderwyk whispered.

McDaniel checked his team. The deputies had taken up security positions at either side of the clearing. Hendry stood by, three or four steps behind and to his left. Vanderwyk had moved around to the side of the house. McDaniel could just make out his shadow against the backdrop of trees.

"There's a path here," he said.

McDaniel and Hendry followed him around the side of the house. The path looked well worn, almost seeming to glow in the ambient light. Three concrete steps led up to another porch, this one smaller than the front. A screen door with a sprung frame hung by one hinge. No plywood covered this entrance. McDaniel could make out the glimmer of a doorknob.

Vanderwyk climbed the concrete stairs. McDaniel and Hendry flanked him on the ground and whistled for the deputies to move in closer. Vanderwyk drew his H&K .40, stood to the side of the door, gently slipped his left hand around the knob, and twisted. It didn't budge. He gave the door a shove. It didn't so much as wiggle in its jam.

"Locked," he said in a low voice.

McDaniel moved up and, covering his flashlight lens with his hand, directed a tiny beam of light on the doorknob. It's bright brass and silver keyhole showed not the slightest hint of wear or corrosion. Just above the knob, an equally new looking deadbolt had been installed. The door, itself, was a steel slab, a security door, though the wooden jamb had not been replaced.

"That didn't come with the house," Vanderwyk whispered.

"Shit," McDaniel whispered. "We're going to need a warrant to get in there."

"Exigent circumstances," Hendry said. "You think there's kids endangered, you can bust down just about any door that stands in your way."

"We need more," McDaniel said. "We *think* she came from here, but… Hendry, you called in our twenty, right?"

"Sure," he said.

"Based on that tip from Griggs? Run back to your truck, try to get Griggs, or Rourke, or whoever you can reach, ask them to start pulling any available info on this property. Who owns it? Has it changed hands recently? Is the house officially condemned? Any permits for restorations? And then see if you can get someone to start working up a warrant for us."

"I ain't running," Hendry said. But he turned and moved briskly back toward the gravel drive.

McDaniel moved toward the back of the house. The trampled path ended at the side door, so McDaniel had to stomp down the tall grass, thistles, and sticker bushes. His heavy rubber boots served him well, and he was thankful for them, but they had worn blisters into his heels and every step was a stab of pain.

He had to squeeze between two maple trees to get into the back-yard. Judging by their thickness, the trees had to be at least fifteen years old. They grew right up alongside the house's foundation. If anyone had been living in the house, or even doing regular main-tenance, those trees would not have been allowed to grow there. The roots would destroy the foundation – probably already had – and the leaves would clog the gutters and ruin the roof. This house had deteriorated past the point of restoration.

The fringes of the city were dotted with these abandoned homes left to sink back into the earth. McDaniel's real estate agent referred to a house like this as a "scraper," because the only thing you could do with them was to get a bulldozer, scrape it down to bare earth, and start over. There was no good reason to install an expensive new security door on a scraper.

"He might be right," Vanderwyk said, right behind him. How he squeezed between those trees, McDaniel couldn't guess. "That brand-new door on this collapsing heap has all kinds of creepy written all over it."

"Yeah, I'm thinking so, but still, we can't for sure tie our girl to this place," McDaniel said. "Maybe the owner just wants to keep the squatters out. For liability reasons."

"Then why not just board it up, like the front door?"

McDaniel had been thinking the same thing. He was also thinking that the place looked abandoned. If a trafficking group had been using this as their base of operations and had moved out after their girl escaped, he didn't want to taint any evidence they may recover here by going in without a warrant or just cause.

The back looked as decrepit and forlorn as the front had. There was no back door. All three windows had been boarded up. The electrical meter had been smashed so long ago that weeds had grown out of it. The power cable sloped down from its connection at the roof and disappeared under the overgrowth.

An odd glimmer caught McDaniel's eye while he was examining the failed electrical system. Nearly obscured by weeds, a four-by-six post stuck about three feet out of the ground near the foundation. A new electrical meter and circuit box were mounted on the post.

"What is up with that?" Vanderwyk asked.

"It's a temporary," McDaniel said. "Only supposed to be used to get construction underway. But it looks like this one has been here a while." Moss coated the top arc of the glass and a vine of some sort crept up and over the post.

As McDaniel and Vanderwyk moved in for a closer look, something else caught their eyes – the very thing they had come here looking for.

A pair of cellar doors lay flat in the weeds and tall grass of the darkened back yard. A fat brass padlock secured a chain through the steel handles of the cellar doors. The doors were painted white, which could have been a coincidence. Thousands of doors in Whatcom County were painted white. But, unlike those other doors, these were secured by a chain that matched the one they found around their victim's ankle.

And a shred of white cotton fabric dangled from the splintery wood. It matched their victim's dress.

CHAPTER 18

"**K**ICK IT IN," McDaniel said, staring at the lacy bit of cotton, tangled and limp between the wooden splinters. "Kick it in!"

He heard Vanderwyk on his handheld, passing the find on to their team back at the station, requesting backup and forensics, informing of their intent to perform a welfare check on any occupants who may be held against their will inside the house.

The best way to avoid a gun battle or, worse yet, a hostage situation, would be to take the occupants by surprise and in overwhelming force. Ideally, the three police officers and two SO deputies would pile through the door and spread out in under a second. Unfortunately, the tiny raised porch only allowed one officer on the door at a time.

Vanderwyk volunteered to run point. Being the largest, he had the best chance of knocking the door open on the first try. But neither Vanderwyk nor McDaniel had brought their body armor on their long trek through the woods. Both SO units were wearing vests, and Lindell guaranteed he, too, could get through the door with a single kick.

The two SO units would go through the door first, followed by the detectives. Hendry admitted that he had a vest "somewhere" in his truck, but couldn't be bothered to go get it. McDaniel asked him to hang back and watch the exterior in case anyone tried to escape after they had made entry.

"How they going to get out?" Hendry asked. "Everything's boarded up." But he moved toward the front of the property, disappearing into the darkness at the edge of the driveway where he had a plain view of the front and far side of the house.

All their preparations turned out to be unnecessary. Lindell kicked the door and, true to promise, it flew open, splintering the frame. Not only did the deadbolt tear through its jamb, but all three hinges also ripped out of the old door frame. Rather than swinging inward, the steel door fell flat like a giant domino, sending up plumes of dust and fluttering papers.

All four officers charged through the opening, yelling, "Police," or "Sheriff's Department." McDaniel and Lindell went to the right, Vanderwyk and Meyer to the left. Their high-intensity LED flashlights dispelled the darkness with startling suddenness. What the light revealed chilled McDaniel to his marrow and froze him in place. Every one of his burn scars, the suction cups on his octopus tattoo, tingled, tightened.

"Bomb," he whispered, backing away.

"Bomb!" Lindell bellowed. "Fall back, fall back!"

They had entered what had once been the kitchen. No appliances remained, though stains on the wall indicated where a refrigerator and range once stood. The brown-and-orange-patterned wallpaper hung in shreds from cracked and buckled plaster. At the head of a hall leading deeper into the house waited a line of gas cans, seven or eight five-gallon cans, as well as a larger blue diesel can. A wad of duct tape secured a road flare, a nine-volt battery, and a disposable cell phone to the side of the cans.

The fuel did not ignite, but in his eye of memory, McDaniel saw a bright red can explode, spraying molten plastic and fire. That explosion, so many years ago, still burned bright in his consciousness. His skin blushed with the heat, a convergence of memory and premonition. Then he felt Vanderwyk dragging him backwards, out the door they had entered.

He spun on his heel and followed.

CHAPTER 19

"HOLY SHIT!" LINDELL barked. The team had run halfway up the drive before stopping to regroup. "Holy shit! Did you see that shit? He's got sixty gallons of gas set to blow. I can't believe we didn't set it off."

"It's cell phone activated," McDaniel said.

"There could be other triggers as well," Vanderwyk said.

McDaniel knew he was right, but he doubted whoever had set it up had triggered the only working entry door. The wear on the path seemed to indicate that someone had been visiting this property regularly, had been coming and going through that door several times a week. The chained cellar doors and the boarded up front door showed no such wear.

"We need to go back in," he said.

"Fuck that," Lindell laughed.

At that moment, Hendry hustled into the circle. "What in the hell is going on? You all piled in there, then you turned tail and ran like you just found the devil himself."

"We need to go back," McDaniel said again. "We kicked that door in on the belief that there may be endangered children being held in there against their will. We still have just as much evidence to support that belief. The only difference now is, if there are children in there, we know *for sure* that they are endangered."

"Will someone tell me what the fuck is going on?" Hendry shouted.

"There's a big, fat bomb…" Meyer started.

"Incendiary device," Vanderwyk interrupted. "There's forty or fifty gallons of gasoline and diesel, set to ignite if that cell phone rings. It's not intended to explode, just start one hell of a blaze."

"To destroy any evidence," Meyer mused.

"What about the children you all were here looking for? You just left them in there?" Hendry asked. Then he turned around and started walking back to the dilapidated house. "Don't worry, I'll go get 'em."

"Whoa, hold up," McDaniel said, "I'm coming, too."

"Wait!" Vanderwyk shouted. "You can't go in there. Department policy is clear about this. That's a bomb, or incendiary or whatever you want to call it. The point is, you have no way to know what is going to set that thing off. You can't go in there until Hazardous Devices clears it."

"Look," Lindell said, "you crossed into the county about a quarter-mile ago, so this is my jurisdiction, and our policy is just as clear as yours when it comes to IEDs. No one enters the structure until it has been cleared."

"You and your policy can rot," Hendry said.

"What about the cellar door?" McDaniel said. "We know she got out that way without setting off that device…"

"Yeah, but she got out without opening those doors beyond the reach of that chain," Vanderwyk said. "You think you can squeeze through there?"

"It doesn't matter where or how she got out," Lindell said, "nobody's going *in,* through any door, until the bomb squad gives you the go-ahead."

"What are you going to say if that thing goes off and we start hearing children screaming in the basement, or in cages in those back rooms? Huh?" McDaniel demanded. "And you're wrong about jurisdiction, this is still in city limits…"

"It doesn't matter. The policy is the same on either side of the line," Vanderwyk said.

"Look, man," McDaniel said, "the door is already open and it didn't blow. It's a cell-triggered device. I'm going in to look for additional victims…

"The hell you are!" Lindell roared.

"I'll be in and out in under five minutes, then we'll have all night to sit and wait for the bomb squad. I just need to know that there's no one else in there," McDaniel said.

Vanderwyk ran his hand over the close-cropped wool on his scalp. "Okay, fine, let's do this."

"No fucking way," Lindell said, moving to intercept the two.

Hendry blocked him. "You need to brush up on your map skills, hoss. This is inside city limits by at least ten yards. You want to make yourself useful? Go call the bomb squad, get them rolling this way."

"This is bullshit, man," he said as he reached for his radio to make the call.

"Not here!" Hendry said. "Get your ass back, away from the device. You two, give me your radios and cell phones, and anything else you got that might emit a signal."

The detectives handed over their equipment. The chance of a stray radio signal detonating a cellular activated device was slim, but it was an easy precaution so they took it. They had been so focused on the argument with Lindell that they had not noticed Meyer missing. She returned now and handed a pry bar to McDaniel.

"You might need this," she said. "And I already called your bomb squad. They said it would be about forty-five minutes. Your Lieutenant Osen told me to tell you, in no uncertain terms, not to go into the structure until they have arrived and authorized you to enter, but I forgot to tell you that part until after you came back out."

"Right," McDaniel said, smiling. "Thank you."

CHAPTER 20

TWO ARCHWAYS OPENED off the kitchen. One led to a dining area, the other to a hallway. The detectives cleared the dining room first. It, too, was completely empty. Even the light fixture had been removed. The flooring planks had separated, and a few had curled where rain had leaked through the roof. Vanderwyk put his light on the ceiling, revealing cracked and sagging plaster. The whole interior stunk of decay and rat droppings.

At the far end of the dining room, another archway opened onto a living room and entry area. Here they saw the inside of the front door. It had had a window in the top half, but most of the glass lay in shards on the wooden floor. They could see the inside of the plywood that now covered the opening, as well as the boards covering both windows. An orange and green floral patterned couch moldered against one wall. A console style television with a busted tube lined another. Otherwise, the room was empty.

They moved back through the kitchen, giving the bomb a wide berth. McDaniel noted eight five-gallon gasoline cans and a ten-gallon diesel can. He reached for his cell, intending to snap a picture of the device for future reference, then remembered he had left it with Hendry. He hoped the bomb squad would be able to preserve most of it for their investigation.

A bomb tells a great deal about its maker. From McDaniel's quick inspection, he determined two things about the device – it seemed very simple, and it was overkill on a grand scale. So far, the house looked about as deserted and empty as it was possible for a house to be. He wondered what was so important, so incriminating as to require that much fire to ensure its destruction.

The second archway off the kitchen opened onto a hallway which had been carpeted, unfortunately. The carpet had been yellowish-green once, but had faded to a dusty, undistinguishable gray-beige. The first room off the hall they encountered had once been a bathroom. The sink and tub were gone, but the toilet remained, a monument to the era of monkey-puke-green porcelain.

McDaniel tried the door across the hall from the bathroom but it was locked. On closer inspection, he found its doorknob and deadbolt to be an exact match with those on the door Lindell had kicked in.

"This is what we're looking for," McDaniel whispered.

Vanderwyk nodded, then thrust his chin down the hall, toward the last two open doors. McDaniel agreed. A quick sweep of the rest of the house would guarantee no surprises. The rooms at the end of the hall had been bedrooms. They moved quickly into and out of both, finding them as sad and empty as the rest of the house.

Back at the locked door, McDaniel asked, "You ready?" He slid the pry bar deep into the gap between door and jamb, just below the deadbolt.

"Do it," Vanderwyk whispered.

McDaniel cranked the bar back, springing the handle lock. Then he let up on the pressure and reset the bar deeper into the gap. He got ready to crank it again, but Vanderwyk said, "I got this." He put his foot on the bar and pushed it forward with all his weight. The jamb splintered and the door popped open, revealing newly constructed sheetrock walls and a sturdy staircase descending into darkness.

On the sheetrock to the right, McDaniel saw a light switch. He flipped it, realizing a moment too late that the switch might have been a trigger, detonating the gas cans. His breath caught, but nothing exploded. Light bulbs glowed on the stairway and in the cellar below. He turned and raised an eyebrow at Vanderwyk.

"Come on, man," Vanderwyk said, "We're supposed to be in and out, quick like." But McDaniel could tell his partner was eager to investigate.

They descended into the well-lit space, noticing a heavy pine scent. At the base of the stairs, a concrete slab extended across about one-third of the basement. The concrete was from the modern era. McDaniel guessed it to be less than ten years old. The remainder of the floor was dirt.

Atop the slab, a room had been framed in with fresh yellow two-by-fours. The lumber was exposed on this side of the walls, but the inside had been finished with drywall. A door stood in the wall, sporting the same knob and deadbolt as the other two doors they had thus far encountered. A section of drywall between a pair of two-by-fours had been busted out. A mangled umbrella lay in the dirt, just outside the hole.

McDaniel felt his pulse quicken as he left the stairs to investigate the newly-constructed room. He took a quick glance around the cellar to ensure there were no other rooms or areas. At the opposite end, he saw the concrete stairs that led up to the flat double cellar doors. His eyes traced the path from there back to the hole in the drywall. He saw what he expected to see, tiny footprints. Her socks had picked up sheetrock dust which she had transferred to the dark cellar dirt as she walked across it.

He pointed this out to Vanderwyk, then knelt at the edge of the concrete to examine the print more closely. Something about the dirt floor disturbed him, but he couldn't immediately identify it.

"In and out, man," Vanderwyk urged. "We'll come back for a better look when we are not at risk of being burned alive." With that, he lifted his foot and kicked the locked door. It swung open, tearing the frame out of its opening.

The two stood, bewildered, for several seconds. This room in the cellar was so incongruent with the rest of the house that its existence down here jarred both detectives. The first thing they saw was a princess style canopy bed in the center of the room. Pink plastic posts held gossamer silk scarfs and curtains above and around the bed. White lace and pink satin pillows covered the bed itself. The walls were painted with glitter paint, a cheery yellow, with giant, amateur murals of unicorns and castles on the largest wall.

Two plastic pink chairs lay overturned on the lush pink carpet. A plastic tea set was scattered about the floor, as were several stuffed animals. A huge dollhouse, bolted to one wall, was occupied by several scale-appropriate dolls. Beside it, a television played Dora the Explorer, the volume muted.

On the opposite wall was a kitchenette area with sink, mini-fridge and microwave. The appliances were bolted to the wall, the bolts painted with pink glitter paint. Beside the kitchenette, a door stood open, revealing a tiny cubicle with a toilet and sink.

Vanderwyk let out a breath he had been holding since he last spoke. "No one here, buddy, lets…"

"Look," McDaniel whispered, "near the floor to the left of the bed." He pointed to a hole in the wall. Concrete dust powdered the carpet beneath it.

"Shhhh…shit," Vanderwyk breathed.

"She was here," McDaniel said. "God only knows how long. And all that gasoline up there…"

Vanderwyk's breath caught in his throat.

"…she was the secret, the evidence, that bomb was built to conceal. Whoever did this…" McDaniel's vision rippled, as if obscured by a heat mirage. He again felt the scars on his back tingle as if the skin had its own memories and was now replaying them. He heard the screams in his head – his screams and the others, the ones who didn't survive – and smelled, again, the choking fumes and suffocating, nauseating black smoke.

"As good as booked," Vanderwyk said. McDaniel heard the urgency and possibly worry in his partner's voice. "But there is no one here now and we need to get the fuck out. I think you're right, that thing up there was supposed to have gone off already." He was pulling McDaniel up the stairs now. "No idea why it hasn't yet, but I sure as hell don't want to be down here when it does."

CHAPTER 21

TWENTY-FOUR MINUTES AFTER McDaniel and Vanderwyk emerged from the rotting house, the Bellingham Police Department's Hazardous Devices Unit arrived on scene. Hendry used bolt cutters to remove a padlock from the gate so that the bomb squad would have easy access to the front of the house. Two marked units had also arrived, Bev Conklin and an officer named Gavin Honcoop, though at the moment there was nothing for any of them to do but wait. McDaniel had thanked Deputy Meyer and released her. Deputy Lindell had left on his own as soon as Hendry had shown him that they were, in fact, still within city limits.

The Hazardous Devices Unit's large white panel truck stopped at the gate but did not enter the driveway. Detective Jennings stepped out of the back and introduced himself. He was a detective with the Family Crimes Unit, most of the time, but tonight he was the lead bomb tech. The Bellingham Police Department encountered a few dozen events each year that required the bomb squad. Four officers were specially trained as bomb techs and responded to these events as needed, but they spent most of their time assigned to regular police duties.

"What can you tell me about the device?" Jennings asked.

"It looks real simple," McDaniel said, "a cell phone, a road flare, a battery and a whole lot of gas."

"We didn't see any wires coming off the device connecting it to anything else," Vanderwyk added, "though we didn't spend much time inspecting it."

"This is related to that dead girl you picked up this morning?" Jennings asked.

"It appears she was held here," McDaniel said. "There is a room in the basement...a great deal of evidence down there I would like to preserve."

Jennings pursed his lips and nodded. "I think I can accommodate you. So long as the cell is the only trigger, it should be pretty simple. You ever see the robot in action?"

"Not on a real call, just parking lot demos," McDaniel said. The robot was a favorite PR tool which the department liked to display for Boy Scout troops or middle school field trips. "Will it be able to get up the porch steps?"

"Oh, yeah," Jennings said. "This puppy can climb stairs no problem. Only thing is, it is painfully slow. You're looking at probably half an hour to get it down the driveway, and another half hour to get it up the stairs and through the door. From there, another ten minutes or so to line up the shot."

"Line up the shot? What is your plan?" Vanderwyk asked.

"I've got this little C4 charge and a quart of water," Jennings said. "It's basically the world's coolest Super Soaker. There is a chamber on the front of the bot that holds the C4. In front of that is a specially-shaped canister to hold the water. When I detonate the charge, it fires the water through a nozzle in a razor-thin fan at several thousand p.s.i. If I line it up just right, it'll slice the cell phone off the rest of the device without damaging any of it.

"Then I'll use the robot's arm to drag each can out, one at a time, allowing us to verify that there are no other triggers and ensure everyone's safety. I'm guessing you're looking at two to three hours before anyone is cleared to enter. You may want to go grab a bite to eat while you wait."

McDaniel knew that last line was a subtle hint. The robot was remote-controlled via a joystick and monitor inside the Hazardous Devices Unit's truck. Everyone on site would want to be crowded around the operator, looking over his shoulder, commenting on everything from his driving skills to comparisons with the Mars Rover. Jennings's own crew knew better, but he still had to order them out on occasion. With fellow detectives, he tried to be more tactful.

"Both our rides are back at the bus stop," Vanderwyk said. "But don't worry, we'll wait out here. Won't bug you too much."

Jennings gave him a grateful nod, then went to work. It was, indeed, a grueling study in patience. Jennings had parked his command center on the dirt road, just around the corner from the driveway. This put nearly one-hundred yards, and several thick trees, between himself and the device. He insisted that everyone else remain even farther away, in case the cans contained something more volatile than gasoline.

The distance ensured their safety, but the robot's slow, deliberate movements made McDaniel want to pull his hair out. Its treads clinked along over the gravel like game show music, making each minute feel like five. Once it had turned the corner from the road to the driveway, it disappeared behind the trees, but the clinking continued, fading slowly as it made its way toward the device.

More and more officers continued to arrive, mainly out of curiosity. McDaniel directed a few to block off the dirt road far enough away in either direction that no one would be able to get a view of their operation. Vanderwyk sent two of the officers to retrieve his and McDaniel's vehicles. Sheriff's Department vehicles cruised by every so often to check their progress. Lieutenant Osen called twice, probably wanting updates, but the spotty cell reception limited those conversations. The rain fell. The night darkened. Somewhere around the bend, the little robot tread kept clinking along.

CHAPTER 22

McDANIEL WAS STARING into the trees, walking through the case in his mind, stacking up and evaluating each of the pieces they had so far discovered, when Vanderwyk interrupted his thoughts.

"You froze up back there," he said, "when you first saw those gas cans."

"What's that?" McDaniel asked.

"I said, you kind of lost it for a minute when you saw the gas cans," he said. "Never seen you lose your cool before. Is everything alright?"

"Sure. It's just, me and fire don't get along too well," McDaniel said, leaning against the side of a Tahoe.

Vanderwyk moved up next to him, staring through the trees in the direction of the robot's plodding sounds. "You know, I've heard you tell the story about your octopus tattoo at least twenty times. Never in the time that I've known you have you ever said how you ended up in that fire."

"And you think I ought to tell you now?" McDaniel asked.

"I don't know, man. It's no big deal, but it ain't like we've got anything else to do at the moment," Vanderwyk said. "To tell you the truth, I'm feeling a little shaken. I could use some distraction. This whole thing is just disturbing on a level I don't ever want to get used to, if you know what I mean."

McDaniel knew. Whoever built that room in the basement had gone to the extreme, trying to create a dream-come-true fairy-tale atmosphere, a place no child would ever want to leave. The little girl who had been trapped there nearly pulled her foot off and then walked through a cold, sodden hell to escape it.

He thought of his own childhood, how his mundane existence had been turned into an adventure he could only have dreamt of, and then how that dream ended in the terror and pain that had defined his teen years and branded his skin to this very day.

"When I was a kid, we lived in Alaska. My dad was a fisher-man," McDaniel began, still facing the trees. "He owned a 45-foot fishing trawler. Had a crew of guys. I don't remember how many. He inherited the boat from his dad, and I guess he expected to pass it on to me. He ran that boat all up and down the coast between Alaska and here.

"Sometime in the 80s there was a downturn, environmental regulations, international trade deals, natural cycles, who knows? Whatever. But the fish just weren't there anymore. He had to let some of the crew go, then more of the crew. The bills kept piling up. It got to the point of either losing the house or losing the boat. Dad kept the boat. Said that's where the money came from."

"I bet your mom was thrilled about that," Vanderwyk said.

"Oh, you have no idea," McDaniel said. "That whole month was a nonstop scream fest. But in the end, the bank took the house. We moved onto the boat, me and my four siblings, with Mom and Dad. We crewed the boat. Dad listed us as 'home-schooled,' and taught us how to run a failing fishing business into the ground."

Vanderwyk chuckled, but it was an uneasy sound, nothing like his typical good humor.

"We worked at the mercy of the tides," McDaniel continued, "which meant up at all hours, sleep when you can. Dad was determined to get back on his feet. Mom was a basket case even then, even before the fire. I think losing the house just broke her. I was the oldest, 17. I had two brothers, 16 and 14, and twin sisters who were 12. Nobody slept, ever, or at least that's how it seemed.

"Dad started drinking instead of eating, said it was the only way to keep his fingers warm. And he kept mom drunk as much as possible, too. She was easier to manage when she was comatose. When we ran out of money for booze, dad started distilling it himself, to keep in supply. Nobody really believed this was going to have a happy ending." McDaniel paused for a moment, listening to the drone of the robot and steeling himself for the rest of the story.

"October 3rd, 1987, at about three o'clock in the morning, we were anchored out in the Salish Sea. I was racked out on my bunk.

I have no idea what I had been doing earlier, but I was sleeping pretty hard just then. I woke to my little brother punching me in the arm and side, screaming about a fire. I ran up on the deck and the whole boat was ablaze, fire just everywhere. We had gasoline onboard for some of the equipment. We had diesel engines and plenty of spare diesel stored here and there. Before we lost everything, dad had always been extremely careful with that stuff, a place for everything and everything in its place, you know, but by 1987, he just didn't care anymore, I guess."

Two fire engines rolled past, looking for a wide spot in the road to set up. Vanderwyk didn't seem to notice.

"I remember several occasions he'd be pouring gasoline into a pump with one hand and lighting his cigarette with the other, almost like he was daring fate. I don't know what started the fire, not really for sure, but I think it was inevitable."

McDaniel's throat tried to close on him. He cleared it and kept talking.

"There was a dinghy at the back of the boat. My brother and I started heading for it, but I saw my mom and sisters up near the bow. I told Mike to get the dinghy in the water. I was going to get them. I'd be right back.

"Mom and June, my sister, were wrapping up my other sister, Amy, in this huge life jacket, and trying to get her to wake up. We didn't know it then, but Amy was already dead. Just as I reached her, one of those plastic gas cans ruptured, sprayed me with molten plastic all up my right side. I was just wearing boxer shorts at the time, so it got me good.

"The pain was beyond words, I just screamed and grabbed onto my mom. She was holding onto the twins. The four of us went into the water then. We could hear Mike yelling for us, but we never did see him. I guess he didn't make it to the dinghy. It was still attached to the boat when the divers went down looking for the rest of my family."

He cleared his throat again, and shuddered as he did. He could see Vanderwyk pretending not to notice that, either.

"A fire like that can be seen for miles. Help came quick, quick enough to rescue Mom and June and me. But the seas were high, and a storm was coming in. Coast Guard did everything they could, but none of the bodies were recovered, none except Amy. Mom scattered her ashes over the place where it happened.

"After that, we had a little bit of insurance money, and I made money anywhere I could. Mom never recovered. We had always lived in Alaska, but the night of the fire, we had been here," McDaniel pointed west, over the trees, in the general direction of Bellingham Bay.

"There wasn't much left for us in Alaska. Dad burned all his bridges long before he burned his boat, and probably for the same reasons, I guess. We hung around here, seems like forever, hoping somehow somebody would find…" McDaniel flapped his hand, dismissing the idea that they had actually expected to find anything.

"Anyway, mom ended up renting an apartment in town. She lived there with June and me, for a while, but one day she was just gone. She left a note saying she was going to look for Mike and

John, my brothers. We searched for her. Filed a missing person report and all.

"There was a detective back then named Spivey. He found she had taken a cab to the marina. A small runabout was stolen that same day. About a week later it was found washed up out on Lopez island. He left the case open, I think to protect me, but I had known from the moment I saw that note what she had done."

When McDaniel finished speaking, the night fell silent. It took Vanderwyk some time to respond.

"Good God, man," he finally said. "Next time I ask you for a story to cheer me up, just tell me to go fuck myself."

"You asked," McDaniel said, finally turning from the trees to look at his partner. "Do you know what entropy is?"

"Entropy, sure, the tendency of all ordered systems to move toward disorder, unless acted upon by an outside force," Vanderwyk said. "It's the shit's fatal attraction to the fan."

McDaniel said, "It is the infinite black void that will eventually swallow up all light and all heat and everything good about being alive. It is a law of our existence." He stared at his partner. Vanderwyk looked as if he wished his partner would return his gaze to the trees. "The only thing holding it at bay is that 'outside force,' the artists and poets and teachers, the architects and builders of order. The lovers and the givers dispelling the darkness, sharing their warmth so our lives can be worth living one more day.

"And then you have this," McDaniel turned and lifted his head in the direction of the house. The robot's monotonous clinking could no longer be heard. "Some motherfucker went to great lengths and expense – spent considerable creative energy – to *welcome* the darkness, to draw it right down out of the void and plant it in my backyard.

"I never wanted to be a cop," McDaniel said, "never wanted to spend my life with one foot in the abyss. But order and beauty are precious. And terribly fragile. And the chaos is voracious. Someone has to stand between the two. Someone has to protect the light."

Vanderwyk looked at him for a long time, seeming unsure how to respond. Eventually he said, "Are you sure you're okay?"

"I'm just getting my head straight," McDaniel said, "reminding myself why I'm out here instead of home with my family."

"Well," Vanderwyk said, "for what it's worth, I'm glad you chose to be a cop, but you would have made one hell of a philosopher."

"And you'd have made a fine plumber," McDaniel said, turning back to the trees. "You've definitely got the ass crack for it."

"*Aaand*, he's back," Vanderwyk said, chuckling, his ubiquitous smile returning.

"We're going to get this guy, Brent," McDaniel said, "and every other motherfucker who was involved with this. We're going to get them and put them in a hole so deep, God won't even know where they went."

"As good as booked," Vanderwyk said.

CHAPTER 23

McDANIEL AND VANDERWYK didn't speak again for several minutes. One of the officers who had gone to retrieve their vehicles returned, parking McDaniel's unmarked Crown Vic just outside the yellow crime-scene tape. McDaniel swapped out his rubber boots for a pair of running shoes from his trunk. A few moments later, the other officer arrived in Vanderwyk's vehicle. He had stopped to pick up a half dozen cheeseburgers from Five Guys, which he now distributed among the detectives and officers.

McDaniel pushed a twenty into the officer's palm and took a burger back to his car. He pulled out his laptop and started typing notes for the reports he would have to write in the morning. It was 7:30. Haverstock, Rourke, Spooner, Frodo, and Sam would all have gone home by now. Their reports appeared in his email in-box. Another email waited for him. It was from Katheryn. He clicked that one first.

> *Hey,*
>
> *Just wanted to know if I should make a plate for you or if you'll be having dinner out. I tried to call, but it went straight to voice mail.*
>
> *Love you*

He looked at his cell. It showed no service. A grin lifted one side of his mouth. His brows lowered and moved together. The incendiary device had failed, he realized, because the trigger was a cell phone and service here was unreliable. He suddenly had a much clearer picture of the person who had done this. His quarry was asymmetrically intelligent. Brilliant in some regards, dangerously naive in others.

As he thought these things, the stillness of the woods was broken by a dull *pop*. McDaniel lifted his eyes to the direction of the house. All was dark. The echoes faded and the stillness returned. He held his breath. It would take a minute for the robot to realign its camera so that Jennings could evaluate the effectiveness of his shot.

No orange fireball burst into the night sky, which was a good sign, but if the shot had not separated the trigger from the fuel, Jennings would have to roll the bot all the way back to his command vehicle, reload it, and start over from scratch. McDaniel didn't know if he could handle another two hours of waiting.

He typed a quick reply to his wife, letting her know he had eaten and would likely be out of cell range the rest of the night. Then he started going through the other emails. His laptop connected to a high-gain antenna on the Crown Vic, allowing him connectivity in many areas out of range of other networks. Even so, the connection was tenuous. McDaniel clicked the link to download Frodo's report, then watched the progress bar creep across the screen at a pace to rival the bomb squad's robot.

Before the file opened, his police radio crackled, transmitting Jennings' voice, "All units, be advised; the shot was good. The device appears to be disarmed. I will now begin removing the fuel."

McDaniel relaxed a little. He still had a long wait ahead of him, but the removal was progressing. He thought about asking Jennings to have the robot retrieve the phone first so he could attempt to process it, but that would require him driving the bot all the way down the driveway and back again, delaying the rest of the investigation by at least forty-five minutes.

Instead, he unwrapped the aluminum foil from his burger and took a bite, waiting for Frodo's file to open. As soon as it did, he clicked Doctor Haverstock's file to get it loading while he read over Frodo's. The work she and Sam had done earlier in the day had been invaluable to his investigation so far, verifying Doctor Haverstock's fear that there had been multiple victims and sending McDaniel's search in the right direction.

The full report he received now, however, didn't seem to contain much else of use. The dress his victim, Seong, had been wearing had been sold at Target stores. Thousands had been sold throughout Washington State the previous spring. The socks were even more anonymous. The chain and clamp could have been purchased at just about any hardware store in the state.

They had sent a few bits of the litter they had collected to a lab for analysis, but the results wouldn't be back for weeks, and even then, they didn't expect it would turn out to be connected to the case. Frodo had sent her various blood samples from the clamp out for analysis but, that too would take weeks to return. She had conducted a second set of tests on those blood samples and had confirmed that there were three separate blood types present on the clamp.

Where are the other girls? he wondered. He realized he had assumed the others were girls, but he felt comfortable with that assumption, at least until the lab results were available. He supposed it was possible that the girl's captor may have worn the manacle himself as part of some depraved fetish – though, McDaniel doubted it would have fit on an adult's ankle.

Even if her captor had worn the manacle, at least one other person had worn it as well. And not just worn it, but worn it and struggled against it to the point of shedding blood. He felt quite sure that there were other victims, victims who had been chained in that basement. Where were they now?

The doctor's full report was a gut-wrenching catalog of injuries, malnutrition, and abuse. He had found no evidence of surgical or dental procedures that may have helped identify the girl or her origins. He found evidence of prolonged sexual abuse, but it appeared that the most recent assault had occurred three to four days prior to her death. He was unable to locate any foreign DNA on her body. The superficial injuries to her extremities contained foreign matter – mud, thorns, splinters – that corresponded to her long trek through the forest.

He ruled the cause of death hypothermia and the manner of death homicide. The official report was followed by a personal note reiterating Haverstock's prior assertion that the girl was likely just one of several victims, and a less than subtle admonition that McDaniel pursue this case with that in view. The admonition wasn't necessary, but McDaniel appreciated it none the less.

He had saved Spooner and Rourke's report for last. The other two reports solidified what was already known but did not add much. He hoped the two officers' work might contain information that would drive the case forward. Seong's body, and items found with it had been their only evidence up to this point. With the discovery of this house, that had all changed. The property was now the key to progress in the case.

Spooner and Rourke had followed up on the information Griggs had passed to the sheriff's deputies. The property was owned by a Canadian man named Geoff Bamford. He had purchased all the property from Spring Creek to the county line in 1998, intending to develop it. Market fluctuations and Bellingham politics never aligned to make the project feasible, and in 2013, Bamford had suffered a debilitating stroke. He had been in a care facility since that time. His heirs, two sons and a daughter, would inherit the property upon Bamford's death, but at this time it was still held in his name.

Rourke had contacted U. S. Customs in Blaine, Washington and ascertained that neither Mr. Bamford nor his wife or adult children had entered the United States at any time in the last two years. He had further learned, from talking with Mrs. Bamford, that both of their sons lived in Toronto, over twenty-six hundred miles away. She further stated that she had actually forgotten about that property – Geoff had bought so many – and that her accountants handled all of that ever since her husband's stroke.

Rourke noted that the property records had been amended four years ago. He could not say for certain what had been changed, because he would not be able to access the original records until Monday morning when the archives reopened, but he thought he had a pretty good guess. The current record indicated that the property contained no structures, condemned or otherwise. Griggs had shown Rourke photocopies of the 1976 records which indicated four houses on various parcels of the property.

McDaniel knew it was possible that if the structures were uninhabitable, they could have been removed from the records to reduce property tax liability, but typically there would be some sort of notation indicating that a structure had been there at one time. The current records had no such notations.

McDaniel sat back in his seat and looked in the direction of the house. He couldn't see it from where he was parked, outside the cordoned-off area. In his rearview, he noticed Vanderwyk in his own vehicle, lit by the glow of his own laptop. He considered the person or people who they now sought.

Deputy Lindell had told McDaniel that he and Meyer checked the other three locations Griggs had suggested. Two of them had smooth concrete slabs that had been foundations for small homes, but the homes themselves were long gone. The third showed no evidence of ever having been built upon, though Griggs's records indicated it had been a residence. This probably meant a mobile home had once been there but had either been hauled away or had been destroyed by fire or some other agent of entropy.

Whoever had held this girl captive here had had the records altered in a manner that would hide the existence of this structure, and he had done it in such a way that if it ever was discovered, it would appear to be a simple and innocuous clerical error.

"Cunning little bastard," McDaniel said. He looked again in his rearview and this time saw Vanderwyk looking up at him. The burger still sat on a paper towel in McDaniel's lap. He had forgotten about it after that first bite. It was cold now, but he was hungry. He peeled the foil wrapper back a bit more and took another bite. The cold, soggy lump was delicious, but only because he had burned twice as many calories on his hike as he had eaten all day.

Jennings came over the radio, informing them that he was now working on removing the final fuel can. McDaniel acknowledged Jennings' transmission. The Crown Vic's dash clock read 9:47. He crammed the rest of the cold cheeseburger into his mouth and stepped out into the night.

CHAPTER 24

"**Y**OU READ ALL the reports?" Vanderwyk asked as they stood outside the Hazardous Devices Unit command vehicle watching the robot drag the final fuel can away from the house. This one was blue rather than red, a diesel can.

"I did," McDaniel said. He was itching to get inside the house again, but the sight of the fuel cans sent a cold shudder through him. His own history aside, the cans showed that CDK had thought this through, very carefully, systematically, logically. But with utter disregard for his captive.

The diesel disturbed McDaniel the most. Any arsonist could buy a can of gas and torch a building. Criminals often douse a crime scene in gasoline to destroy evidence. It burns bright and hot and fast. By contrast, diesel burns slowly, but it burns for a very long time. A gasoline fire can burn itself out before engulfing a structure. With 40 gallons, McDaniel didn't think that would have happened here, but CDK wasn't taking any chances. He had thought it all the way through, adding diesel to the mix to ensure that if something went wrong, the house and the girl in it would be completely incinerated.

"Not much to go on, huh?" Vanderwyk said, referring to the reports.

"I think we've got a hook in him," McDaniel said, "maybe two or three. Just got to reel him in."

"What are you thinking? Someone in county records?"

"Or someone who knew how to manipulate those records. What I'm thinking is somebody paid the power bill," McDaniel said. "Somebody paid to have this gravel delivered. There are only four or five gravel companies who operate out here. They'll have records. I think we are going to find prints in there," he nodded to the house, "and more DNA evidence than you want to think about. My guess is he felt safe inside there. That's the point of the bomb, and the hidden gate, and all the rest."

"Are we going to push through all that tonight?" Vanderwyk asked.

McDaniel heard the weariness in his voice. He was beginning to feel exhausted as well. The long hours, the long soggy hike in bad boots, and the emotional strain of the day weighed heavy on them both. But this was tempered by the anticipation of what they might find within, and the knowledge that CDK would almost certainly bolt the second he realized they were on to him.

"There's too much here to process it all tonight," McDaniel said. "Even if we were fresh, I'd be leery of starting something like this after dark. We'll do a preliminary walkthrough with the forensics team, pick up the big pieces and then call it a night. First thing tomorrow morning, we see what they came up with and start running down leads."

Jennings exited the command vehicle, his eyes bloodshot from staring into the tiny black and white screen for the last three hours. He blew out a relieved breath. "I've isolated the fuel cans. Assuming they contain nothing other than gasoline and diesel, you'll have nothing to worry about. The problem is, I can't make that assumption."

He pulled a cigarette out of his breast pocket and lit it up. "You could have anything in there. Really. Back in the 70s and 80s, soap companies put phosphorus in laundry detergent – makes your whites look whiter. These Bevis and Butthead anarchist types would distill the phosphorus out, then dissolve that and Styrofoam into the gasoline. The idea was, it would form this goop that would stick to a victim and continue burning even if submerged in water. Real nasty stuff, in theory. Not sure if it actually ever worked in real life. Could be a mixture like that."

McDaniel needed to steer his mind away from that vision, one that felt too much like memory. He said, "Or, it could be ANFO,"

"It could be ANFO," Jennings nodded. "In which case, it could kill everyone in a thousand-foot radius." He took a long drag on the cigarette. "So, we're not taking any chances. After my smoke break, I'll have the bot pop the tops off and collect a sample from each can. Then it'll bring them back here for analysis."

McDaniel fought to keep the frustration from his face and voice. "Analysis? How long is that going to take?"

Jennings fixed him with a long stare. He took a final, deep drag on the cigarette and flicked the butt to the side. It hissed out on the soggy duff. "You know protocol in a case like this?"

McDaniel did.

"Burn it in place," Jennings said. "I could have been back home an hour ago, paperwork and everything finished."

McDaniel put his hands up to shoulder height, palms out.

"I'm a detective, too, remember," Jennings said, "when I'm not out here playing with this thing. I understand the evidentiary value of that place. And I understand the importance of getting to it quickly. I'm cutting all the corners I can. By analysis, I mean the bot is going to light a sample from each can. As long as it burns, and doesn't do anything else, you're golden…but you're going to be waiting for another hour, at least." He paused, then smiled, "Draw up search warrants or something."

CHAPTER 25

McDANIEL WASN'T UPSET at Jennings. He had no desire to get blown up again, but the warrant crack annoyed him. Warrants had already been the next item on McDaniel's to-do list, but now as he compiled the forms, he felt like he was following Jennings' orders rather than running his own case. It was stupid and petty, he knew that. He also knew the feeling was more from his exhaustion and triggered memories than anything the bomb tech had said, but that didn't do much to alleviate the annoyance.

The initial search of the house could be justified under exigent circumstances, and Jennings' activities were allowable under the same principle, but any further evidence gathering required a warrant. McDaniel had already written up a warrant to search the house. He had emailed it to the judge, who had emailed the confirmation back to him. The house was fair game as soon as Jennings gave the word, but several more warrants were still needed.

McDaniel didn't expect to find much evidence on the burner phone that had been intended to detonate the fuel, but under a recent Supreme Court ruling, he would need a separate warrant just to look at the thing. He would need another warrant to access call records for that phone, once he learned who the provider was. Another would be needed to access electrical bills from Puget Sound Energy. He would not necessarily need a warrant to review the records of gravel companies who may have done the work on the driveway, if they were willing to cooperate, but he added it to the list, anyway – one less time-suck out of the way.

He divided these between himself and Vanderwyk, and they went to work. He left the subject's name blank on the warrants for the gravel company and the phone records. He'd fill these in when and if he got that information. As an afterthought, he also drew up a warrant for an unnamed company, whoever had installed the gate, on the off chance they could find a sign or plaque indicating who had installed it.

Every ten to fifteen minutes, a bright orange flame rose and danced above the driveway, about halfway between the command vehicle and the house. McDaniel counted these flashes, making little tick marks at the top of his yellow notepad. There had been eight fuel cans. As soon as he saw the eighth flash, he would know it was time to move again.

As the seventh flash popped, someone tapped on his driver's side window. He rolled it down and Bev Conklin extended a large Starbucks cup through the opening.

"Sargent Stevenson sent a couple rookies to get coffees. I saved one for you," she said, smiling. "It's just coffee, none of that fancy stuff you hate."

McDaniel felt his spirits lifting just looking at the cup. "Thanks, Bev," he said. Then, "You back already? Didn't you just get off shift a couple hours ago?"

"Well, it was a little longer than that, but not much," she said. "I slept fast."

McDaniel took a long, slow sip of the coffee. It was strong, and very thick, but had cooled a bit on its journey from the pot to him.

"This is where they kept her?" Conklin asked. The levity had left her voice.

"Yeah," McDaniel said.

"And you didn't find the other victims?"

"If there are other victims, they're not here. Did your sergeant tell you what we did find in there?"

Conklin nodded. "These people, they're real monsters. Do you have anything on them yet?"

McDaniel smiled, not a friendly smile. "I don't think it's a group. This is starting to feel more like a single individual. And, yeah, we've got a few things on him. When Jennings gives us the go-ahead to enter the house, I think we'll have a whole lot more."

As if on cue, the radio chirped. Jennings announced, "All units, be advised, the scene is clear to enter…but stay sharp. Keep eyes out for a secondary device, trip wires or what have yous."

"Well, that doesn't give me a warm fuzzy," Conklin said.

Vanderwyk had walked up behind Conklin. Before McDaniel could answer her, Vanderwyk spoke his line for him, "If you want a warm fuzzy, go stick your teddy bear in the microwave."

"Oh, you've heard that one, too?" Conklin asked.

"If you've spent more than a few days in the car with this guy, you've heard that one," Vanderwyk said.

The three watched the white CSI van roll slowly up the drive to the house. If it had been Sam and Frodo, the detectives would have wanted to brief them before they started collecting evidence. But Sam and Frodo worked the 8:00 a.m. to 4:00 p.m. shift, remaining on-call until 8:00 p.m. The night shift CSI's were Gable and Sanders. Unlike Sam and Frodo, Gable and Sanders were sworn officers, not lab techs. Both were long-time veterans, though neither were quite as old as Hendry. They tended to resent input from the detectives and were good enough at their work that their self-sufficiency was justified.

Behind their backs, they were known as Gobble and Sandwich. The two men despised each other, and pretty much everyone else on the force. But they worked well together and though their personalities left much to be desired, their work never did.

Both had the seniority to have made detective years ahead of McDaniel and Vanderwyk, but discipline problems had assured that would never happen. James Gable A.K.A. Jimmy Gobble's issues stemmed from his lack of self-control around pastries. The rank and file believed he had dedicated his career to single-handedly keeping the cop-and-doughnut meme alive. His excess weight required his uniforms to be special ordered and had caused him to fail his yearly physical more than once.

Sanders was a different story. He had caught a bullet in his hip in the early 90s, while detailed to a Tacoma-based gang task force, and still walked with a hitch on that side. He had been out of service almost a year after getting shot. Since his return, he gravitated towards assignments away from the front line. No one blamed him for this, but it clearly weighed on his self-esteem. He compensated by over achieving in whatever duty he had been assigned, and by being a complete ass to anyone junior to himself.

As far as public knowledge went, Sanders was a good, hard-working, honest cop. Whatever he had done to land himself on the permanent shit list was a mystery, and thus the subject of much gossip. The most common theory was that he had been caught in an inappropriate relationship with a captain's daughter, or a hot young cadet.

McDaniel figured that was just titillating tabloid-style bullshit, backed by as much fact as the latest bigfoot sighting. When he looked at Sanders, he saw an emptiness behind the man's eyes. McDaniel couldn't grasp what exactly that look signified, but it made him think of a man just biding his time while waiting his turn to board the next train to hell.

"You going to go talk to them?" Conklin asked.

"Nah," McDaniel said. "It's their scene now. We'll let them take charge. Once they have established dominance and leadership, they'll call me and I'll tell them what to do."

CHAPTER 26

McDaniel GOT THE call from Officer Sanders over his vehicle radio. McDaniel could hear the irritation in his voice. Sanders was the type who liked to hoard information, only sharing when absolutely necessary, and then only with as few people as possible. Using the radio sent his words to every cop in the city. McDaniel assumed he had tried his cell at least twice before resorting to his handheld.

"Papa-30, copy echo-103, I'm starting on this bedroom in the basement, gonna work my way out from there. You see anything in here you want me to focus on?"

"You don't need me to tell you how to work a scene," McDaniel said into the mic. He winked at Vanderwyk. Vanderwyk rolled his eyes at Conklin. She smiled at them both.

"Ten-four," Sanders replied, "Y'all can come on up whenever you're done doing whatever you're doing out there."

"You done sitting on your ass for hours on end?" Vanderwyk asked McDaniel.

"Just about," he said. Then into the mic, he said, "Echo-103, Papa-30, there was a cell phone detonator on the fuel tanks. Bomb tech shot it off. I'd sure like to have a look at that if you can locate it."

"Gonna need a warrant to look at that," Sanders said.

"I don't need a warrant for you to drop it in a baggie for me," McDaniel replied.

Sanders keyed his radio but said nothing.

"You want to go take another look?" McDaniel asked Vanderwyk.

"I think we'd better," Vanderwyk said.

Conklin said something about helping Jennings pack up his equipment. McDaniel figured it was her way of avoiding Sanders and Gable. He didn't blame her.

The first thing McDaniel noticed upon reentering the house was the smell of gasoline. The water cannon, which had cut the trigger off the device, had also sliced through one of the hard-plastic cans. Several ounces of gasoline had leaked out, spreading across the cracked linoleum. His skin crawled. His scars tingled.

Vanderwyk was watching him, no doubt worried. McDaniel refocused his awareness, forcing himself to return his attention to the task at hand. He now had a better understanding of the house's layout. The incendiary device had been positioned directly above the girl's room in the basement.

Whatever other atrocities CDK had perpetrated against this girl, Seong, it was the gasoline and diesel that shook McDaniel.

He tried, but could not manage to keep the image out of his mind. CDK had chained this girl to the wall, had sexually abused her, and had left her all alone in the basement of a rotting house in the middle of a secluded forest. He was probably the only other person she had seen, possibly for years.

But, in addition to all that, as a last-ditch fail-safe measure, he had constructed a device designed specifically to incinerate her the moment he feared she might be discovered. If the device had been activated, liquid fire would have poured through the ceiling of the pink room, drenching and engulfing the little girl chained to the wall. McDaniel could feel the black void of entropy sucking at the fabric of his existence, as if this house sat not in a dark wood, but on the precipice of the abyss.

His reverie was broken by a fat-fingered, gloved hand thrusting a plastic evidence bag in his face. Gable said nothing, just grunted. The bag contained the disposable cell phone. A ribbon of duct tape still clung to it, as did a few beads of water, but the phone was intact. The old-school LCD screen indicated a full battery and one bar of service. McDaniel assumed that one bar was more about marketing, and perhaps optimism, than an actual indication of available cell service. He took the bag and thanked Gable.

"I'm working this floor, Sanders's got the basement," Gable said. "The charger for that thing's still in the wall. I'll collect it after I get a few more photos."

"Thanks," McDaniel said, "No rush on the charger. This is what I need for now."

Gable did not respond. He returned to snapping photos. McDaniel took a quick visual tour. Gable and Sanders had set up four mobile halogen spotlights, showing the house to be even more dilapidated than it had appeared on his first encounter. A worn path was now obvious, leading from the exterior door directly to the basement door. The accumulated dust and mold of several decades had been worn away, leaving an almost clean trail across the yellow linoleum.

It did not appear as if CDK had spent any time on this floor other than to pass through it. The main level was camouflage and nothing else. Once Gable had documented and collected what remained of the bomb, there would not likely be anything else for him to do on the main floor. McDaniel knew that the peculiar division of labor was because Gable was worried that either the basement stairs couldn't handle his weight, or his knees couldn't handle the stairs.

Vanderwyk was already through the basement door. McDaniel followed. As soon as he began to descend, he again noticed the strong pine odor. It was unnatural and sharp, like a cleaning solution or air freshener rather than an actual pine tree. He felt his stomach sink just a little.

"You smell that?" Vanderwyk said, from the bottom of the stairs.

"Yeah," McDaniel said. He scanned the basement again from his elevated position on the stairs. There were no rooms other than the one in which the girl had been held. An old oil furnace and a new electric water heater stood against the wall to the side. Beyond that, the basement was empty. "Maybe he was just trying to cover the mildew stench."

"Maybe," Vanderwyk said, but his eyes said he didn't believe it.

Sanders's voice came through the hole in the sheetrock wall. "You two stay out there," he said. "And don't ask me for anything. I'm going to be here 'till tomorrow just processing this one damn room." After a pause, he added, "I fucking hate pink."

"Hey, Sanders," McDaniel called, "did they brief you on this before they sent you out?"

"Yeah. Little girl chained to the wall in a basement."

"We suspect multiple victims," Vanderwyk said. "Anything you could tell us about that would be helpful."

Sanders poked his head through the hole and looked at Vanderwyk. "Multiple vics? No one mentioned that. All I see in here is one bed, one shitter, one bolt-hole in the wall where her chain used to be. This looks like single occupancy to me."

"We thought we'd find more children," McDaniel said. "Now we're thinking maybe there were others before her."

Sanders let out a long, exasperated sigh. "I'll get fingerprints going first. Those process a hell of a lot faster than DNA...but I'm sure I'll find plenty of that as well. You two wait out there. And tell that fat fuck not to even bother coming down. Not enough room in here for his fat ass." With that, Sanders disappeared back into the pink room.

Vanderwyk and McDaniel exchanged a look. Fingerprints could be a slam dunk or completely useless. CDK had an obvious level of sophistication, being able to get power hooked up to a property that he didn't own was a trick, getting all trace of the house he did not own removed from county records was also no easy feat.

But, setting up a cellphone-triggered bomb in an area that had only intermittent cell service suggested that CDK hadn't been involved in something like this before. These things led McDaniel to believe that CDK was not likely a regular guest at the county lockup. It was very possible that he had never been arrested. If that were the case, even if they found his prints here, they would have nothing to match them with.

On the other hand, if there had been multiple victims, if other girls had been held here before Seong, it was possible that *they* had left prints behind. Any prints small enough to be made by a child could be compared against Seong's. McDaniel's mind flitted back to the message scrawled in the dusty glass of the bus stop, the little girl's name, and six lines, hash marks. Had there been six other girls? Had Seong met them? Perhaps, if he could find those other girls, they could tell him about Seong, where she came from, how she came to be in this basement, who had put her here.

"Look, man," Vanderwyk said, "it's going to be several hours before these guys have anything for us to run with. What do you say we knock off for the night, get three or four hours of sleep and hit it fresh in the a.m.?"

It sounded good to McDaniel. The warrants they would need to start their day tomorrow had been approved. The judge had signed a warrant for PSE. He had agreed to sign the phone warrants once McDaniel had the phone in hand and could name the carrier. It would be a busy morning. The two would pursue the warrants separately. They only needed one to come through with an address or a name. Once a clear target was identified, both men would chase that lead down together.

McDaniel wanted to solidify the images in his mind before he left, let them float around inside his head for the few hours of sleep he might catch before returning to the case in the morning. He walked along the edge of the concrete slab, looking into the hole that had been busted out of the sheetrock. He let his eyes travel to the tattered and twisted umbrella that lay on the dirt part of the basement's floor. It was covered in white powder, drywall dust, apparently. It was clear that the umbrella had been instrumental in Seong's escape.

McDaniel wondered about the chain. He had seen the bolt-hole on his first sweep of this room while waiting for the bomb tech. He would have liked to examine it more closely, try to understand how she escaped from that part of her dungeon, but getting a peek at the bolt-hole was not worth pissing off Sanders, nor was it worth slowing down the investigation to indulge in a shouting match over crime scene jurisdiction. He would wait until tomorrow to investigate that.

He let the scenario play through his mind. Somehow Seong had freed the chain from the bolt-hole. She had had no luck opening the door, so she turned her attention to the wall. Most people, when they see a wall, take its finality for granted. Few would think to attack it as a means of escape. McDaniel wondered what had inspired Seong to break through the sheetrock.

Knocking a hole in the wall had scattered bits of sheetrock, and great quantities of white dust, all over the floor on both sides of the hole. Seong had tracked this dust, leaving a clear trail of tiny white footprints in the dark soil. The prints showed that she had walked along the edge of the concrete slab, paralleling the wall, until that wall met the exterior concrete wall. She then walked along that wall until she came to the stairs.

McDaniel only wondered about this for a second. The reason she had walked along the walls, rather than making a beeline for the concrete stairs, was because she couldn't see those stairs. McDaniel had turned the light on, during his first sweep of the basement. Assuming CDK had not been here since she escaped, then the light would have been off when she exited the pink room. He wanted to see it as she would have.

Overhead, the floor joists creaked and groaned as Gable moved around the main floor. Thin lines of dust drifted down from above. McDaniel keyed his handheld radio, "Echo-104, Papa-30, Hey, can you turn out the lights down here? The switch is at the top of the stairs."

Gable didn't answer, but a few seconds later the basement fell into darkness. Pinkish light spilled through the hole in the wall, splashing across the dirt floor. McDaniel's stomach seemed to both tighten and sink at the same time.

He again crouched down by the hole, making himself approximately the same height that Seong would have been. The oblique lighting and McDaniel's new angle of view accentuated the dirt floor's subtle contours. He let out a shuddering breath. The distinct, oblong mounds, in this odd lighting, appeared as six parallel lines. The six lines, McDaniel now understood, that Seong had drawn on the bus stop wall bore witness of these six graves.

CDK's other victims.

CHAPTER 27

A T 1:57 A.M. McDaniel lost the coin toss. At 1:59 a.m. he called Lieutenant Osen. The man answered on the fourteenth ring, but when he did finally pick up he sounded fully awake. McDaniel guessed the first ring woke him and he had spent the intervening time exercising his voice to give the impression he had been awake and awaiting the call.

"This is Osen."

"Sir, it's McDaniel."

"You found something?"

"Sir, we found what we believe to be six bodies buried in the cellar."

There was a long pause. McDaniel could almost hear Osen's mind processing the information, visualizing the consequences and repercussions tumbling one after another like dominoes. Finally, Osen said, "Believe to be?"

"Sanders ran the Ground Penetrating Radar. Gable is on his way back with gas probes, so we'll have those results shortly, but the GPR indicated results consistent with buried human remains."

Osen let out a long, disgruntled sigh. Bellingham was known for several things - its art, culture, history, and progressive ideology to name a few. No one in city governance wanted *serial killer* to be added to that list. But even more importantly, Bellingham was a college town, home of Western Washington University. A killer on the loose could lead to all sorts of problems on campus, from students leaving the school to attend elsewhere, to staged hoaxes, to protest marches that turned to riots.

Eventually, Osen said, "You know I'm going to have to turn this over to State, right?"

"Give them the scene, but keep Vanderwyk and me on lead," McDaniel said.

"They have the manpower to handle something like that," Osen continued.

"Sir, whoever this guy is, he's already hustling to cover his tracks. He's got to be," McDaniel said. "We are up to speed. We've got some solid leads. If you dump this on State…"

"I'm not 'dumping' it anywhere!" Osen said, his voice a harsh whisper. "You are telling me we have six bodies buried in the basement of a condemned house in the middle of nowhere, and I'm telling you we don't have the resources to handle a scene like that."

"If you turn this over to the State Patrol, their team of forensic anthropologists will spend two weeks picking that place apart," McDaniel said. "We'll get every piece of the puzzle, except for the who-done-it piece. Because he'll be long gone by this time tomorrow."

"McDaniel, it's two o'clock in the damn morning," Osen said, "I'm not pulling you off this, not yet anyway. I'm not making *any* decisions right now. Are Gable and Sanders working the scene?"

"Yes, sir,"

"Good," Osen sighed again. "Tell them their work will be turned over to the State's team, so make it look professional. Tell them to document the GPR and gas probe results, but beyond that, stay clear of the graves. Get the rest of the scene processed as they normally would."

"Okay, sir," McDaniel said, "I got it."

"You and Vanderwyk wrap up whatever you're doing and get out of there. I will set up a conference with the State investigators tomorrow morning. I want you two fresh and ready to present everything you have compiled so far."

"Sir, I have warrants already signed and ready to go. This guy is going to run. If there's any chance of catching him, it is tomorrow morning. That's not going to happen if we're all sitting on our thumbs in some conference room."

"God damn it, McDaniel!" Osen shouted into the phone, then his voice dropped back into the harsh whisper. "I know that! I know how to run an investigation. That's why I haven't pulled you already. And I'm not going to argue with you about this. At this moment, you are lead on the case. You will remain lead unless and until I give it to State, at which point you will no longer be lead. But for right now, unless you are doing something that will solve this case in the next fifteen minutes, get your ass home, get some rest so that when I call you to present your material, you won't be asleep on your feet. You got that?"

"Yes, sir," McDaniel said.

This time when Osen sighed it sounded more like an apology, or at least a concession. "Look, who have you been working with in-house? Spooner?"

"Yes, sir, Spooner and Rourke were doing the inside work for us," McDaniel said.

"You call him, tell him to come in early and compile the notes. I still want you here, to present, but I'll push the conference to late morning, maybe early afternoon. Spooner can get them started. If you can catch this psycho by lunch, well, I guess we'll all be happy. Otherwise, you come in, present your material to the State team, and we'll decide how to proceed from there."

"Yes, sir."

"I will call you tomorrow, once I have a time."

"Yes, sir. Thank you, sir." McDaniel hung up.

"How long we got?" Vanderwyk asked.

"Noon tomorrow, best case," McDaniel said. "But we're under orders to go home and sleep. In the a.m., we either find this guy or hand it over and walk away."

Vanderwyk looked down and shook his head. "He's gotta play it that way. You know that, right?"

"No, I understand, but we are going to run this asshole into the ground, at least as long as they let us," McDaniel said. "If State does take it, that'll slow things down. We are going to bust our butts between now and then to compensate."

"After a nap," Vanderwyk said.

McDaniel finally smiled, "After a nap."

CHAPTER 28

AFTER RELAYING THE orders and exchanging unpleasantries with Gable and Sanders, McDaniel trudged up the long driveway and down the dirt road to his car. He consulted with Conklin as to how to drive out of the woods and back to a paved road. As isolated as this place was, CDK's kill house was less than three miles from the main drag as the crow flies, only a bit farther by road.

Vanderwyk followed him out. The bright lights in McDaniel's rearview annoyed him. He wished Vanderwyk would back off, or just turn his lights off. It wasn't like he needed to see anything other than the back of McDaniel's car. He got so distracted by Vanderwyk's headlights that he missed a turn and nearly went nose-first into a ditch when the road he was on dead-ended.

When he finally got the car turned back around, he wanted to take off in a cloud of dust and be out of sight before Vanderwyk could get his own car turned around. He knew it wasn't really Vanderwyk, or his lights, that were pissing him off. He just really needed some sleep, and the prospect of losing the case just as he had started to gain traction was not easy to accept.

His nerves were wound tight as guitar strings. His jaws ached and he realized he had been grinding his teeth. The muscles at the base of his neck and between his shoulder blades ached, not from use, but from tension. Detective Griggs's flask was still in his coat pocket. A shot of whiskey would go a long way to improving his mood, and he was off the clock, after all. Vanderwyk would see it if he took a swig. He'd probably want some, too.

McDaniel grinned at the thought of he and Vanderwyk showing up hungover, or still drunk, to the conference with the State investigators. It would embarrass the hell out of Osen, which would almost be worth the two-week suspension.

His tires finally bumped up onto hardtop, leaving the rough dirt road behind. Without the potholes, washboards, and flying gravel, it was suddenly very quiet in his car. The hum of tires on fresh asphalt had a calming, lulling effect. He'd be home in less than five minutes. He figured he could hold off on the whiskey until he got there.

His thoughts were completely erased by a sudden, loud *beep beep beep beep*. Light flashed to his right. McDaniel's heart leaped so hard he thought someone had punched him in the chest. The thing flashing on the passenger seat was the cell phone in a plastic evidence bag.

His first half-asleep thought was that the thing was about to explode. He flinched, hard, swerving half-way across the road.

The *beep beep beep beep* continued, pulsing four times, resting for a beat, then pulsing four more times.

Vanderwyk came over the radio, "Papa-30, ten-eighteen?" it was the ten-code for *are you okay?*

McDaniel pulled to the side of the road, not responding to his partner. A message was flashing on the phone's display. By morning, he would have a warrant to search this phone, but if it was password protected, it could take hours or days to crack it open. The current activity on the screen was fair game, even without the warrant because it was in plain view. But if the screen went dark before McDaniel captured the info, he might never see it again.

With each four-beep sequence, a new message flashed across the screen:

> MISSED CALL
> NUMBER BLOCKED
> 06:37 p.m.

> MISSED CALL
> NUMBER BLOCKED
> 06:38 p.m.

> MISSED CALL
> NUMBER BLOCKED
> 06:40 p.m.

MISSED CALL
NUMBER BLOCKED
06:42 p.m.

McDaniel watched as the missed call messages scrolled down the screen. This was their quarry, and he was panicking. It took more than a full minute before the messages stopped. CDK had called forty-seven times, trying to detonate his bomb, before giving up.

Had he known the device failed? McDaniel tried to imagine the scenario. What had CDK expected to hear when he put that call through? What had he been thinking? And where had he been when he called? In the woods, watching?

A thumping on his window pulled him out of his imaginings. Vanderwyk stood outside, looking worried. McDaniel rolled his window down.

"Hey, man, you okay?" Vanderwyk asked. "Falling asleep?"

"He called it," McDaniel said. "CDK called that bomb, forty-seven times, trying to detonate it. Just after we hit the paved road we crossed back out of the dead zone and this thing started going nuts, picking up all the calls it missed out there."

"Shit," Vanderwyk whispered.

"Exactly," McDaniel said. "Step back." When Vanderwyk did, he pushed his door open and exited the car. "Here, check this out. I didn't see the first couple missed calls, but it appears he started calling sometime between six and six-thirty."

"He saw it on the six o'clock news," Vanderwyk said.

McDaniel nodded, "Yeah, sounds about right…So, he sees the news, and what do they actually report?"

"You want to call Osen back and ask him?" Vanderwyk said.

"No, I'd rather keep my job, thank you," McDaniel replied. "What could they have reported? Dead girl at bus stop with a chain on her leg, two detectives going into the woods…that's all we had at six."

"Unless Osen made something up," Vanderwyk said. "This guy sees the news, figures we're going to find his little cottage, and decides to pull the pin. So, he makes the call and, what?"

"I guess he would have expected to hear it ring, then the line would go dead, right?"

"Only, the call doesn't go through. It just says...what? Call failed? Or would it just keep acting like it's ringing?"

"Either way, he figures it didn't go through, so he keeps calling. And it keeps not going through."

"So, then what does he do?"

"What time did we go into the woods?" McDaniel asked.

Vanderwyk pulled out his notepad, "Looks like about two-thirty."

"And we got to the house just before six. So, he was actually calling that phone while we were waiting for Jennings--"

"No," Vanderwyk said, "he was calling that phone while you and I were inside that house, looking for his other victims."

McDaniel inhaled sharply. Not just at the revelation that if the cell network had been a bit more robust, he and Vanderwyk would have burned to death, but also at the mention of other victims.

He slumped against his cruiser. This day suddenly felt like it had been forever long. Believing that the other victims were still alive had been optimistic. He had adopted that belief because it added urgency to their search and justified more aggressive investigative decisions, like entering the house without a warrant, like continuing the search even after finding the incendiary device.

But now, the knowledge that those other victims had been buried beneath the floor this whole time sucked the enthusiasm out of him. He had wanted the story to be that Seong's courage had saved the others. But it was too late for that. They'd never had a chance to save any of the victims.

Eventually, McDaniel said, "And then, he stopped calling. The last call was at 8:03. What did he do then?"

"We were already set up at the site by the time he knew we were on to him," Vanderwyk said. "The officers out there working perimeter recorded five or six vehicles that drove by while we were out there. We'll start running those down in the morning."

"So, either he tried to go out there to burn it down manually and was turned back by the perimeter guys, at which point he would go to Plan C, or he didn't drive out there and went straight to Plan C."

"What's Plan C?" Vanderwyk asked.

"That depends, I guess, on whether he thinks we can find him, and how long he thinks that will take."

"If I was him, knowing what I know, I'd have been on a plane to Uganda as soon as I realized that bomb didn't go off."

"That's a pretty good Plan C," McDaniel said. "But if he has roots here, connections, family, he might not be willing to give all that up. If he thinks he can distance himself from this, if he believes he can throw us off his scent, he might stay put, try to act normal."

"But either way, he's moving fast, and probably panicking," Vanderwyk said. "He's going to be making mistakes that will leave him vulnerable, but only if we move faster."

"Whatever we can't get done by noon tomorrow isn't going to get done, anyway, whether he splits town or not. What are our two best leads? You take one and I'll take the other."

"This phone is our best lead. With the warrant, we can get that blocked number. It's probably a burner, too, but we should be able to ping it, find out where it was when he called and where it is now."

"I agree. If it is a burner, he might have ditched it by now, but it will get us close if nothing else, McDaniel said. "I think our next best bet is that electrical meter. That bill is going somewhere. You run with the phone thing, I'll go see the folks at Puget Sound Energy. It's sneaking up on three a.m. Let's say we meet at the office at seven a.m., try to have a target location before that conference."

"Well, I'll check my calendar…" Vanderwyk was still smiling, like he always did, but it was an exhausted smile.

"You do that," McDaniel said, "I'll see you at seven."

CHAPTER 29

McDANIEL ARRIVED HOME just after 3:00 a.m. He left his car in the driveway. The garage door opener was loud and slow, and he wasn't planning on staying long. He let himself in through the garage's side door, then slipped into the laundry room. He stripped off his muddy pants and dropped them in a bag for the cleaners. The jacket he hung up and the rest of his clothes went in the washer.

There was a bowl of salad with grilled chicken in the fridge. He picked out a few bits of chicken and washed them down with a shot from Griggs's flask. The whiskey burned all the way down. It was cheap rot-gut liquor, but by the time the burn had bottomed out in his stomach, the knots at the base of his neck loosened.

He stripped out of his shirt and slacks in the downstairs bath. It seemed to take way too much effort. He could smell the sweat from the long day, and the gasoline stanch had lodged deep in his nasal passages. More than anything, he wanted to crawl into bed, but not like this.

His hand shook as he reached for the shower knob. Then the water was running. He stood in the spray, letting it wash over his face. He bowed his head, leaning it against the wall. The hot water flowed over his neck, over his shoulders, over his scars. All his scars.

He might have fallen asleep, standing there, enveloped in steam and exhaustion and dark memories. Making the decision to turn the shower off seemed to take an effort of willpower. He dried off, then wrapped in a towel, intending to head up to bed. He opened the door and nearly screamed.

Katheryn stood there waiting for him.

She didn't say anything, just wrapped her arms around him and pulled him close. He embraced her, feeling her ribs through her silky nightgown. She smelled like jasmine or honeysuckle or something. He didn't know what it was, but it was wonderful. Her warmth against his body, her head on his chest, his face nuzzled into her hair. He breathed deeply, filling his lungs with her scent. There was peace here, and order and contentment. The balance in his world centered him, acted as an anchor and a shield, relaxing him far more than the whiskey ever could.

After several minutes, Katheryn turned her face up to his and kissed him firmly. She drew back just a bit then looked up at him, a twinkle playing in her sleepy eyes, "Why do you stay out drinking all night when you could be home in bed with me?"

He ran his hand down her back and pinched her on the bum. She squeaked a giggle and tried to pull away, but he held her tight.

 "Why are you so mean to me?"

"Somebody has to do it," she said. She rested against his arms, hanging away from him just a bit, tracing the circular scars on his back with her fingertips. The laughter left her face. "You're working that creepy doll thing, aren't you?"

He nodded.

"Is it bad?"

He nodded again. "Yeah, it's bad."

"Do you want to talk about it?"

"No," he said.

She looked up at him with her sad, beautiful smile. "Okay."

"I have to hit it early tomorrow. Anywhere around here I might find a quiet place to get some sleep?"

"Follow me," she said, taking his hand and leading him up the stairs.

CHAPTER 30

H E DREAMS …

A swirling, sucking void, an emptiness so immense that the whole of the universe could be swallowed, and yet the void be no less empty. An infinite blackness devouring all life and light, all structure and purpose, all order. He falls through this void where children scream for their mothers and mothers scream for their babies. No scream is ever answered and the lost are never found. Where misbegotten horrors beyond sane imaginings peel back the walls at the edge of time and peer through the darkness at him with a gaze, blank and pitiless as an imploded sun. Scavengers, devoid of form and without substance, sift through the tattered ghosts, picking apart the shredded spirits, yearning for one last morsel of innocence to consume, and yet finding none. Their lifeless eyes, too, fall upon him.

Far below, a tiny cube of radiance calls to him. He is both thrilled and terrified. He knows what it is and longs to reach it, but to see it here, in this place, terrifies him. No light, however pure, can endure long in this place. The cube of light rushes up at him as he falls toward it. And then he is there, inside his home. Its walls bathed in soft ivory light, a fire in the hearth, lit candles on the mantle. Outside, the wind howls. Katheryn and Robyn stand side by side, smiling at him. The light that illuminates his home radiates from them. They have no fear of the things beyond the walls, the things that even now rush toward them with greedy eyes and infinite appetite.

Someone has broken a hole through the wall behind the two women. As he looks through this hole to the dirt floor beyond, a ghastly pink hue bleeds through the cream-colored walls. Katheryn and Robyn continue to smile, but the trust in their eyes now turns to pleading. The chain around their ankles is bolted to the concrete wall. Pink light spills through the hole to the dirt floor beyond, bathing the graves in its unnatural glare. The dead ones there are impatient, unwilling to wait for a proper exhumation. They begin to unbury themselves.

And now he knows where he is and what waits just above their heads. Looking up through the ceiling to the dilapidated rooms above, he sees them. He sees can after can of gasoline, just waiting for the signal to ignite and incinerate the last bit of life in the eternal abyss. He sees the cell phone, its battery full, its single bar of service. Then it has two bars, then three. He reaches for it, but his hand is chained to the wall. The empty inhabitants of the void howl in anticipation. The dead watch through the hole, their eyes glimmering in the pink light.

The screen glows with all five bars lit. And it begins to ring.

Beep Beep Beep Beep Beep

CHAPTER 31

Beep Beep Beep Beep Beep…

McDaniel flailed in the general direction of his alarm clock four or five times before actually hitting it. The beeping stopped, though he didn't know whether he had hit *off* or *snooze*. The clock showed 5:45 a.m. He was in his bed. Katheryn was not there, and her side was cold.

The howling from his dream persisted upon waking, eerie and disturbing. As his mind extracted itself from sleep, and the dream, he finally recognized the awful howling for what it was – Robyn's music, alternative grunge punk turbo yodel something or other. He couldn't remember, but she always blasted it in the shower. She said it helped her wake up. McDaniel figured being doused with a bucket of ice water would be a more pleasant way to accomplish the same thing, but he never said so. He didn't want to be one of *those* kind of dads.

He was dressed and downstairs by 6:30. Robyn and Katheryn were in the kitchen, planning their day. In the living room, Katheryn's pillow and a spare blanket from the linen closet lay folded neatly on the longer of their two couches. A fire burned in the gas fireplace and two candles glowed on the mantle.

"Hey, dad!" Robyn called from the kitchen.

Darren turned and smiled at her, doing all he could to shake off the memory of his dream. "Hey, squirt." He wanted to hold her, but feared the intensity of that embrace might scare her.

"I see you kicked mom out of bed, again," Robyn said. She wore a black tee from some band called Birthday Massacre. Its illustrations looked like caricatures of the things in his dream. Her light spirit made them appear far less threatening, made his dream feel as insubstantial as a morning mist that vanishes before the first coffee break.

He looked over her shoulder at Katheryn, who was still in her night gown and a plush house-coat. She put on a tired smile for him, but the worry showed through. He immediately felt guilty and wanted to apologize, but she turned away as soon as she recognized this in his eyes.

To Robyn, he said, "Well, you know how bad she snores sometimes."

"I do not," Katheryn said, at exactly the same time Robyn said, "She does not."

Robyn laughed at the synchronicity. It was an infectious sound. Darren chuckled. Katheryn didn't laugh, but the worry seemed to lift a bit.

"What are your plans for the day?" Darren asked Robyn.

"Classes all morning," she said, standing on tiptoe to reach a mug on the top shelf. "Then, after lunch I'm heading down to Fairhaven to drop off applications." She scrunched her nose, suggesting some trepidation about her job hunt.

"Are you catching a ride with Neil?" Katheryn asked, not trying to hide her suspicious tone.

"If I was 'catching a ride with Neil,' *mom,* I'd have told you I was going to study at the library."

"Nobody studies at the library anymore," Darren said.

"Exactly, dad, you should be a detective or something." She kissed him on the cheek as she moved around him toward the brew station.

"So, if Neil isn't taking you, how are you getting to the library?" Katheryn asked as she gathered up her breakfast dishes. The edginess in her voice surprised Darren, though Robyn didn't seem to notice. Good-natured breakfast banter between the three of them was a longstanding tradition. He wondered what, exactly, had happened after he fell asleep last night.

"Aunt June is taking me," Robyn said, smiling brightly, "and I'm not going to the library. We have one of those on campus."

"She's not bringing that nutty friend of hers, is she?" Katheryn asked, sounding even more suspicious now than she had when the subject had been Robyn's boyfriend.

"Probably. Elli and Aunt June are inseparable," Robyn said, then, just to tease her mother she added, "Maybe I should call her *Aunt* Elli."

June was Darren's sister, his only surviving family member. The two of them had endured much hardship in the wake of their parents' deaths. It had taken its toll on both of them, in different ways. Darren had nightmares; June had addictions. Her friend, Elli, was her NA sponsor, but might as well have been her sister. Darren trusted Robyn with them, completely. And, he completely understood Katheryn's unease.

"Maybe you shouldn't," Darren said, then tried to narrow his eyes at Robyn in such a way as to indicate that this wasn't a good morning to tease her mother.

She looked at him funny, and mouthed the question, *What?* Then, out loud, to her mother she said. "I *am* going out with Neil tonight, after dropping off applications, but only for a quick bite. I'll be home by nine. I promise."

Katheryn carried her dishes to the sink, giving Robyn a disapproving look, her lips pressed into a thin line. "You know I don't like that one." She said, but without much resolve.

"Dad likes him," Robyn said, wrapping her arm around him and flopping her head onto his shoulder. She batted her eyelashes at him comically, "Don't you, dad?"

"No, I think he's a weasel," Darren said, wrapping his arm around his daughter. "I told him that last time he was here."

"*Dad*," Robyn said, pulling away.

"But I'm confident you will figure that out on your own, sooner than later, and if he wants to buy you dinner sometimes between now and then, that's his business." He kissed Robyn on the top of her head and let her go.

Katheryn began washing her dishes in a manner that suggested she wasn't as comfortable with the situation as her daughter and husband seemed to be. Darren guessed her unease had more to do with last night than with anything Robyn had planned for today.

Her back was to him now, as she fussed over her plate in the sink. He moved up behind her, putting his hands on her waist, and whispered into her ear, "I'm sorry, Kat."

She turned and looked into him, her eyes darting back and forth between each of his, as if searching for something. Her expression shifted between worry, fear, annoyance, and hurt. They were not emotions he was used to seeing on her face, and he again felt the pang of guilt.

He was about to apologize a second time, but she stopped him. She reached behind herself and turned on the faucet so that the sound of the water would ensure that Robyn did not overhear her. "Some of the things you say, Darren," she whispered, "when you get like that…" She shook her head and sighed. "You scare me."

He broke eye contact, not knowing how to answer. The window behind her was still dark. The sun would not rise for another hour. He turned and looked at Robyn.

"Okay, I get it," Robyn said, "I'll go to my room so the adults can talk about the adult things. You don't have to waste water on my account."

When she was gone, McDaniel turned the faucet off. He still didn't know what to say. *I'm sorry* felt trite and empty. There was a deep ache inside him that defied expression. Katheryn made his life perfect, or almost perfect. Everything she could not make perfect, she made tolerable. He wanted to do the same for her. Having chased her from their bed with his nightmare rantings made him feel defeated, and even more tired than he already was.

"It would help me if we could talk about it," Katheryn said, "so I can understand what's going on in here." She brushed her fingers through his hair.

"If I was a garbageman, I wouldn't bring my work home with me," he said, "and this is far worse. I don't want you two exposed…"

She wasn't buying it. Her eyes narrowed and her lips pursed.

Darren sighed. "That sounds like a brush-off line, huh?"

She nodded. "It is a brush-off line. Even if it's true."

He sighed again, at a complete loss. Finally, he said, "There's darkness out there. It's like acid. It… once it gets on you, it leaves scars. I don't want it here. I don't want it to know about this place…" He trailed off.

"I don't understand…"

"I don't *want* you to understand," he said. "The type of person who can do that…" He stopped and swallowed, then took a breath. He tried again. "After the fire, I had to learn how to live with the understanding of…of our…fragility. I had to come to grips with the knowledge that we are suspended between consuming fire and icy sea. We live on this thin ribbon of light, perfectly balanced between two oblivions. Even a slight misstep can disrupt that balance. I learned this. I know it. I can live this way, and I know you could, too, but I don't want you to have to. You don't want to know what's out there. All you need to know is that I will keep you safe from it."

"That's what scares me, Darren," Katheryn said. "I know you can handle anything this world throws at you. You are a survivor. But you have to let me in. And you have to let me make my own decisions. I am an adult. We are in this together. We share our lives. If you wall off sections of your life to protect me, you are walling off parts of yourself. You are stealing my husband from me. And if *we* fall apart, *you* will fall apart. You know that. Then what will happen to all those walls?"

Her last line struck him, dislodged something inside. The dream images flashed through his mind, the walls cracking, the dead eyes peering through, glimmering in the pinkish light. He shuddered, looking to the place on the living room wall where the cracks had appeared in his dream.

Her eyes followed his gaze. Her brow wrinkled in confusion, then she turned back to him.

He nodded. "I know, on some level, that you are right. I also know, the stuff out there, I can't let it in here…" In his pocket, his phone buzzed, an alert that it was time to leave. Vanderwyk would be waiting for him.

Katheryn heard it, too.

"You have to go," she said, clearly disappointed. "Robyn made a bagel for you, and I think she started a coffee…"

He pulled her close. "I'm sorry, Kat, for keeping you awake, for being aloof, for having to leave in the middle of our talk. I'll make it up to you." He kissed her forehead and squeezed her, then started to turn for the door.

She pulled him back and kissed him full on the lips, making sure he knew she meant it. "I know you will," she said. "Now, go find that son of a bitch, so I can have my husband back."

CHAPTER 32

McDANIEL MET VANDERWYK at the police station just after 7:00 a.m. It was still dark outside. The thick, low-hanging clouds would probably prolong the appearance of night long after the meteorologically calculated sunrise at 8:03 a.m. Icy drizzle fell through a fine mist that hung in the air.

The detectives' desks faced each other beside a wall of windows. Four other pairs of desks, similarly configured, filled the bullpen, but none of the other detectives had yet arrived. The door to Lieutenant Osen's office was closed and the blinds drawn. Whether he was in or not, McDaniel couldn't tell. He hoped to be gone before finding out.

"Spooner and Rourke should be up here by quarter after eight," Vanderwyk said. "They are still assigned to us, at least until State shows up. What do you want them working on?"

"As soon as the sun is up, send them up to the site to search the exterior and grounds. See if they can find any litter from the yard," McDaniel said. "You've got the cell phone thing?"

"Yeah, I'll start on that now. If we're lucky, I'll have something for you by noon," Vanderwyk said. "But more likely it'll be next week."

McDaniel nodded.

"If I hit a dead end, I'll start working with city housing records, see if I can figure out who altered the property to show no house there," Vanderwyk said.

"Good," McDaniel said. "I'm going to camp out in front of the PSE office on State Street until someone shows up, see if we can't get the billing address. Have you heard anything from Gable and Sanders? Did they get anything good at the site last night?"

"I'm just pulling up my email, now. Looks like I got something from each of them."

McDaniel would have the same emails, but he wasn't going to be here long enough to log on and load them.

"Uh, looks like Sanders found several hundred fingerprints, most of them child-sized but more than enough adult prints to make a match. Says he has run all the adult prints through IAFIS, but didn't get a hit on any one of them. He started running the child prints, but he had so many he didn't get through them all. He collected 'stiff patches' from the bed sheets, which he expects will contain DNA. He also swabbed every smooth surface, including inside and outside the toilet. When Frodo and Sam come in, they will finish packaging those samples and send them to the state forensics lab."

"One of them needs to finish running all those prints," McDaniel said.

"They aren't going to be happy about that," Vanderwyk said. "That's tedious grunt work. You sure you don't want to keep Spooner in house today to run those so Sam and Frodo can focus on the cool DNA side of things?"

"If they run the prints, results will be back today. The DNA could take months," McDaniel said. "And I want both uniforms up at the site looking for anything else we may have missed. He may have dropped his wallet in the driveway for all we know. Crazier things have happened. Or maybe a receipt blew out of his car, or he left a footprint somewhere."

Vanderwyk said, "Got it. I'll let them know."

"Gable didn't have anything to report, did he?"

'Hmm… let me check." Vanderwyk clicked the next email and scanned it. He then clicked icons to open three attached pictures. "Shit," he muttered under his breath.

McDaniel raised an eyebrow, then started to move around behind Vanderwyk so he could see the pictures.

Vanderwyk laughed, very quietly, in a way that expressed both relief and disbelief, then muttered, "There *was* a trigger on that door."

"What?" McDaniel asked, moving around the desks more quickly.

"That side door we came through was rigged to blow the fuel," Vanderwyk said, a bit more confidently this time. "It had a contact plate set up so that if the door swung open more than halfway… boom!"

Vanderwyk clicked through the pictures so McDaniel could see. "The only thing that saved us was that Lindell kicked the damn thing right off its hinges. It fell flat rather than swinging open."

The first picture showed a brown wire snaking out from under the door. In the next photo, the door had been moved away, revealing a metallic device bolted to the floor, connected to the wire from the first shot. The final picture was taken from just outside the door, looking down at a sharp angle. A narrow triangle of clean linoleum on the otherwise filthy floor showed that CDK only ever opened the door that wide. The contact plate waited about six inches beyond that triangle.

McDaniel shook his head, covering a tremor with a scoff. "Wow."

"Yeah," Vanderwyk said.

After a moment to grasp how close they had come to obliterating the entire scene, and possibly themselves as well, McDaniel forced a chuckle, then said, "Well, now we know one more thing about this dipshit."

Vanderwyk looked up at him, thinking, then looked back at the final photo and got it. "He must be very thin."

"Skinny as a rail," McDaniel agreed. "I might have been able to squeeze through that opening without setting it off, but it would be a very close call. Too close for comfort if I was visiting on a regular basis."

Vanderwyk's albino eyebrows lifted, "I'd have been toast."

CHAPTER 33

THE PUGET SOUND Energy office was about a five-minute drive south of the police station in old-town Bellingham. McDaniel arrived just before seven-thirty. The sign on the door said they opened at 8:00, but he tried it anyway. When it didn't open, he tapped on the door. Through the glass, he could see a reception area, opening to rows of cubicles on one side and offices on the other. No one was in sight, but the lights were on.

He thumped harder on the glass door. A head popped out from behind the cubicle wall, a blonde woman in her early twenties with messy hair and flushed cheeks. She had a seriously annoyed look on her face and pointed to an illuminated *closed* sign hanging in the window.

When McDaniel held up his badge, the expression on her face changed to surprise, then fear. She quickly raised a finger to say *one minute*, then ducked back into the maze of cubicles. McDaniel heard voices – one male, the other female. He couldn't tell what they were saying, but he could guess. A smile lifted the friendlier corner of his mouth.

A second later, she moved out from behind the cubicles and came to the door. One of the buttons on her blouse was misaligned. Her smile was Oscar-worthy, but when she cocked her head to the side and mouthed, "Can I help you?" through the glass, McDaniel felt she had overplayed the sweet-and-innocent bit.

"Yes, ma'am," McDaniel said, loudly enough to be heard on the other side of the door, "You can help me by opening the door. I am a Bellingham Police detective. I have a warrant."

She feigned shock that he wanted her to open the door, her acting going from over-the-top to half-baked-ham. She pointed at the lock and cocked her head again.

McDaniel nodded.

She made an exaggerated, "Oh!" with her lips, then finally turned the lock. She opened it a crack, then stuck her face through and said, "We're closed until eight."

McDaniel fixed her with a stern look.

Another moment passed, then she said, "But, if you have a warrant…"

He held it up to her and smiled his most pleasant smile. "I just need a peek at some billing records. I will be out of here as quick as it takes you to pull those up for me."

She started to shake her head, but he gently pushed his way past her and walked toward the cubicles. "Is this your workstation back here? You've probably got a computer on your desk, right?"

"Oh, no, sir, the uh…the public isn't allowed--"

He held the warrant up.

"That has to go through a supervisor. I just do…" She continued to move around him, positioning herself between the detective and whoever she had hidden in the cubicles. McDaniel allowed this, but made her work for it.

"When will your supervisor be here?" McDaniel asked.

"Normally, he'd be here already, but, um, well there was this regional meeting today… in Seattle," she said. "I think he'll be back by noon? You know, depending on traffic."

"Is there someone else here who can help me?" McDaniel made a show of standing on tiptoe, trying to look over the cubicle wall.

"No!" she said, then with a self-conscious giggle, "No, no, it's just me. I'm here all alone. For now."

McDaniel smiled and looked at her until she blushed and started fiddling with frilly things on her sleeve. "Well then," he finally said, "I guess I'll have to wait around until your supervisor gets back from Seattle."

More self-conscious laughter from the girl.

"It's going to be a few hours, I guess," McDaniel continued. He drifted toward a row of steel and Naugahyde chairs that lined one wall of the reception area. Then he turned abruptly back toward the cubicles. "Say, do you have a bathroom back there?"

She squeaked and stepped in front of him again. "No. It's, um, out of order."

From far back in the cubicle maze came a stifled cough.

McDaniel raised an eyebrow at the young woman.

"It's a cat," she said, twisting her fingers in and out of each other. "Um…what was it you needed?"

"Well, you said I'd have to go through your supervisor. I have a warrant to look at billing records, but I wouldn't want you to get in trouble," McDaniel said. "You know, that didn't really sound like a cat to me. Maybe I should go check…"

"Oh! Well, if it's just billing records…"

"I don't need account numbers, just an address," McDaniel said.

"Oh! Well that's easy," she said, beaming a brilliant smile. "I'm so sorry, I thought you needed account numbers. If it's just addresses, I can handle that for you."

"All I need is a single address. The service location is here," he said, handing her a slip of paper with the address of CDK's kill house and the meter number. "Get me the address where you send the bill for this account and I'll be gone."

CHAPTER 34

IT WAS FIVE minutes to eight when McDaniel walked out of
the PSE office with a copy of last month's power bill for CDK's
kill house. The name on the account was Bob Roberts. The
receptionist said the records showed he had paid that bill, and all
others in recent months, via money order. Mr. Roberts's mailing
address was a house in an area of Bellingham known as the Let-
tered Streets, because each street name consisted of a single letter.
The neighborhood was full of well-kept older homes, many dating
from the early 1900s. Mr. Roberts's house was on G Street.

McDaniel punched the address into his laptop and waited for
the Google map to load. He'd gotten away with putting a little
pressure on the PSE employee to speed things along, but he knew
that wouldn't be wise with the folks down at the County Assessor's
Office, nor with the judge who would be reviewing his warrant

request for the G Street address. Neither would be in their offices until a few minutes after eight. McDaniel knew it would be best to wait at least half an hour beyond that.

That would give him time to type up the warrant and get a look at the G Street address. The map loaded. McDaniel zoomed in on his target. It was a newer home than many around it, a 1970s-style ranch house with a single car garage at one end. The backyard had a tall wooden fence all the way around, but McDaniel noticed a rear parking pad. It appeared to connect to the alley that ran behind the house. He considered driving past the property, but decided against it for now. He felt confident that he would see it soon enough. He clicked out of the map and started working on the warrant.

At 8:20 a.m., he decided to risk a call to the County Assessor's Office. He got ahold of Melinda Peters and told her what he was looking for. He listened to the story she told him every time he called about how much easier things were these days with computers doing all the thinking and filing, and how much harder it was when she first started there because everything was on real paper, in real files, in real metal filing cabinets. All the while, her fingers clacked away on her keyboard.

Her fingers stopped clacking. McDaniel knew she had the information for him, but he would have to wait until the end of her story. She was now at the part about breaking nails when the filing cabinet drawers jammed. Next would be the part about paper cuts. He knew if he tried to rush her, she'd get her feelings hurt, and she'd send all the information to the wrong email address.

While he waited, he thought about emailing the warrant request to the judge's office, but decided to look at the information from the Assessor's Office first.

He was glad he waited. When Melinda finally said goodbye, she emailed him the current property owner's name and address – Adam Ecclestone from Victoria, British Colombia, another Canadian. McDaniel didn't know if this was relevant or not – much of the investment property in and around the Bellingham area were owned by Canadians – but having both properties that were linked to CDK owned by Canadians seemed too much of a coincidence.

Ecclestone's number was listed in the file Melinda had sent. McDaniel dialed it. The man who answered had an exceptionally polite demeanor, while at the same time expressing a subtle superiority. He confirmed that, yes, he did own the property in question, but he certainly did not know anything about anyone named Bob Roberts.

"That sounds like a made-up name to me, if I am to be honest with you," Ecclestone said with a chuckle. "But perhaps that is why you are calling?"

"Perhaps," McDaniel replied, trying to put a smile in his answer. "Sir, is the home currently occupied?"

"Well, I should hope so, but I cannot say for certain from one day to the next," Ecclestone said. "I try to keep my fingers out of the day-to-day managing of my holdings. That's what I have accountants for."

McDaniel felt the spike of adrenaline, could almost see the electricity firing across his synapses. Ecclestone's answer was nearly word for word identical to Mrs. Bamford's. He kept his voice as calm and jovial as it had been. "Would you mind telling me the name of your accountant?"

"What is this regarding, detective?" He detected a hint of apprehension in Ecclestone's voice now.

"Mr. Ecclestone," McDaniel said, "we have reason to believe an individual may be using that address to commit mail fraud, having bills forwarded to your house and the like. I want to put a lid on this quickly to ensure you don't end up on the hook for someone else's debts."

There was a long pause on the other end. McDaniel began to wonder if Ecclestone might know more than he was letting on. Finally, Ecclestone said, "If it's not one thing, it's another. Please feel free to contact my accountants, Schechter & Polakoff, there in Bellingham. I will contact Mr. Schechter and instruct him to cooperate with your investigation."

McDaniel couldn't help but smile, Schechter & Polakoff was a local accounting firm. They were probably very good at their work, but the comically bad commercials they ran during the news at eleven made them the butt of many jokes.

Schechter was the younger of the two, probably in his early thirties. He had fat lips and beady eyes. His black hair, greased and parted at the center of his crown, curled up, down, and back up at the ends, causing it to look like a large plastic mustache balanced just above his forehead. Polakoff was mousey and balding, with only thin wisps of gray hair hovering around his scalp. He wore round, wire-rimmed glasses and a tweed suit that probably had leather patches at the elbows.

Thinking of the two awkward men staring into the cameras to deliver their sincere and urgent message about fiduciary duty distracted McDaniel to the point that he almost missed Ecclestone's last comment. Then, as the words played over in his mind, he caught it.

"Mr. Ecclestone," he said, "if you don't mind, hold off on contacting anyone for the time being. Let me make sure I have all my facts straight before we go making any unnecessary calls. I appreciate your willingness to help. If it turns out we need to talk with your accountant, I will let you know, but for now please do not mention this to anyone else."

Another long pause, then, "Detective McDaniel, there is more to this than mail fraud, obviously. I will keep quiet for now, but I do not appreciate being lied to. And I will be in contact with Mr. Polakoff on the first of the month, at which time I will ask him about the tenant in that house and any suspicious bills that may have arrived."

"Mr. Ecclestone, at this time, the only thing we know for sure is that bills associated with a known criminal are being mailed to your G Street property. I did not lie to you about that. We do suspect there may be more criminal activity associated with that address, but none that I can discuss now. I am looking to protect your interests, and when I know more, I will be happy to share it with you."

"Then I look forward to hearing from you soon. Is there anything else, Detective?"

"No, sir, thank you--" McDaniel stopped when he heard Ecclestone hang up.

He made a quick call to the U. S. Customs office in Blaine and asked if Mr. Ecclestone had recently entered the United States. The Customs Officer found a record showing that Mr. Ecclestone had flown into New York the prior summer, but found no record of his crossing the border into Washington State anytime in the prior twelve months.

Next, McDaniel pulled a notebook out of his breast pocket and flipped through it until he found Mrs. Bamford's phone number. He had not talked to her before; the information he had on her came from an interview Officer Rourke had conducted while he and Vanderwyk were waiting on the bomb squad. When she answered her phone, he was struck by her similarity to Ecclestone. She spoke with the same lofty, detached politeness. He wondered if they knew each other, and jotted a note to pursue that in the future if none of his current leads panned out.

Mrs. Bamford wanted McDaniel to know that she thought Officer Rourke was very professional, and that she thought he had had a nice voice, and how she wished all American police officers showed the same level of courtesy. She then wanted to be sure McDaniel knew how upsetting this whole situation had been and how much she appreciated his efforts towards resolving the matter. Eventually, McDaniel had an opportunity to address the reason for his call.

"Ma'am, you told officer Rourke that you have an accountant who handles your properties here in the States?"

"Yes. That is correct."

"Which firm is that?"

"Oh, I never do remember their names. They have odd names. I know this is silly, but I always think of them as Shyster and Polack. They are on the tele all the time--"

"Is it Schechter & Polakoff?" McDaniel asked.

"Yes!" she said, laughing. "Schechter and Polakoff. I must really try to remember that."

CHAPTER 35

McDANIEL FELT THE surge of excitement that always came when a case was starting to break. The two properties CDK had been connected to were owned by Canadian investors. That could have been a meaningless coincidence, but both properties being managed by the same accounting firm was too coincidental to be meaningless.

He tapped the trackpad on his computer, intending to look up Schechter & Polakoff. When the screen came on, it displayed the email he had been preparing containing his search warrant request. It also showed the time, 9:22 a.m. The excitement he was feeling suddenly compacted, becoming something closer to anxiety. He had good leads, and a new break, but he might run out of time before he could chase them down. As soon as he stepped into that conference room, all his momentum would be lost. CDK was scrambling to cover his tracks, the call log on the trigger phone proved that. McDaniel had to scramble faster.

He quickly added the new information he had gleaned from the County Assessor's Office, and from Ecclestone, to the Probable Cause statement on the warrant, then hit *send* on the email.

He had cc'd the email to Vanderwyk. Two minutes after sending, his partner was on the phone.

"You're not going to believe this," Vanderwyk said. McDaniel could hear the same giddy anticipation in his partner's voice that he himself felt.

"If you're going to tell me that you got something off the cell phone in only two hours, then you're right. I'm not going to believe you."

"No, we're locked out of the records for at least a week, probably more like three weeks," Vanderwyk said. "The cell provider for this phone is GoFish."

"Go fish, like the card game?" McDaniel asked.

"No, in the card game the emphasis is on 'fish.' With this cell carrier, the emphasis is on 'Go,'" Vanderwyk explained. "*Go*Fish, not go *fish*. Got it?"

"I understand what you are saying to me. I don't get what that has to do with anything."

"Nothing, really, it's just that GoFish is like a subcontractor. They don't have their own network, they run calls through the large networks, but only for burner phones. They run a kind of shell game. Basically, they provide an extra layer of protection for people who don't want us to find them.

"We have a warrant that says we get to look at those cell records, but in order for that to happen, the request has to work its way through the usual maze of red tape. But once the request has made it through all of GoFish's roadblocks, they send it over to the major carrier, and it starts all over again at the beginning. So, we are looking at three weeks before we get any records from them."

"Okay," McDaniel said, slowly. "Then what are you so excited about?"

"He fucked up," Vanderwyk said. "All the calls you and I saw were blocked. But the first two calls he made were not blocked. He gave no thought to it because he expected everything to be vaporized when his bomb went off. It wasn't until the second call failed that he realized he was in deep shit."

"So, we know what number he called from," McDaniel said.

"Exactly! Now, that one is a GoFish phone as well. So, we are just as screwed with that one as we were with the other, but check this out – Remember Agent Hostetler?"

"The FBI agent?" McDaniel asked.

"Yeah, I called her."

"And she answered?"

"Cute," Vanderwyk said. "Now pay attention, because this is cool. I explained to her what this case is about, got her pretty pissed off at our guy. Then, I told her about the cell-detonated incendiary device. She said it was a bit of a stretch, but she had an idea. Half an hour later she calls me back and says she managed to open a file on our guy, classified him as a possible domestic terrorist."

"Does *that* get us access to his phone records?" McDaniel asked.

"Yeah," Vanderwyk said, "in three weeks. GoFish has their system set up so that even if we got a court order and physically raided their facility we still wouldn't get records any faster than that. So, that is still a no go."

"Then what are you all excited about?"

"Hostetler did some poking around. It turns out that the FBI is already keeping tabs on CDK's phone – not directly, but as an associate of a key player in a different investigation. She wouldn't tell me anything about that other investigation, only that there have been several calls between their target's phone and CDK's phone.

"Since they were already in the GoFish system on their target's phone, they have access to the information about any call between CDK's phone and their target's phone. Right now, not three weeks from now."

"Okay, that sounds good," McDaniel said. "Are they willing to play ball with us?"

"Well, Hostetler said the agents running that other investigation are unwilling to share anything from their files with us. Whatever they're onto, it's big. They are afraid of leaks in local law enforcement. But she said she would work with those guys to try to track CDK's movements over the past week or so. She'll redact anything that relates to their guy and forward whatever she can about CDK to us. I hope to hear from her within the hour."

"Dicks," McDaniel said. "Let me guess, you had to give them access to our case files?"

"Yeah. I felt it was a good trade," Vanderwyk said. "If they give us something that helps us nail this guy, we give them his file."

McDaniel would have done the same thing, but it irked the hell out of him. "You know they're going to offer him a deal, right? If they're after a big fish and CDK has dirt on their target, they'll give him whatever he wants."

"Darren, he's got six dead girls in his basement. It doesn't matter who he has dirt on, they're not going to let him walk. Worst case, he'll go to some fancy resort hospital, which might happen anyway, but he will be behind bars. Forever," Vanderwyk said. "And the FBI would have gotten to him eventually, even if I hadn't made the deal."

"Yeah, no, you did the right thing. I'm not busting your balls," McDaniel said. "But we are running out of time. If Osen decides to turn this over to State, they'll be starting from zero. By the time they are up to speed, CDK will be on the wrong side of long gone."

"I explained all that to Hostetler. She said she'd call back before 10:00," Vanderwyk said, sounding a bit deflated.

"Hey, it's good," McDaniel said. "We're going to get this guy, one way or another. Did you see the warrant application?"

"I saw that you sent it. Haven't had a chance to read it," Vanderwyk said. "Do you think the judge will sign it?'

"It's not a slam dunk. Could go either way, I guess."

"Or he could sit on it for a while," Vanderwyk said.

"Right. Tell you what, if we don't get the warrant by 10:30, how about you and I just go knock on the door and see who answers?"

An obnoxious beeping cut through their conversation.

McDaniel said, "Hold on, got another call coming in." He hit his phone's "hold & accept" option.

"McDaniel, where are you?" It was Lieutenant Osen.

"I'm parked outside PSE, where are you?"

"Don't be an ass," Osen said. "I have arranged the conference for 12:30. If you want lunch today, eat before you come in. This will take a few hours."

"Got it," McDaniel said.

"Anything new I need to know about?"

"I've got an address, warrant has been applied for, we have a possible lead based on both property owners using the same accounting firm, but I haven't had time to run that down, yet. Vanderwyk expects to get some information within the hour about CDK's movements based on cell data. That's about it."

"So why do I have an FBI agent requesting the CDK file?"

"That's a longer story than I have time to go into right now," McDaniel said. "But whatever you do, don't give it to him. Not yet. They have information we need. Vanderwyk made a trade. If their info helps us nail our guy, we give them his file. *After* we nail him. The Feeb is just trying to make an end-run around the deal he made so he doesn't have to share anything with us." McDaniel's lip curled up, he couldn't always play Osen, but he knew which button to push this time. "He doesn't want to give us anything because he thinks you've got a leak."

There was a long silence on Osen's end of the line. A beep alerted McDaniel that Vanderwyk had hung up on the other line. When Osen finally spoke, McDaniel heard what he had hoped to hear, the man was incensed. "Vanderwyk called that Agent Hostetler, didn't he? Is she the one suggesting I have a leak in my unit?"

"Hostetler is the agent helping us," McDaniel said. "I don't know which agent made that allegation. Probably the one who called you trying to get a peek at the file. You didn't show him anything, did you?"

"He didn't want a *peek*, he wanted the whole damn file. He's pushing to take the case from us," Osen said. "And, no, I didn't give him anything. Tell that Vanderwyk he can hit on feebs all he wants on his free time, but sharing case information with anyone – *anyone* – for personal reasons, like trying to get laid, is a violation of professional standards of conduct--"

"Sir," McDaniel cut in, "sir, we need the information Vanderwyk is getting from Hostetler. We might even get a current location on our guy if he's still using the same phone. Vanderwyk made a good trade, just don't give up the file until we get our end of the bargain."

"I'm not giving them anything," Osen said, and swore under his breath. "You understand the first thing the Feebs do in a case like this is catalog every error the local agency has made? That way, if they fail to solve it, they can blame that failure on us. If they succeed, their line is, 'we solved this case in spite of the fucking mess we inherited from the locals.' I don't want them anywhere near this!"

After several deep breaths, Osen continued, a bit calmer now. "You have about three hours before the conference. What are your plans between now and then? Anything new you expect to bring to the table?"

"If the search warrant for the G Street house gets approved--"

"No," Osen said, emphatically. "You don't have enough time to execute a proper search of that property and be back here ready to present the case to the State investigators."

"Then have Spooner or Rourke present. They have the notes up--"

"I want *you* here. I will not be embarrassed by calling in top investigators from the State Patrol only to have *my* two investigators missing because they are off fucking around in the field and flirting with the Feebs!" Osen roared into the phone.

Perhaps McDaniel had hit that button a bit too hard.

"Besides, Spooner and Rourke are still collecting evidence out at the kill house." Osen continued, his voice taking a shrewd twist. "In fact, I just got off the phone with Spooner, and guess what?"

McDaniel waited.

"He had no trouble with his cell phone out there at all. It worked just fine," Osen growled. "So, you and Vanderwyk can drop the 'I'm-sorry-sir-my-phone-is-cutting-out bullshit!"

"Sir--" McDaniel started, thinking he was about to try to explain what "*intermittent* cell coverage" meant.

"Stop," Osen said. "I don't want to hear it. You have three hours to wrap up whatever you're doing out there. I want your ass in the conference room at 12:00 sharp. The only thing I want to hear from you now is 'yes, sir.'"

McDaniel knew Osen had bumped the deadline from 12:30 up to 12:00 just to bait him into further argument. He didn't take the bait. "Yes, sir."

Osen clicked off.

McDaniel dialed Vanderwyk back. When he picked up, McDaniel asked, "Are you still at the station?"

"Yes, but I was about to leave. It's getting tense around here."

"I hear you," McDaniel said. "Good Girl Bad Girl?"

"Perfect," Vanderwyk said. "I'll be there in ten."

As McDaniel pulled up to the curb outside Good Girl Bad Girl, his phone dinged, indicating a new email. It was a reply to the emailed warrant request. The message from Judge Culverson was simple, "Call me."

McDaniel did.

The judge picked up immediately. "I can't approve this warrant, detective," he said, without any preamble. "You present compelling and suggestive evidence, but there just isn't enough here for me to sign off on a full search of this property."

"Your honor, the seriousness of the crime and the speed with which we believe the subject is attempting to destroy evidence--"

"Detective, you did a fine job detailing all of that in the warrant application. But every citizen of this country is guaranteed the right to be free from unlawful search and seizure of his person, house, papers, and effects. I am extremely curious as to what you might find in that house. I *want* to sign off on this warrant. But you just don't have enough PC here," Culverson said.

"Your Honor, the fourth amendment is in place to support the whole of the constitution, which is in place to support the promise that every citizen has the right to *life*, liberty and the pursuit of happiness. CDK has deprived at least seven people of those most basic rights."

"Detective, I am aware of the purpose of the fourth amendment. I am aware that this CDK person needs to be apprehended with all haste. But all you have given me is an electric bill and a coincidence," Culverson said. "Look, if you want to shop this around, you might find another judge willing to sign it, and it won't hurt my feelings. Like I said, this is almost enough, and I want you in that house. But, I need a little bit more. Or, your other option, go talk to the occupant of the house, develop more solid probable cause, then resubmit the warrant. If it shows up in my inbox with good, solid PC, I will expedite it."

McDaniel took a deep breath. He saw Vanderwyk cross the street and duck into GGBG. "Thank you, Your Honor," he said. "I hope to be in touch soon."

Judge Culverson express a similar sentiment, then ended the call.

Inside the café, Vanderwyk had taken his favorite table near the back corner, tucked half under the stairs, near the end of the counter. It ensured frequent contact with Karri and Noreen, but limited contact with the other customers. Both sisters worked behind the counter, making coffee drinks and breakfast sandwiches. The bad-girl half of the operation was not yet open for business at 9:45 on a Monday morning. McDaniel ordered a black Americano with an extra shot and a chocolate croissant.

Vanderwyk grinned broadly as McDaniel approached. He had some sort of flaky pastry full of jelly and slathered in cream cheese frosting. His notebook lay open in front of him, covered in crumbs and scribbled notes.

"I got the cell data from Hostetler," he said as McDaniel sat. "It tells a story."

"I hope it's a good story," McDaniel said. "Culverson just shot down our warrant and Osen nixed the search even if we had one."

Vanderwyk hunched over the table, closing the distance between them and bringing his head down to the level of McDaniel's. "Oh, yeah, it's a good story. It's a great story. Sit back, enjoy your plain old black coffee and listen up."

McDaniel sipped the Americano – it was still too hot to gulp – and settled back in his chair. "Tell it, brother."

"We've got CDK's movements for the last 24 hours. From before our victim died, right up until about an hour ago. He might be running, but he's marking his trail at every turn," Vanderwyk said, beaming. "We're gonna nail this bastard to the wall."

"Save the vulgarities for upstairs, Detective," Karri said in a dismissive, I-shouldn't-have-to-be-telling-you-this voice. She was collecting dirty dishes from the table next to theirs.

"Sorry, Karri," Vanderwyk said.

"But between you and me," she said, whispering. "You better nail him to the wall." Her voice dropped lower. She leaned close,

"And when you do, I hope you cut his balls off. I'll put them in a pickle jar on the counter upstairs."

Vanderwyk's red face turned a shade redder. McDaniel smiled, cleared his throat, and said, "I'll see what we can do."

Karri smiled and straightened up. In her perky good-girl voice, she asked, "Can I bring you gentlemen anything else?"

Vanderwyk shook his head.

McDaniel said, "I think we've got all we need for now."

Karri smiled again and headed to the back with her stack of dirty dishes. Vanderwyk watched until she disappeared behind the curtain.

"Good girl? Bad girl? Which one do you think *she* is?" he finally asked.

"She's the one who's going to be spitting in every coffee she ever serves you from now on if we don't catch this guy. Tell me what you've got, man."

"Right," Vanderwyk said. He opened his eyes wide, blinked twice, then focused on his notepad. "Okay, I'll walk you through it. The FBI is tracking this phone, here." He tapped a number on his pad, not the actual cell number, but a code the FBI had assigned to that number. "I'm just going to call this guy 'Target,' so I don't confuse myself.

"What Hostetler gave me is a list of calls made *from* Target phone to CDK's phone, or calls from CDK *to* Target. They are not up on CDK's phone, so if he called anyone other than Target, we won't have those calls. We do have the calls made to the trigger phone because we have that phone and can read them out of the call log.

"So, night before last, at about 6:37 p.m., Target calls CDK. At the time of that call, CDK's phone is only pinging off one tower, meaning his phone is only in range of one tower. That means we can't triangulate an exact location, right?"

"Sure," McDaniel nodded.

"But that tower is the only tower you can hit from CDK's kill house, and only about half the time. So, he was somewhere in a five-mile radius of that tower when the call came in. We can eliminate more than three-quarters of that radius, because if he was in those areas, he would have hit more than one tower. You with me so far?"

"What you're saying is that we can be reasonably certain that CDK was at his kill house when that call came through."

"Yes!" Vanderwyk said pointing his pen at McDaniel. "Now, Target was in Los Angeles when he placed this call to CDK. The next call is from CDK to Target. This is a little over four hours later, at 11:04 p.m. And, guess what? CDK is now calling from LAX. He hopped on a commuter plane and flew out of Bellingham Airport to LA. That's the only way he could have gotten there that fast."

McDaniel felt his lips tightening into his predatory grin. He understood Vanderwyk's giddiness. "There's only going to be one flight from Bellingham to LA on a Saturday night. And there's only going to be a handful of people on that plane."

Vanderwyk lifted his Grande Latte Macchiato in a toast to his partner. "Exactly. Our suspect pool is that plane's passenger list. But wait, there's more." He took a long, slow swallow of his coffee.

Several drops leaked out from under the lid and dripped on his tie. McDaniel knew Vanderwyk kept a rack of spare ties in his cruiser for this exact reason.

Vanderwyk continued, "So, according to our timeline, CDK gets this call from Target, flies to LA. Sometime during the four hours between that call and his arrival in LA, our victim--"

"Seong," McDaniel put in.

"Um, right, our victim, Seong, manages to escape from the pink room. She, um… Well, we get the call at 4:37 a.m. the following morning when Leslie High finds the body. Now, there is no activity on either phone until 6:14 p.m. that evening."

"Just after the news goes live about us finding Seong," McDaniel said, nodding.

"Right," Vanderwyk said, "then CDK starts mad dialing the bomb. The first two calls he makes, he's just panicking, not thinking anything other than 'burn it down,' then he realizes the calls aren't going through, or something, and decides to block the number, but by then it's too late. All these calls come from L.A."

"So, he's still down there?" McDaniel asked.

"No, he's back," Vanderwyk said. "The final call between Target and CDK was at 8:22 this morning. CDK's end of that call pinged to Bellingham airport."

McDaniel sat back in his chair, pursing his lips. "He gets a call and immediately hops a flight to L.A. Seong gets away. He hears about it and tries to burn the house, but fails, so he tries to fly back, but can't get a flight until this morning." He nodded his head, staring into the blackness of his coffee. "Wow."

"Right?" Vanderwyk said.

"But, if he was on a plane into Bellingham… we just need to grab a passenger list of all flights coming into Bellingham from LAX this morning, cross-reference it with the list of passengers heading to L.A. Saturday night, and we've nailed him."

Vanderwyk nodded, smiling like he'd just won the Lotto.

"So, what is he up to now?" McDaniel asked. "He had an emergency in L.A. He went there to take care of that, whatever that was. Then he has an emergency back here. What is he doing to take care of this? He's got to be trying to separate himself from that property somehow."

"Yeah," Vanderwyk said. "You had some stuff about that in the warrant. I didn't read it all. What did you find out about the property?"

"The electric bill goes to this address on G Street," he tapped his own notepad. "Some rich Canadian owns the property."

"Just like the kill house," Vanderwyk said.

"Right," McDaniel said. "And just like the kill house, the owners of the G Street house use an accountant to manage their properties down here."

"The same accountant?"

"The same accountant," McDaniel said. "But it gets better. It's not just any accountant. It's Schechter & Polakoff."

Vanderwyk burst out in surprised laughter. Several other café customers turned and looked at the detectives. Vanderwyk got control of himself, for the most part, then leaned in and lowered his voice, "No fucking way. You're talking about *the* Schechter

& Polakoff…as in 'We put the douche in fiduciary' Schechter & Polakoff?"

Somewhere behind him, McDaniel heard Karri making a *tsk tsk* sound. He said, "Sorry, Karri." Then, still chuckling, he said to Vanderwyk, "None other."

"Holy shhhhh…"

Karri stood over the table, hands on her hips. "You two want me to open up the tattoo parlor so you can carry on up there? Or do you want to watch your darn language?"

"Sorry, Karri," Vanderwyk said, "It's just…" he shook his head.

"You can go upstairs if you want. I'll open it up for you," she said. "But if I do, one of you is getting ink."

"I think we were about to leave," Vanderwyk said, blushing again.

"We've got until 12:30," McDaniel said. "That's plenty of time. I'm thinking a nice, tribal neck tat would really set the right tone for the conference."

"Yeah," Karri mused, her voice playful. "I've got time for a quickie." She ran her fingernail in a spiral pattern on Vanderwyk's neck. "How about right here?"

Vanderwyk's face had turned as red as his tie and looked like it might pop. "No, nope, nope, nope. Stop it!" His eyes bugged out and his fingers turned white from gripping the tabletop.

"Karri," McDaniel said.

"Sorry," she smiled sweetly and patted Vanderwyk on the top of his head.

"I promise we'll be good," McDaniel said, "but we really do need our privacy for the next few minutes."

"Of course," she said, and walked away, looking once back over her shoulder at Vanderwyk.

Vanderwyk blew out a long, ragged breath, his cheeks blazing. "Where were we?"

"You okay, buddy?" McDaniel asked. He realized he was feeling almost high. CDK was not in the bag, but they had his scent and were hot on his tail. This was the fun part, the carnal impetus to hunt and chase. Once CDK was cuffed and booked, the emotional fallout from the pain he had caused would hit, and all semblance of fun would be gone. But this moment, this adrenaline rush of knowing his prey was his to catch if his game was on point, was almost as rewarding as finally capturing his quarry.

"Yeah," Vanderwyk said. "I'm fine, how 'bout you? You look kind of funny when you grin like that."

"Oh, I'm feeling good, man. We got this guy."

"You think it's one of those accountants?" Vanderwyk asked.

"I bet my next paycheck they know who it is, or at least have an idea," McDaniel said. "I'll get a warrant typed up to go through their client list, see if anything pops."

"What about G Street?"

"I'd really like to do a knock and talk, but if there is anything of value there, it'll probably go sideways on us. We just don't have time to set it up right," McDaniel said. "For now, I guess I'll head in to the office and start compiling notes. Osen wants everything looking spot-on for the big pow-wow."

"I think I'll go with you," Vanderwyk said. "I feel like we've worn out our welcome here…"

Vanderwyk's phone rang. He answered as he stood up from their table. "Vanderwyk…uh huh…yeah…Yes! Yes, G Street!… Holy shhh…shhh…okay, wow, thanks, Patti. Thank you. Yes, we're heading over. Yes, we're going right now." He emphatically nodded his head toward the parking lot.

McDaniel got up and followed him out, handing a five-dollar tip to Karri as they passed.

CHAPTER 36

"P atti?" McDaniel asked, smiling.

"That was Agent Hostetler," Vanderwyk said, shoving through GGBG's door.

"What did Agent Patti have to say?" McDaniel asked, jogging to keep up. GGBG's door jangled closed behind him.

"CDK just called Target," Vanderwyk said, smiling too broadly for his own good. "Guess where he called from?"

"Your mom's house?"

"The G Street address!" Vanderwyk said. "He's there right now!"

No further discussion was needed. Vanderwyk dashed across the road and hopped into his cruiser. McDaniel slid into his own Crown Vic and gunned the engine. He heard Vanderwyk on the radio requesting any units in the area to assist. Two patrol cars were close enough to arrive at the address at about the same time as the detectives. When that radio traffic cleared, McDaniel called Vanderwyk on his cell.

"Hey, there is an alley behind the property," McDaniel said. "I was checking it on Google earlier. He's got a parking area off the alley. I think you and I should check that out before we go in the front."

"Yeah, ten-four," Vanderwyk said. He was just ahead of McDaniel and was having a hard time keeping his cruiser to a reasonable speed. "We've got two uniforms showing up, I'll have them stage out front. They'll hold back until we're in place."

The phone beeped in McDaniel's ear. He looked at the screen and saw an incoming call from Osen, but decided Osen could wait. The address was seven blocks north of GGBG. At their current rate of speed, they would be there before he could even explain the situation.

"Good plan, but you need to slow down," McDaniel said. "It would suck to miss CDK because my partner wrapped his car around a light pole."

"Hey, Osen is calling me," Vanderwyk said, rocketing up Halleck Street. "I think I'll let it go to voice mail, exigent circumstances and such."

"Good call," McDaniel said. "Now drop it to 30. A speeding Crown Vic will spook him faster than anything else."

Vanderwyk crammed the brake and hung a left on F Street. McDaniel followed. They were one block up and one block over from their target. Vanderwyk rolled forward at under 20 miles per hour, which now felt like a snail's pace. At the next intersection, he pulled to the curb and parked.

McDaniel parked and hopped out of his vehicle. The houses on either side were well-kept. Their lawns featured eccentric yard art and compact urban gardening motifs. Gingerbread molding laced the houses themselves. Three dog-walkers paused in their strolls to eye the detectives. One of them produced an iPhone and held it up, a sure sign the detectives would be somewhere on YouTube by the end of the day.

McDaniel popped his trunk and grabbed his body armor. The patrol officers radioed that they were staged, one at the east corner of the block and the other at the west. McDaniel donned the armor then put his sports coat on over it, not a great disguise, but it was at least a little less conspicuous. Vanderwyk had done the same. They jogged around the corner and ducked into the alley.

"Which one is it?" Vanderwyk asked. "They don't have house numbers in the alley."

"It's a single-story ranch. Should be yellow," McDaniel said. "Should be that one up there with the high fence." The rear gate in the high fence was open. The nose of a shiny black SUV jutted into the alley. As they drew closer, McDaniel heard the motor running. Its rear hatch was open, the door sticking up above the board fence.

Vanderwyk whispered into his radio, "Unit at the west corner, move your vehicle half a block south and pull into the alley. He's got a black Escalade back here. Don't want him sneaking out the back."

"Ten-four, we're in the front yard, waiting for your signal. It'll take me a minute to get back to my car."

"Ten-four," Vanderwyk said.

Through the slats in the fence, McDaniel saw a small, older man carrying a cardboard file box from the house to the trunk of the Escalade. He nodded through the fence and whispered, "Let's go have a chat."

As they rounded the corner of the fence, they caught a brief glimpse of the man's back as he walked through an open door into what appeared to be the back of the garage. To the right of the door, and at a slightly higher elevation, was a sliding glass door, then two aluminum-framed windows. The yard was empty except for the Escalade and a clothesline. Vanderwyk notified the other officers that they were about to make contact with a subject in the backyard and to keep their eyes peeled.

When the two detectives were halfway between the Cadillac and the garage door, the small man emerged again, carrying another box. When he saw them, his eyes bulged behind wire-rimmed glasses. McDaniel thought he was going to drop the box, but instead, he wrapped his arms around it and hugged it to himself, staring over it at the detectives. His gaze flicked to his SUV, then to McDaniel, then to Vanderwyk, then back to his SUV. The three of them seemed frozen, as if that instant spanned several minutes.

Vanderwyk opened his mouth to identify himself. The man, still clinging to his box, spun on his heel and darted back through the garage door. Vanderwyk charged after him, yelling, "Police! Stop!"

McDaniel thumbed his mic and called, "He's running! Subject is five-five, slight build, mid-fifties, glasses, balding, tan jacket…"

He plunged into the back of the garage and saw Vanderwyk chasing the subject to his right. The older man leaped up two stairs and through a door into the kitchen. Vanderwyk was almost on him, but as the little man passed through the door, he turned and dumped his file box on the stairs.

Reams of glossy 8X10 black-and-white photos of naked children spilled down the steps and across the garage floor. Vanderwyk's feet slipped out from under him on the slick paper. The big man stumbled, but regained his footing just as fast.

McDaniel was right behind him, but Vanderwyk's bulk blocked the doorway. The door started to swing closed on its spring-loaded hinges. Vanderwyk kicked enough of the awful pictures off the stairs to be able to climb them without tripping, then barreled into the doorway. At the same time, a crashing sound reverberated through the house, the front door splintering open under the heavy boot of the uniformed officer.

Vanderwyk bellowed, "Stop! Police!"

McDaniel hopped up the stairs, drawing his gun. Then the smell hit him, a stench of gasoline so thick he gagged on it. He wanted to yell, *fall back*, but his throat seized up and vertigo overtook him. He stumbled to the side, eyes rolling. Scattered across the kitchen and dining room floor, a half dozen five-gallon gas cans lay overturned, their caps off, their contents spilling in glistening, noxious pools.

His skin, head-to-toe, erupted in sweat and goose-pimples simultaneously, and each of the round scars up his right side puckered. He turned back to Vanderwyk, who was drawing his gun and yelling.

The little man in the wire spectacles snatched a squared-off machine pistol from the countertop. The Uzi came alive in his hand, spraying bullets like a loose fire hose. The little man looked terrified. McDaniel couldn't get a clean shot because Vanderwyk stood between them, stumbling and jerking.

At that same instant, McDaniel saw what the little man held in his other hand.

A road flare.

The panic in his mind burned twice as bright as that flare would. The co-mingled memory and expectation of pain hit him in a flash, sharp and hard. He fought his overwhelming instinct to bold, instead, lunging forward, grabbing Vanderwyk's collar.

He managed to get his voice working and screamed, "Fall Back!" though he had lost sight of the uniformed officer. He thrust his gun up with his right hand while pulling backwards on Vanderwyk with his left. As they stumbled into the garage, he squeezed off several rounds. He hadn't much chance of hitting the little man, who he could no longer see, but hoped to at least provide some cover fire.

Then the kitchen exploded.

CHAPTER 37

A BLACK-ORANGE FIREBALL ERUPTED into the garage, slamming into McDaniel like a giant's fist. The sensation was horribly familiar. He and Vanderwyk tumbled across the floor. Angry, voracious flames poured upward out of the kitchen door and across the garage roof.

McDaniel got to his hands and knees and grabbed Vanderwyk's shoulder. "C'mon, man! We got to move!" The door leading out of the garage was less than five feet from the door into the kitchen, which belched and spewed flames in all directions. Within seconds, their exit would be cut off.

"Motherfucker got me," Vanderwyk said, his voice expressing nothing other than surprise. "That funny little shit actually hit me."

"Least of your worries right now, partner," McDaniel said, helping Vanderwyk roll up onto his hands and knees. He tried to yell, *let's move*, but ended up coughing instead. Thick black smoke rolled across the bottom of the flames, dropping lazy, toxic tendrils.

Vanderwyk shuffled on all fours along the back wall of the garage, hacking and coughing as he went. McDaniel followed. He realized he no longer had his gun, but had no intention of going back for it. Just before he made it out the door, his hand slid across the glossy photos. He grabbed a handful as he shuffled into the backyard.

As soon as they had cleared the garage, they collapsed together to the ground. McDaniel's eyes burned and filled with tears. He heard Vanderwyk yell, "Stop!" then begin coughing so hard McDaniel feared he'd lose a lung.

Across the yard, the little man was yanking on the door handle of his SUV. His knees were bleeding through rips in his suit pants. He was coated in soot and actual smoke rose off the back of his jacket. The Uzi was nowhere in sight, but he clutched a tablet of some type in the hand not yanking on the door handle.

McDaniel looked back toward the house and saw that the sliding glass door had been blown out, probably by the spray of bullets, giving the man a way of escape.

The Escalade's door popped open.

McDaniel jumped to his feet and charged. He had to trust his legs to do the work because his head still spun with vertigo and it felt like he was running sideways. He hit the mic on his radio and yelled, "In the alley, block the alley!"

The little man jumped into the seat just as McDaniel reached him. McDaniel grabbed for him, trying to get a hand around his neck but only getting his shoulder. The man threw the SUV into drive and stomped the gas. McDaniel held on as the vehicle lurched forward. He dug in with his fingers, gripping the man with all his strength as the Escalade pulled him off his feet.

Out the front windshield, he saw the marked, Bellingham Police cruiser brake and slide to a stop directly in front of the Escalade. The little man floored the gas, slamming into the cruiser with a horrible crunch as glass shattered and sheet metal twisted. McDaniel's face was thrown forward against the inside of the open driver's door. Then he was on the ground, staring at the undercarriage.

The Cadillac flung gravel as its tires spun. McDaniel rolled away, trying to get his bearings. He was in the alley, now sitting on his butt, back against the fence. The Escalade had pushed the Police cruiser all the way through the fence on the far side of the alley and now appeared to be stuck.

Its front wheels spun in reverse. Gravel flew from under its tires, showering the side of the police cruiser like machinegun fire. Behind the Escalade, the yellow rambler blazed, flames licking out of every window and door. Vanderwyk had crawled away from the house but now lay on his back in the yellow grass, gasping and wheezing.

McDaniel struggled to his feet. He saw the officer in the police cruiser sit up. Blood ran down the side of his face. He made eye contact with McDaniel, looking first dazed then, as that cleared, angry.

He drew his weapon and turned toward the Escalade. McDaniel tried to run forward, but only managed to shamble. The little man must have seen the officer's gun, because he abruptly ducked below the dash. The officer fired several times through the windshield and grille of the SUV.

The little man either suddenly remembered that his SUV had four-wheel drive capacity, or he saw the switch while he was ducking. Whichever it was, the back wheels lurched to life, spinning only briefly before the SUV jumped backward.

Its front bumper tore free, still lodged in the side of the cruiser. The Escalade's front wheels turned as it reversed, swinging its front end around. Its rear bumper shredded the neighbor's board fence.

McDaniel threw himself back to the ground to avoid the front end as it swung. The officer in the cruiser continued to fire through the side of the Escalade, but he was having trouble holding the gun steady. The transmission made a *chunk* sound as it slammed into drive and the vehicle lurched down the alley, spraying gravel as it went.

McDaniel managed to get his feet under himself again and stood. He could feel his face swelling and blood trickling from one nostril. There was blood in his mouth, too, and a hard, sharp thing that turned out to be a tooth.

He looked to the smashed patrol car. It was high-centered on a mess of concrete and wrought iron. The officer was still pinned inside it. He had holstered his weapon and was now talking into his radio. McDaniel realized his own radio was missing, probably ground to bits under the Escalade's tires.

Sirens wailed, converging on their location from all directions. He held up four fingers to the officer in the crumpled Crown Vic and raised an eyebrow. It was a question, *code four?* common police code meaning *everything under control?* He then recognized the officer as the red-haired Irishman from the day before. The officer raised one finger in the common code meaning *fuck you.*

He nodded his head, then made his way over to Vanderwyk. Thirty feet away from the house, the heat was nearly unbearable. Vanderwyk lay on his back, staring up at the low-slung clouds, a big stupid smile on his face, as he gasped for breath. He held his left bicep with his right hand. Dark blood oozed slowly between his fingers.

"We got to get you away from the fire, partner," McDaniel said, crouching low to stay under the heat.

Vanderwyk gritted his teeth. Through them he said, "It is taking every ounce of my will-power…" he paused as if concentrating, "will-power not to laugh…"

"It's okay, man, help is coming," McDaniel said.

"No…I'm fine, I… I just don't want to laugh 'cause it hurts."

McDaniel opened Vanderwyk's jacket and saw two lead slugs embedded in Vanderwyk's vest.

"It hurts to laugh, but…" he chuckled, wincing as he did, then got control again. "I cannot believe I just got Uzi'd by Schechter & Polakoff!"

McDaniel crouched lower, the heat baking the skin on his face. "I'm going to buy you a tee shirt with that on it. It'll be your Christmas gift. 'I got Uzi'd by Schechter & Polakoff in Bellingham, WA.'"

Vanderwyk broke out in a coughing, laughing fit, clutching his ribs as he did. "Stop! Stop making me…" He coughed again. "Fucker! Stop making me laugh!"

"Then get up and move away from the fire." McDaniel hooked an arm under him and helped him roll up onto his hands and knees. "You stay here and I'm going to start with the accountant jokes."

"Asshole," Vanderwyk coughed, laughing. He spat a glob of blood in the grass as the two of them crossed the lawn on hands and knees. "Look at that," he spat again. "I'm coughing up blood and you think it's funny."

"You're the one laughing," McDaniel said. "You probably just have a bruised lung. It'll feel better as soon as it stops hurting."

"Man, you should have seen the look on his face," Vanderwyk said. He burst into laughter again and collapsed to the ground, tears cutting lines through the soot on his face. "That little shit's eyes were bigger than those douchy little glasses he wears. Classic spraying-and-praying. I cannot believe he got me."

"Up we go," McDaniel said, helping Vanderwyk to his feet. They were far enough away from the fire that the heat was tolerable. They crossed the cement pad where the Escalade had been parked. Lying in the grass to the side of the parking spot was the iPad tablet the accountant had been carrying. McDaniel must have stripped it from his grasp as the man made his escape.

Vanderwyk hummed the Christmas tune, *Do You See What I See?* then chuckled. Then coughed.

"I see it, partner," McDaniel said. "We'll get it bagged."

Four paramedics were dragging two gurneys towards the detectives. Police officers, EMTs, and firefighters swarmed the alley. Firefighters were using a hydraulic jack to peel open the door of the police cruiser. Inside, the Irish cop was drinking from a slightly crumpled soda can as he waited. McDaniel became aware of his cell phone having seizures in his jacket pocket.

"Looks like we're going to miss that conference," Vanderwyk said.

"That's what I like about you, partner," McDaniel said as he helped Vanderwyk onto one of the gurneys, "always looking on the bright side."

CHAPTER 38

THEY DID, INDEED, miss the conference. Both detectives were taken to Saint Joseph's Hospital. McDaniel was treated for smoke inhalation and a minor concussion, along with various scrapes and contusions. The second worst part of the day was the forty minutes it took a nurse to dig the gravel out of his knees, palms, and elbows.

The worst part was waiting for news about Vanderwyk. Body armor can stop a bullet, but often the bullet will dimple the vest, penetrating the body up to an inch beneath the skin. Two rounds to the chest, even with armor, could inflict grievous injury. And Vanderwyk had also taken a round to the left bicep.

The doctors suggested that McDaniel stay overnight for observation, but that was probably because three other officers were spending the night and the police department was footing the bill. The Irish cop, Murphy, had a concussion, broken ribs, and a broken left arm. The officer who had stormed through the front door had second-degree burns on his legs and hands.

After McDaniel's treatment in the emergency room, he was taken up the elevator one floor to a semi-private room. Hospital policy required him to make the trip in a wheelchair. He caught a glimpse of the ER waiting area as the nurse rolled him down the hall. It was filled to standing room only with family and off duty police officers. When they reached his room, the nurse told him that the other bed had been assigned to Vanderwyk. But when he asked how his partner was doing, she said there had not been any word.

The room was dark and quiet after the bustle of the emergency room. Most of his injuries had been anesthetized locally, and he had been given a heavy dose of ibuprofen. There wasn't any pain, but he felt slight, throbbing pressure in his knees and palms where the gravel had been embedded. The side of his face had collided with the inside of the SUV's door as it slammed into Murphy's cruiser. He'd broken off an eye-tooth right at the gum line and had a black eye. His face had swollen and now felt puffy and numb, as if there were a layer of neoprene glued to his cheek and forehead.

They had stripped him down to his boxers in the E.R. to assess his known injuries and check for unknown injuries. (In high-adrenaline situations, even serious injuries can go unnoticed until much later. It is rare, but not unheard of, for a police officer or soldier to walk away from a gun fight and only later discover they had been shot.) They didn't find any holes on McDaniel that he hadn't been born with, though he did receive many comments on his octopus. Most were favorable.

His clothes had been unceremoniously dumped in a heavy-duty white plastic bag that now hung on the handle of his closet door. The pants had been shredded during the encounter. His jacket hadn't fared much better. The paramedics who brought him to the hospital had checked his wallet, badge, body armor, and cell phone with hospital security. His gun was somewhere under a pile of smoldering rubble on G Street.

The nurse had helped him into the bed and insisted he rest. He was not to get out of bed, talk to anyone, or even sit up. As soon as she was out of the room, he stood and walked to the window. He had a nice view of the first-floor roof and part of the parking lot. At least seven patrol vehicles were parked there. He walked to the door. A uniformed officer sat in a chair in the hall, a standard precaution for officers injured in the line of duty. He greeted McDaniel and asked if the detective needed anything.

"Is Officer Murphy here?" McDaniel asked. "Have you heard how he's doing?"

The nurse at the desk across the hall cleared her throat disapprovingly. She stood up and glared at him. McDaniel smiled and held a hand up to her.

The officer said, "Yeah, he's here. Pretty banged up, but nothing permanent."

"Can you do me a favor? When you get relieved, head down to the gift shop and have them send some daisies to his room, from me? I'll pay you back when I get out."

"Sure, I can do that, but he won't be too happy about it."

"That's the idea," McDaniel said.

The nurse cleared her throat again, more loudly, then started walking toward them.

McDaniel said, "Thanks," to the officer, then said, "Sorry," to the nurse, and slipped back into his room.

He walked to the window, then to the bathroom, then to the closet, then back to his bed. He sat on the edge, then sat in the chair instead. He looked at the clock. A little over an hour and a half had passed since they had arrived. Vanderwyk had been awake and talking during the ride to the hospital. In the E.R, McDaniel had heard him start laughing once, but that had ended in a painful-sounding cough. He hadn't heard anything since.

A phone sat on the table by his bed. It had clear plastic cube buttons. Its yellowish-white color reminded him of cheap motels. A sticker glued to its side told him to dial 9 for an outside line. So he did. When he heard the dial tone, he punched in his wife's number.

She answered halfway through the first ring. "Hello?"

"It's me."

"Are you okay?" There was a sternness in her voice accompanying the concern. It said *you damn well better be.*

McDaniel smiled, which felt very awkward and lopsided. "Yeah, I'm alright," he said, relaxing a bit, "but you wouldn't know it by looking at me."

"Oh, God," she said, "how bad is it?"

"Think: 1980's-T.V.-detective-bar-fight, only with smoke inhalation," he said. "Where are you?"

"Darren." She sighed, disapprovingly, then said, "I'm just closing up the shop. They sent a pair of officers to tell me that you were hurt. They didn't say how bad, then I saw the smoke downtown…"

"Hey, it's okay. It's really not that bad. You don't need to rush," he said. "Listen, you have time to call around, see if you can get one of your girls to come in so you don't have to close early--"

"Hush!" she said, harshly. "My husband is in the hospital. I'm going to be there."

He smiled and settled back into the chair. "Could you do one thing for me?"

"Whatever you need," she said.

"Swing by the house and grab me a change of clothes. Mine are toast."

There was a pause, then she said, "Fine, but you are not leaving there until the doctor gives the okay."

They said their goodbyes and McDaniel hung up. He paced the room again a couple times before settling back into the chair and flipping the television on. Two women were pretending to be near-orgasmic over a piece of jewelry encrusted with fake gemstones while the *DIAL NOW!* numbers scrolled across the bottom of the screen. He flipped over to the local network news. One of the reporters who had chased him across the grassy park yesterday afternoon stared into the camera with sincere intensity, just as fake as the Rhinestone Network ladies.

"... details are still flooding in. What we have so far is multiple accounts of automatic gunfire and explosions in the middle of this quiet downtown neighborhood. Behind me, you can see the line of police cruisers blocking off the entire area. Residents are saying they have been forcibly removed from their homes as the area has been evacuated..."

The view cut away from the reporter at the roadblock to an aerial view from a helicopter circling over the G Street address. It gave McDaniel an eerie sense of *deja vu*. The picture looked almost identical to the google satellite image he had been looking at just a few hours ago. The only difference was, in this view, the yellow rambler was now a smoldering black rectangle stamped into a patch of lawn.

The reporter's audio feed continued, "We have no official word yet, but many residents speculate that both of these explosions are terrorist-related..."

Both? he thought, then the view switched to a split-screen, showing a second location, a parking garage with flames billowing out through the openings and thick black smoke rolling skyward. A stamp at the bottom of this image said, "Filmed Earlier."

The bed-side phone rang. McDaniel hit mute on the remote and answered.

"Hey, buddy. It's Spooner, how you doing?"

McDaniel hadn't been called 'buddy' in at least two decades, and he had never heard Spooner call anyone else by that name. "Spooner, I'm fine, really."

"Oh, okay." He sounded a bit more like himself. "What about Vanderwyk? I heard he got hit."

McDaniel ran a hand over his mouth and chin. He took a breath, then said, "Yeah, he got hit. His vest took the worst of it, but I haven't heard how he's doing."

"Shit, man, we're all praying for him," Spooner said.

McDaniel grinned. His mother would have said, *with that mouth?* but McDaniel didn't. Instead, he said, "I assume that you are calling instead of Osen because he doesn't want to talk to me?"

"He isn't *talking* to anybody," Spooner said, "just yelling. He gave your case to the state investigators."

McDaniel guessed this was as much to punish him for the fallout as for any legitimate reason, but at the moment, it didn't really bother him. He might feel differently once the painkillers and concussion wore off.

"Osen told the State investigators, 'We were out of our depth, to begin with, and now I'm down two senior detectives,'" Spooner said. "What he didn't tell them is that we already did all the work for them. All they have to do is go scoop the guy up. And that should be easy since the idiot has been running those stupid adds for a decade. Everybody in the state knows what Anton Polakoff looks like."

"He's still in the wind, though, right?"

"For now. But you guys fucked him up. You took down his kill house and whatever that G Street house was. He's bleeding… oh, they recovered his glasses near the alley, smashed to shit. So, whatever he is doing, he isn't perving on children anymore. He's probably holed up in a culvert or a vacant house."

"It shouldn't be too hard to find that Escalade. Front end damage, bullet holes…"

"We found it," Spooner said. "Even easier than you think. He switched vehicles a few blocks away in that parking garage behind the Herald Building. He dumped the Escalade, then torched it. Not too tough to guess the blazing Escalade was the one we were looking for."

"I'm starting to think this guy has a thing for fire," McDaniel said.

"Yeah," Spooner said, "he's probably a bed wetter, too."

"Aren't they all?" McDaniel said, then asked, "Hey, Spooner, what does the evidence from the kill house tell you? Is this our guy? I mean, we know Polakoff is good for several counts of aggravated assault, arson, weapons charges, and we can link him to Seong and the bodies at the kill house, but do we know he was the one who actually killed them? Or is it possible that he was just some sort of cover-up guy?"

"Well, you know as well as anybody that anything is possible, but it's looking like he's the guy," Spooner said. "We recovered hundreds of fingerprints in that pink room. About half of them were from children, Seong, mainly. But all the rest match Polakoff's prints we got off of that iPad you recovered. There were no other adult prints at the kill house."

McDaniel shook his head and let out a humorless chuckle. "'The Creepy Doll Killer.' He's not at all what the media portrayed, is he?"

"Yeah, as soon as you start calling someone by three initials, they take on a larger-than-life super-villain status," Spooner said. "There was no evidence to suggest anyone else had been in that kill house. I'm gonna say Polakoff is your man, but we'll know for sure in the next few days. Before Osen called us back from the kill house to cover your seat at the conference, thanks for that by the way…"

McDaniel smiled and nodded.

"…before we left, we found cameras mounted in a dummy smoke detector, in the microwave clock, and behind the television. They were all wired into a digital video recorder. We didn't get a chance to view any of the footage, which doesn't hurt my feelings at all, btw. State has the DVR now. That will probably answer any lingering questions about what went on in there."

"I think we know what went on in there," McDaniel said, no longer smiling. He felt a greasy nausea crawling through his gut, but didn't know if it was a result of the concussion or the details of the case. "That house and the pink room feel right for Polakoff, but he doesn't strike me as the criminal mastermind type. I feel like we are missing a piece of this."

"What do you mean?" Spooner asked.

"So, he's got this girl chained to a wall, bodies buried in his basement, and he likes to start fires. That's one profile, fits with loner, sexually-deviant sociopath. But on the other hand, he's got a full-auto Uzi, which he had obviously never fired before. You can't just flash your accountant's badge at the local gun shop and pick up one of those guys," McDaniel said. "Makes me think someone gave it to him. He's got that Escalade, plus a second vehicle he had staged at the parking garage. He's got all those file boxes. And he's got a connection to a mystery person in L.A. that the FBI is hunting."

McDaniel paused, then asked, "You said you got prints off the iPad. Did you find any useful data on it?"

"It was busted, not bad, but the screen is cracked and it wouldn't turn on. Frodo took a quick look at it and said she was pretty sure the state's computer forensics guys would be able to restore whatever was on it, but they don't have the stuff from G Street yet. That's all still in our evidence locker."

"What else did you get from G Street?" McDaniel asked.

"Well, for starters, that dipshit left his license plate embedded in the side of Murphy's cruiser, so that helps. It's not his Escalade, by the way, belongs to a holding company in Canada. There was the iPad, with some of Polakoff's blood on it, which suggests maybe one of you guys put a hole in him. We can hope. There were about a dozen photographs scattered across the lawn. Some of them were nothing but charred and bubbled scraps, but a few survived…" Spooner paused.

McDaniel guessed there was more to tell, so he waited.

After a beat, Spooner continued, "It's a good thing we recovered those, but I wish I had never seen them. Glad the state is handling that aspect of the case. The front of each photo is a naked child, the back has a chart listing age, gender, height, weight and a column marked 'special.' There are serial numbers on each. No names."

McDaniel remembered grabbing the photos as he stumbled out of the blazing garage. He remembered their slick, almost greasy feel in his fingers. A pump bottle of hand sanitizer sat on his bedside table. His hands had been thoroughly scrubbed and bandaged during the gravel removal, but he squirted out some of the alcohol solution anyway.

"Hey, Spooner," McDaniel said, "thanks for keeping me in the loop. I doubt Osen would have given me anything."

"Yeah, no problem, man. And just so you know, Osen is pissed because of the public response to gunfire and explosions in the heart of the city, but everyone in the station thinks you guys did the right thing. This Polakoff guy, even if he is just some skeevy tweed-wearing accountant, he had to be stopped. You guys stopped him."

"We stopped him for now, but if we don't catch him, he will do it again. Where are we with his partner, Schechter?"

"Joel Schechter is here now, talking to one of State's detectives. It took our guys a while to explain what had happened and convince him it was true, but once that sank in, he came in voluntarily, gave us unlimited access to his office and files. Polakoff's, too. He appears to be cooperating fully. I have not heard much of what is going on in there, but I do know that he expressed fear for his personal safety."

"He thinks Polakoff is going to come after him?"

"Like I said, I didn't hear much of it, but that's not the idea I got. More like someone else might come after him. One other thing you should know, a team from the FBI just showed up. One of their guys grabbed the lead detective from State and took him into an interview room for a private conference. I think there's a good chance the feds will take the case from State."

"If the bodies at Polakoff's came from his L.A. connection, that would make it a federal investigation…"

"Oh, Rourke is heading this way. He just finished a shouting match with Osen, looks pretty pissed."

"Lovely," McDaniel said. Rourke was the union steward. It would be his job to protect McDaniel and Vanderwyk from disciplinary measures if the administration decided to file against them. His typical strategy was to badger and harangue the officer he was assigned to defend, hoping to discover any weakness in the case as early as possible.

"Yeah, well, just remember, he's got your back, and he usually goes easy on the initial interview, but if you hold anything back and he finds out, he'll be on you like white on rice."

"Right," McDaniel said. He leaned way back in his chair, trying to get comfortable despite aching everywhere.

"Detective McDaniel," Rourke said, his voice strained and his tone far more formal than McDaniel was used to.

"Officer Rourke," he said. "Are you calling as Osen's go-between or as my union rep?"

"Osen doesn't have anything to say to you. I won't pass anything you say to Osen, if that's what you're asking."

"How does it look? Is this going to come down on me?"

"Well. Let's see, that G Street rambler wasn't much to look at, but the house just to the east was applying to be added to the Historic Register. It took significant heat damage on the side facing Polakoff's house.

"There are bullet holes in at least two other homes in that neighborhood, no doubt from Polakoff's machine pistol. Thank God he didn't hit any civilians. Where the hell did he get that thing anyway?"

"There's no way to know that until we can run the serial numbers," McDaniel said. "Have they been able to recover what's left of it? He didn't have it with him when he jumped into the Escalade."

"No, the place is still too hot. Gobble and Sandwich probably won't be handling this one. They claim it's better to pick through that mess in daylight hours, which I guess is true. Osen'll probably have a State forensics team out there at first light.

"But back to your original question, the brass will try to hang this on somebody. It just looks like a huge fuck-up and none of them want to be saddled with it. In addition to the fire and bullet holes, there are also two destroyed fences. That statue Murphy ended up straddling – the homeowner is claiming it was an original piece by some activist artist who died in a protest in South America – they're saying it's worth like a half-million dollars or some shit--"

"Wait, hold up," McDaniel said. "They paid a half-million dollars for a statue and they just left it out in their backyard? That's more than the house is worth."

"Didn't say they paid that much, probably bought it for fifty bucks at one of those summer arts festivals before the guy died. But that's not the point. The Herald is probably going to run a front-page sob story about the artist's life and the importance of this piece and the extent of cultural degradation that will be brought about by its destruction at the hands of reckless and savage police officers. You know, like they always do."

"Well, at least nobody reads newsprint anymore."

"They've got a website, smartass," Rourke said. "And look, this isn't just about media relations. There's Murphy's Crown Vic, also totaled. You know they don't make those anymore, right? Once they're gone, they're gone. Pretty soon we're all going to be driving around in Chargers."

"I'm sorry about the car, Rourke."

"It's not just the car. You've also got four police officers hospitalized. Your big scary serial killer monster turns out to be a milk-toast, bespectacled, scrawny weasel of a man. And, best of all, he got away. Can you, maybe, just run me through it real quick? How exactly did this happen? So I can start putting together a defense for you."

"Yeah, sure, we got a tip that our man was at the location--"

"A tip from who?"

"Vanderwyk brokered a deal with his contact at the FBI. I don't know if you want to put that in your defense, but I'm telling it to you straight. We had a warrant, so we had legal access to the info. Getting it from the feebs let us skip three weeks of red tape."

"Okay, fine," Rourke said. "So, J. Edgar calls and says…what?"

"Said CDK's phone was being used at the G Street address. We had that address already, but were holding off on the search until--"

"Until Osen gave the go-ahead," Rourke said. "Yeah, I got that part. So, you get this tip. They say he's there. So, you guys just go kick in the door? Even though Osen said to hold off? Sounds like you're fucked."

"The tip told us two things," McDaniel said, patiently. He knew this was a game, so the other man's bluster didn't rile him. "It told us where the target was – and keep in mind who this target was, a serial killer who preyed on young girls. The tip also told us who was calling him. The last two times this person had called CDK, those calls were associated with the attempted destruction of evidence.

"If CDK was at the G street address, and if he had received a call from that number, we felt it was reasonable to believe that he was destroying, or attempting to destroy evidence."

"But you have no idea who this mystery caller is, right? Because that is an FBI case you do not have access to."

"That is correct, but all the information we have received from this source up to and including this tip had been accurate. We had no reason to doubt this information."

There was a pause in the conversation. McDaniel heard scribbling and assumed Rourke was scratching out notes on a legal pad. The man was making *hmm* and *mmm-hmm* noises as well. When he spoke again, he continued with his hectoring shtick, but with less gusto. He was pleased with the answers he was receiving.

"Fine, so you know your man is at the house. You call in backup, stage appropriately…You should have had one more car blocking the other end of the alley, of course. But that's…mmm…minor point and wouldn't have mattered anyway..." More scribbling from the other end. "Okay, so we get to the point where you knock on the door..."

"Negative. We approached through the alley," McDaniel said. "We observed the subject loading boxes into his SUV. He had both arms wrapped around a file box. He did not appear to be armed or in any position to offer significant resistance. We approached, identified ourselves as police officers, everything by the book. He was in a position of disadvantage. There was no way we could have been expected to know that he had a submachine gun on his kitchen counter. If we had waited longer for additional backup, or for Osen to quarterback this thing, he would have been long gone."

"Sounds like an ideal situation," Rourke said. "Explain to me how it went to shit." This was information he needed, but the tone of the question was more of amazed curiosity than prosecutorial interrogation. "Because there's no denying that it went to shit."

"No, you're right about that," McDaniel mused. "The little weasel ran in through the garage door, up the stairs into the kitchen. I understand now that he was planning to run back out through the sliding door. We followed him. I think I realized what had happened as soon as I was in the garage, but by then it was too late.

"I smelled the gas, knew it was a trap, but by then – I didn't tell you this part, Polakoff dumped his file box on the stairs between the garage and house. Vanderwyk's feet got tangled. I couldn't get around him, and I couldn't get him out of the way. When I smelled the gas, and saw the cans scattered about, my only thought was getting us out before it blew. Then Polakoff pops up with that gun and all hell broke loose. From that point on, it was just act and react."

"Shit, man…" Rourke said, his demeanor now completely reverted to normal. "That is some crazy, crazy shit. This CDK/Polakoff character is extremely dangerous, which gives you extreme latitude in your response. The Brass is going to want to crucify somebody over this mess, but based on this preliminary info, they've got nothing on you. Your actions appear to be reasonable and justified. They'll find a few points of criticism, just because that's the one thing they are good at, but nothing that can really hurt you."

"Alright, bro, thanks for having my back on this. Let me know if you need anything else from me."

"Yeah, sure thing," Rourke said. "Have you heard anything about Vanderwyk?"

"No, not yet," McDaniel said. "But I see my wife up at the nurse's station asking for me, so I'm going to let you go. Call me right away if you hear anything."

"You got it, man. Hang in there."

"You too." McDaniel disconnected.

CHAPTER 39

KATHERYN KNOCKED AND entered the room. Darren felt his nervous energy drain away at the sight of her. The worries about Polakoff and Vanderwyk and Osen suddenly seemed less important, or at least, less pressing. Those things were outside – the world that spun around them, sometimes smoothly, sometimes not. Regardless, at the center of his world, everything was as it should be, and as long as that were true everything else could fall apart and he'd be okay.

She rushed forward and wrapped her arms around him, but gasped when the light fell across his swollen eye and cheek. "Oh, ouch! You're a mess!"

He turned his face, showing her only the undamaged side. "It's just a matter of how you look at it," he said and tried to twinkle his eye at her.

It didn't work.

"No," she said, glowering at him. "Your face looks like hell. And you're supposed to be resting."

"I don't feel like resting." But, he suddenly did feel tired, and calm enough to lie down, maybe even sleep. He let her walk him to the bed. The pain made a brief appearance in his knees when he bent them to sit. This seemed to give notice to his headache and it revived as he lay down.

Katheryn helped him with the covers. She then turned the chair so that it faced the bed and sat, holding his hand. Her eyes studied his face for several minutes. He watched thoughts passing through her mind, indicated by the variations in her expression.

After several minutes, she said, "Tell me about CDK. Tell me about the girl you found, and the house where you found the others."

He looked away from her, to the muted television that continued to flash video of the burning house or the burning Escalade. "Katheryn…"

"Tell me what you dreamed last night, about the cracks and 'the eyes peering through,' Darren," she said evenly but firmly. "I want to hear the very worst of it, every detail."

"Kat, I told you this morning--" he tried again.

"You told me you don't want to let the darkness into our home. Okay, that's kind of weird, but I can accept it. But we're not at our home, and 'the darkness' damn well knows about *this* place already. If you don't believe me, go check out the basement." She gave him a sad smile and a double squeeze on his hand. "The

T.V. is saying 'machinegun fire.' You guys don't carry machine-guns, do you?"

"No," he said.

"That means someone was shooting at *you* with a machine-gun, right?"

He nodded affirmation.

"The doctor says you are being treated for smoke inhalation. That means you were inside the house when it blew up, right?"

Again, he nodded.

"I understand that some of the things that you see and feel and experience have traumatized you and that you feel it is your duty to shield me from that pain. But here's what *you* need to under-stand, it is my responsibility as your life partner to share your pain...and your joy, and everything in between. That's what you need from me and damn it, Darren, I need that from you. You have to let me in, for both our sakes."

She squeezed his hand in both of hers.

"On top of that, I need to understand what it is about this CDK bastard that justifies me letting you run into exploding houses and machinegun fire. You tell me he's a 'bad guy' like were twelve-year-olds playing a game. But this isn't a damn game, Darren. You are in the hospital. Your partner has bullet holes in him. I trust you. If you say you've got to get him, I know you've got to get him. If you feel it is worth risking your life to catch this guy, well, fine. But you have to make *me* feel – not just know – I need to really *feel* how horrible he is, so that when two officers show up at my shop and tell me you are in the hospital – or when you bring your nightmares to bed with you at three in the morning – I can understand why. So that I can send you out the door in the morning hoping you find him rather than hoping you never get within a hundred miles of him."

Darren had been watching her as she spoke but now rolled his head away from her. He looked at the ceiling for a long time, then began to speak. He started with finding Seong and took Katheryn step by step through the whole case. At first, he focused on the details. Not wanting to leave anything out – if he was going to open up, he was going to do it completely – but as he spoke, and as she listened and encouraged him with comments and subtle gestures, he began to speak less about the facts and more about how the facts affected him, about smelling the gasoline and the terror that smell conjured in him, about the nausea he still felt when thinking about the box full of photos, about Seong's desperation and courage and the words he would like to speak over her grave when she was finally laid to rest.

Those were the first tears he shed since his mother's funeral. Katheryn cried, too, and at some point, moved into the bed and curled around him. It was a tight fit, but neither of them minded. When he had finished, she hugged him close to her until he slept. Two hours later, when the nurses wheeled Vanderwyk into the room, they were still asleep, undisturbed by any dream.

CHAPTER 40

DARREN AWOKE TO clatter and commotion, feeling Katheryn move away from him. She had been dozing lightly and at the nurse's polite tap on the door, had slipped out of the bed and now sat primly straightening her hair, a demure smile on her lips.

An orderly wheeled the other bed out of the room, whisking the curtain aside as he did so. A moment later, two orderlies wheeled a different bed into the space. A third orderly helped guide the associated IV pole, oxygen tank, and heart monitor into the room. Two nurses fussed about a sleeping Vanderwyk, ensuring proper head elevation and correct connections to all the equipment. As the orderlies exited, a doctor entered. She was an East Indian woman who appeared to be in her late twenties but was probably older.

She glanced passingly at Vanderwyk, then approached McDaniel and extended her hand. "My name is Dr. Lohda. You are Darren McDaniel, correct?" Her speech had the clipped and lilting accent of her people. Combined with the softness of her voice, it sounded more like singing than speech.

"Yes," he said, shaking her hand.

"I am pleased to meet you. Mr. Vanderwyk asked that I share with you the details of his injuries and prognosis," she said. "Would you like me to tell you now?"

"Yes, doctor," McDaniel said. "Is he going to be okay?"

"He will be very 'okay' for a man who has been shot three times, I think," she said, smiling sweetly. "He is very sturdy. But, as I said, he has been shot three times and that is bad for anyone." She said this last bit as if scolding McDaniel, peering briefly at him over her glasses.

She looked down at her clipboard. "The injury to his arm, here," she demonstrated by pointing to her own left bicep, "was, as you say, a 'through and through.' There is damage to the muscle tissue, but we can expect him to recover at least ninety percent of function, probably more. For a gunshot wound, this is not that bad.

"The injuries to his chest were more critical, or I should say one of these was critical. The other not so much. One bullet struck Mr. Vanderwyk in the center of his chest, over the sternum. This bullet struck the trauma plate on his body armor. Because of this, the armor's backface deformation was minimal, resulting in a large contusion, but likely no other damage.

"Unhappily, the third bullet struck Mr. Vanderwyk's body armor low on the left side, here," again demonstrating on her own body without taking her eyes from her notes. "The armor here is thinner and did not provide Mr. Vanderwyk with the same level of protection. The impact broke one of Mr. Vanderwyk's ribs and this rib then punctured his lung. A punctured lung is very serious. We had to work very hard to keep the lung from collapsing. He also inhaled the smoke, causing inflammation and low oxygen levels, and this also increases the danger for Mr. Vanderwyk if his lung collapsed.

"We were able to stabilize Mr. Vanderwyk." She brought her eyes up from her clipboard for the first time since her explanation began. She looked at Vanderwyk, smiled, then turned back to McDaniel. "He is strong and healthy. I think he will continue to be strong and healthy for many years to come, but today I will need to keep him here for observation."

"I think he'll like that," McDaniel said.

"Darren!" Katheryn said in a hushed voice.

Dr. Lohda looked quizzically at McDaniel, then to Katheryn, then back to McDaniel. Finally, she flipped to a different set of notes and said, "Well, Mr. McDaniel, your doctor has said he can clear you to go home if you feel well enough. Or if you are feeling dizzy or nauseous you should stay tonight and be evaluated in the morning."

"I'm ready to go home," Darren said. Katheryn gave him a look of concern and he smiled reassuringly at her.

"Very well, then, Mr. McDaniel. I will ask the nurse to page your doctor. As soon as you have seen him you can go."

CHAPTER 41

I T TOOK OVER an hour before they were actually checked out
of the hospital. Night had fallen over the city, and it was almost
seven by the time Katheryn pulled her car into their garage.
Darren had been spacing out most of the ride home, thoughts
wandering between concern for Vanderwyk and disappointment
in losing his quarry.

Now, as Katheryn assisted him out of the passenger seat (he
hadn't needed assistance, but he didn't decline it either), his
thoughts turned to food. He hadn't eaten since his light breakfast at GGBG that morning.

Katheryn had other ideas. "Robyn's still out with her friend,"
she said, softly, her lips close to his ear. "You want to see if we can
get a little closer than we did in that hospital bed?"

"Oh, I don't know," Darren said, opening the door between the house and garage for her. "That was pretty tight. I'm not sure you could get any closer than that."

"Oh, I think you'd be surprised just how close we can get," she said, turning to him as he came through the door, "if we can strip away all the layers separating us." She slowly slid the zipper of his coat open, then lifted it off his shoulders.

He shrugged out of the coat as she took it. "It does always seem like something comes between us," he said. "I think we need to find a way through all these barriers." He opened the bottom button on her coat, near her navel, and began working his way up. "But, you're going to have to take it easy on me, I'm feeling a bit fragile."

She ran a hand across his abdomen, then around and up his back, "You don't feel fragile to me."

"No?'" he asked. He slid his hand inside her coat, around her waist, and guided her deeper into the house.

"Doesn't feel like you'd be easy to break at all," she said, letting the coat slide off. She caught it in a graceful twist and slung it over the back of a chair as they moved into the kitchen. She turned back to him, both hands on his chest this time. "But it feels like I'm going to have a lot of fun trying."

Darren was about to come back with a line about Ikea. It was a longstanding, inside joke about breaking and fixing furniture, which always came down to inserting knob A into slot B. Before he could, Katheryn went rigid in his arms. Her eyes bulged and the high color in her cheeks went paper-white.

Darren turned to see what she saw as she breathed out his name.

CHAPTER 42

A NAKED ASIAN BOY stood looking at them, peering out of an 8X10 glossy nailed to their wall. A framing nail had been pounded into the drywall beside the telephone, pinning the photo there. The boy's hands dangled at his sides. His sunken eyes look through the camera rather than at it.

A fat black slash had been drawn across the middle of the photograph. The slash ended in an arrow pointing down. Directly below the photo, someone had hung an old, cassette tape-based answering machine, coated in dust and still bearing a Value Village price tag. Its red light blinked.

McDaniel's hand went to the place on his belt where his gun belonged, then hovered there, unsure of its purpose when it found the spot empty. The house was dead quiet. McDaniel's mind raced. *It* had been here; the darkness had been inside his home. It had left something, and it had taken something. He knew what it had taken, but could not quite allow himself to accept it.

Katheryn had ahold of his left arm with both hands. Her grip tightened as he reached out and pushed the play button on the old machine.

A beep, a pause, then Robyn's voice. She sounded scared, but also very pissed off. "Dad," she said, "It's Robyn. You need to call back this number. Don't call anybody else." The next words she said in a rush, "Two of them…" but the line clicked off.

"Oh, God, Darren," Katheryn whispered. In her eyes, McDaniel saw a reflection of his own terror. He felt his own terror giving way to rage.

He grabbed the phone and punched the last call return button. The reedy, peevish voice that answered was unmistakably that of Anton Polakoff.

"Detective McDaniel," the voice said, quavering as if in pain or exasperated to the last extremity.

"This is McDaniel," he said, concentrating on maintaining a steady voice. "Where is my daughter?"

"*Your* daughter?" Polakoff asked. McDaniel still could not pinpoint the emotion coloring his words, but whatever it was, his voice trembled with it. He could almost see the phone shaking in Polakoff's hand. "*Your* daughter? Detective McDaniel, a man may only claim ownership over that which he has the ability to keep."

McDaniel's jaw clenched. He felt veins pumping in his temples and forehead. Katheryn clung to his arm and, he knew, somewhere near the other end of this telephone call, Robyn clung to him just as tightly.

He said, "What is it that you want, Mr. Polakoff?"

"I want my life back, you son of a *bitch!*" he screamed, losing what little control he had had over his voice. "But it's too late for that, isn't it? You made sure of that. You... You... I am not a monster. You hear me? I am *not* a criminal! You have the T.V. news calling me the Creepy Doll Killer! Do you know... what... *how* that makes me feel?" he sobbed twice, then sniffed. "I never meant for them to die. I rescued those children. I saved them! You have no idea what you've done!"

"Mr. Polakoff," McDaniel said, he mimed to Katheryn for her to call the detective squad on her cell. "I don't understand. Explain--"

"Don't play your stupid fucking games with me, detective. You don't have to try to keep me on the line. Trace this call if you can, I don't care." His voice cracked. "I'm going to tell you where I am when I'm good and ready. But not until you listen and understand. I am not the monster. *You* are!

"You comfort yourself in your privileged normalcy, all of your impulses sanctioned and approved by the society *you* define. Your desires, your needs, you are free to indulge them fully – using them for whatever purpose fulfills you. You are embraced by the society you and your kind have created. They give you titles of honor like 'father' and 'husband' and you think that makes you right and wholesome, but your needs and my needs are just the same. And you all persecute me because I was born with non-normative physiological impetuses. Why is it when you fulfill your need to possess a woman, they call you good, but when I possess a woman they call me a monster? Answer me!"

"I do not *possess* my wife or daughter," McDaniel said.

"You lie to yourself, detective! The first thing you said to me is, 'Where is *my* daughter?' You see her as your possession, but she's my possession now because *I have her*. And I can use her in whatever manner my needs demand."

A tiny snapping sound in McDaniel's ear brought his attention to the telephone handset. He gripped it so tightly that the display window had cracked. Katheryn's hand had slipped down his arm. She held his other hand, but at arm's length so that she could whisper into her cell phone. The frustration on her face told McDaniel all he needed to know about that conversation.

"Mr. Polakoff," he said, feeling steel barriers beginning to wall off his heart, "you have a very limited window of opportunity. *Very* limited…"

"I was a father to those children. I was a husband to them. I saved them and cared for them. I provided for their needs and they provided for my need. Why can't you people understand? Love is never wrong! Regardless of gender or age or race, love is never wrong! For how many years will we continue to call ourselves an enlightened society while we continue to persecute unique expressions of love or family systems outside the conventions?"

"Mr. Polakoff, 'love' does not leave six dead bodies buried in a basement," McDaniel said.

What came next sounded at first like a wail, but soon morphed into a scream, then Polakoff cried, "I didn't mean for them to die!

I didn't mean for them to die! Don't you understand? *You* did that to them! Your rules and laws and judgmental, fundamentalist, sexually repressed, puritanical, despotic… you forced our love underground! We had to hide and…and…"

He heaved several deep, ragged breaths. Then he finally calmed enough to say, "I loved those girls. Every one of them. I loved them and they loved me. I know that to be the truth, and you can never take that from me. I *own* that, Detective McDaniel. I rescued those girls. I took them home and I cared for them." He sniffled, then continued, "But now, because of *you*, I won't be able to rescue any more of them. Now, whatever happens to them… That's on you, detective."

If Polakoff never rescued another child, McDaniel would be very happy indeed. "Is this why you took my daughter, to persuade me to convey your story to the news so that they would stop calling you 'CDK?'"

"She's *my* daughter! Haven't you been paying attention? My daughter!" Polakoff said. He paused, and McDaniel heard a second voice in the background, relaxed but emphatic. When Polakoff spoke again he seemed calmer. "But, I am willing to give her to you, in the same condition I took her from you. I only ask that you return to me the property you took from me. Specifically, you have my iPad. I want it back."

The sudden shift in the conversation confused McDaniel and it took him a beat to catch up.

"Don't bother trying to tell me that you can't get it. I know you can. The evidence you collected today is still in lockup at your station. It has not yet been transferred to the State Patrol Investigations Unit. Between twelve-fifteen and twelve-thirty tonight, the evidence cage will be unlocked. You will retrieve my iPad and bring it to Fairhaven, the South Bay Boardwalk at the end of Taylor Dock. You know the place?"

"Yes," McDaniel said. He suddenly had too many questions to ask, not that Polakoff would answer even if he did ask.

"I will be there at precisely one-fifteen. I expect you to be as well. Do not alert any other law enforcement. Do not bring anyone else with you. I will bring the daughter. When my property is safely returned to me, I will return her to you. That is all." He immediately hung up without waiting for a reply.

Darren set the phone in its cradle, dazed. Katheryn continued to whisper into her cell phone – someone had transferred her to the jail and she was trying to get back to the detective division. McDaniel could hear the officer on the other end of the call saying, "Ma'am, I can't hear you, you need to speak up…"

Darren gently wrapped his hands around hers, closing her phone and ending the call. She looked up into his face, her eyes huge. "What, Darren? Tell me!"

"She's alive. Unharmed," he said, zombie-like. He stared at the place in the wall where the cracks had appeared in his dream, expecting them to break open at any minute. "I'm going to go get her back."

CHAPTER 43

McDANIEL HAD TAKEN Katheryn to the Best Western Heritage Inn. Their home no longer felt safe. Katheryn had called her sister, who immediately headed for the hotel as well. As soon as that was settled, McDaniel took off to the police station. He had armed himself with a gun from a shoebox on the top shelf in his closet, a snub-nose .38, the classic police pistol of a bygone era. The revolver had been a gift from Detective Spivey when McDaniel finished his probationary period and became a full-fledged police officer. This was the year before Spivey retired. The gift had been a symbolic changing of the guard gesture. McDaniel had fired the gun a few times, but that had been over a decade ago. He prayed he would not need it tonight, but felt certain he would.

McDaniel's mind spun faster than the wheels of his car as he sped through the deserted city streets. Polakoff had Robyn, but he was willing to return her. All he wanted was a busted iPad. Why? Why go to the risk of kidnapping a police officer's daughter, then meeting with that officer for an exchange? Obviously, Anton Polakoff was not trying to avoid prosecution by eliminating incriminating evidence. If that was his goal, he had far bigger worries than the iPad. Unless the evidence it contained incriminated someone else, someone Polakoff was trying to protect, was risking his life to protect.

He thought of Robyn's last words to him, *two of them*, and the other voice he had heard in the background and decided that must be it. Polakoff had a partner – not Schechter, the State had placed Schechter and his family in protective custody after confiscating all files and computers from his home and office. Polakoff must have had a secret partner who had known about his 'abnormalities,' and the bodies in the basement.

McDaniel wondered if this partner might be the target of the FBI investigation who had exchanged several phone calls with Polakoff over the past three days. That made sense to McDaniel, but was of little consequence. Something else troubled him on a much deeper level – how did Polakoff know that the iPad was still in the Bellingham Police Department's evidence locker? And even more troubling, how could he ensure that the locker would be open and unattended during the fifteen-minute window he had given McDaniel?

Only one answer worked – Polakoff had someone on the inside. And it had to be a cop. After midnight, there were no evidence techs, admin staff, or facility crew roaming the building. Polakoff's mole had to be a police officer, a dirty copper, a bad penny. It made McDaniel's skin crawl. One of his sworn brothers was taking payoffs to protect a serial-killing child rapist. As he whipped his car around the last corner, approaching the station, his hand went to the grip of his old .38. He started thinking maybe it wouldn't be so bad if he had to use it, after all.

The desk officer sat slouched behind the front desk, barely conscious. He looked young. McDaniel guessed he wasn't more than a year out of the academy. Rookies always got the shit jobs. He watched, with a lazy eye, as McDaniel approached, but snapped awake and nearly jumped out of his chair when the detective slammed both palms on his desk.

"Who is in here tonight?" McDaniel demanded.

"W-what?" the rookie stammered. "They…they haven't brought anybody in. Slow night. What happened to your face? Are you alright?"

The clock over the desk read twelve-twenty. McDaniel had just under an hour before the meeting time set by Polakoff. He wanted to reach across the desk and yank the guy out of his chair by the front of his shirt. Seeing this, the officer sunk lower and slid back.

McDaniel growled, "Not arrests! *Cops!* Which officers are here at the station tonight?"

The desk officer looked left, then right, then back at McDaniel, his hands clamped onto the arms of his chair. "It's just me…I think," he said, his voice wary. "Could be someone came in the back, through the sally port entrance. It's supposed to beep up here when that door opens, but it usually doesn't."

"Pull up the camera feed," McDaniel said, moving away from the desk. "I've gotta run downstairs, but I'll be right back. Let me know who else has been--"

"Can't," the rookie said. "Those cameras are down."

"What do you mean the cameras are down?" McDaniel demanded.

"I mean the cameras are down," the rookie said. "Been down since around eight. We've got a tech coming, but he won't be here 'til morning."

McDaniel wanted to scream and shake the rookie until he coughed up a useful answer. After a moment, he said, "You see anybody else coming or going, anybody other than me, you call me immediately. You got it?"

"Yeah, man, I got it. It's detective McDonald, right?" the rookie said. His voice said, *yo, take it easy, dude.*

"Mc*Daniel*," he said, slapping one of his cards on the desk. "Do not fall asleep. Call me if you see anyone. Coming or going."

"Yeah, sure, coming or going. I got it."

McDaniel was racing down the hall before the rookie had finished speaking. The station was silent except for his shoes slapping the tile as he ran. In the basement, the motion-activated automatic lighting blinked on as he stepped off the stairs, suggesting that no one else had been there for at least fifteen minutes. A door stood between the hall and the wire cage that held all the evidence for current and past cases. Per policy, this door was to be locked at all times. Tonight, a pencil propped vertically between the door and jamb prevented it from locking.

McDaniel entered the room, gun in hand. No one waited for him. This room offered about four feet of standing room between the door and a chain-link fence. An opening in the fence allowed officers and detectives to confer with the evidence tech who manned the lockup during business hours. Only evidence techs were allowed behind the fence. A sign on the fence gate reinforced this policy, "Authorized personnel only." Two cameras watched the gate, one inside the fence and one outside. As McDaniel entered, he saw why the cameras were down. Both had been blocked by lens caps.

A formidable padlock secured the wire fence gate when the room was closed, as it should be now. The lock hung in its spot, and a casual observer would have thought it was secure, but upon closer inspection, McDaniel saw that the hasp was open. He would be in deep shit if anyone caught him inside the lockup, maybe a two-week suspension, maybe terminated, but this thought barely registered before it was gone again.

As he lifted the lock and pushed the gate open, his cell rang. It was the rookie at the front desk.

"What have you got?" McDaniel asked.

"Sir, a cruiser just pulled into the sally port," the rookie said. "Officers Conklin and Fink, bringing in a drunk."

McDaniel grimaced, "Oh, right, okay. Thanks, but, never mind. I think the guy I'm looking for has been here and gone already."

He then realized that someone might question why *he* was on the premises tonight. He was supposed to either be in a hospital bed or his own, he was on administrative leave pending an inquiry because he fired his weapon, and he no longer had an active case.

If the brass decided to come down on him tomorrow for breaking into the lockup, or stealing the iPad, or working while on admin leave, he was fine with that, but what he didn't need was to be stopped and detained tonight. He had to get what he came for and get the hell out before anyone more awake than the front desk rookie caught him here.

Inside the lockup, he found the boxes quickly. Two brown evidence boxes labeled "CDK" sat on the floor just inside the wire gate. A stack of paperwork authorizing, cataloging, and recording the transfer of the evidence boxes to State sat atop one of them.

McDaniel pulled a pair of rubber gloves from a box on the counter and put them on, then popped the top off the first box. The iPad was nestled in a plastic evidence bag with several other plastic or paper evidence bags. McDaniel grabbed it and slipped it inside his sport coat, under his arm. He replaced the box top, locked the padlock on the gate, took the pencil out of the door, pulled it closed, and headed back up the stairs.

He jogged up two flights, taking the stairs two at a time, and slammed through the door into the second floor. Again, darkness met him, but was quickly dispelled by the motion-activated automatic lighting. He crossed the room to his cubicle where a message blinked on his phone. He guessed it was probably a duplicate of the message Robyn had left at his home phone. Polakoff wasn't taking any chances. If it *was* Robyn, asking him to hit the call-back button, then he intended to leave it for evidence. If it was anything else, it was utterly irrelevant at this moment.

He scratched out a quick in-case-I-don't-make-it-back note, sketching the events that led up to him swiping the iPad and heading off into the night without backup to face down a serial killer. He underlined, four times, the part of his note about Polakoff having a mole in the department, then stuffed the note under his desk blotter so that only one corner stuck out. He wrote Osen's name on the piece of the note that remained visible, then moved toward the stairs.

Something caught his eye at the back of the room. He turned to see Osen's office door hanging ajar. A second later, lights inside the office popped on. McDaniel again drew his weapon, moving quickly toward the office. He had never known Osen to be in the building a minute past five unless a major case was in the works. With Polakoff's case now in the State's hands, McDaniel guessed that whoever was in his office, it wasn't Osen.

The door swung open as McDaniel reached it. Detective Griggs stood in the frame, looking startled or confused by McDaniel's appearance. All the pieces came together in McDaniel's mind like a zipper's teeth meshing.

"You son of a bitch…" he whispered.

"What?" Griggs asked, drunk or at least groggy. "What's going on, McD…"

"You son of a bitch!" McDaniel roared, closing the gap between them in a quick, fluid motion, transferring the pistol to his left hand. Griggs's eyes bulged and he tried to step back. McDaniel threw his right fist into Griggs's nose. The older detective stumbled backward, tripping over his feet, and sprawled across a couch at the back of the office.

"What the fuck, McDaniel!" he said, making no attempt to resist or even get off the couch.

McDaniel holstered his gun as he crossed the room. The iPad fell to the floor, but he paid it no mind. He grabbed Griggs by his lapels and hoisted him to his feet. "You piece of shit!" he snarled, slamming Griggs into the wall. "You're finished, man. And if anything, *any*thing happens to Robyn, I'll fucking put you down myself!"

"Whoa! Cool it, cowboy," Griggs said. His hands were up in surrender, but there was an edge to his voice, as if warning McDaniel he had wandered way too close to crossing the line. "I don't know what you think you know, but it sorta sounds like you're calling me a dirty cop. And that's not something you want to say to me."

"Dirty? You're Polakoff's fucking inside man!"

"I think we're about to find out just how much of a badass you really are," Griggs said, his voice cool, his eyes menacing. "You all want to laugh behind my back because you think I'm lazy, that's fine. But you start saying I've turned, and I'll fucking break you in half."

McDaniel held eye contact, trying to stare him down, trying to shake him. It didn't work. He had known Griggs nearly his entire life. He may have been a bit lecherous with the women, but McDaniel could not imagine him as a pedophile, and his standard of living certainly did not suggest he was taking any money on the side. McDaniel began to wonder if he might be wrong.

He still held Griggs against the wall, but loosened his grip. The man's eyes were bloodshot and his breath so heavy with whiskey that McDaniel thought he might get drunk off the smell. "What the hell are you doing here? I thought you were taking your vacation in Mexico."

"Ease up on the jacket," he said, brushing McDaniel's hands away. "I am headed to Mexico. Got a flight to Cabo in about five hours. Having my kitchen floor refinished while I'm gone, but the contractor showed up a day early. The fumes were killing me, so I packed my shit and crashed here for the night."

McDaniel stepped back, taking in the whole scene. A suitcase and a wheeled carry-on sat at the end of the couch. Griggs's suits never looked pressed, but the one he wore now had obviously been slept in.

"You knew this was a sex crime before you even saw the body," McDaniel said. "Making wisecracks about blowjobs. You knew her name. You knew where the kill house was--"

"Oh, for fuck's sake, McDaniel," he said, sitting down hard on the couch. "You find a slant on a chain, it's gonna be a sex crime. Everybody knows that. I hadn't seen the body. I never would have said that if I had known she was a baby, you know? The radio said 'girl.' I was thinking girl like a working girl, not a *girl* girl.

"And as to the kill house, when I was on the meth and marijuana task force in the nineties, we were up in those woods all the fucking time. I've got files on every one of those houses. Fuck, man. Remind me never to help *you* on a case again," he scoffed, then added, "Nice shiner, by the way."

McDaniel stared at Griggs, thoughts screaming through his head, too much noise to decipher. Nothing made sense. No course of action seemed right. The only thing he knew for certain was that he had to be on the boardwalk in twenty minutes to get Robyn. If this man, or the snoring rookie at the front desk, or any other cop was helping Polakoff from the inside, McDaniel would find him and burn him down, but now was not the time.

He pointed his finger at Griggs, stepping away. He had no idea what to say to the man now, so the pointed finger would have to suffice. He grabbed the iPad off the floor, stuffed it back in his jacket and headed for the door.

"They've got your girl?" Griggs asked.

McDaniel stopped but still said nothing.

"That iPad is the one they collected from G street, isn't it? They've got your girl and they want to trade for that iPad," Griggs said, his words coming slowly, like puzzle pieces moving into place. "That's the way it is, isn't it?"

"None of your concern, Griggs," McDaniel said. "Go back to sleep. Fly to Mexico. Whatever. If you're clear of this, then stay clear. If you're already in it, well, maybe you ought to stay in Mexico. But whatever you do, you better not try to stop me." His hand was on the knurled grip of the old .38. He hadn't intended to pull it, but suddenly knew he would if it came to that.

Again, Griggs raised his hands in surrender. "Go do what you gotta do, brother. I was just going to offer to come with, watch your six, like back in the day."

"Don't come anywhere near me, Griggs," McDaniel said, moving through the door. "I mean it."

Griggs sat back on the couch, letting his hands fall to his knees.

McDaniel turned and ran through the detective's bullpen. He took the stairs three at a time on the way down and nearly steamrolled over Officer Conklin on the first-floor landing. She called after him, but he didn't pause or answer her. The front desk officer was standing and talking on the phone as McDaniel sprinted past him and out the front door. He was in his car and peeling out of the parking lot before anyone had a chance to stop him.

CHAPTER 44

THE SOUTH BAY Trail ran for several miles, starting in the historic Fairhaven area and winding its way along the waterfront to downtown Bellingham. Near the middle of its length, the trail connected with Taylor Dock, a public fishing dock that jutted over one-hundred feet into the sound. At the end of the dock, an elevated boardwalk paralleled the coastline, approximately one-hundred feet from the shore and twenty feet above the water. It was here that Polakoff ordered McDaniel to meet him for the exchange.

McDaniel had not thought much about the location as he sped across town to retrieve the iPad, nor as he raced to make the exchange. But now that he had arrived, the chosen location began to bother him. It bothered him more and more as he stepped onto Taylor Dock.

Tactically speaking, this was probably the worst possible place to make an exchange of this sort. The elevated boardwalk was more than a quarter-mile long, and Polakoff had asked to meet in the middle. The shoreline rose in a steep cliff with condos and a hotel terraced into the bank.

He and Polakoff (and Robyn, for that matter) would be fully exposed for several minutes as they traveled the length of the boardwalk. They would all be easy targets for an ambush or a sniper. From the middle of the boardwalk, there would be no way to reach cover if things went bad. Jumping for the water wasn't an option. In most places, it would be too shallow to safely cushion a fall from that height, and if it *was* deep enough, a swimmer would be almost as easy a target as a person standing on the boardwalk.

It enraged McDaniel on an entirely new level. Polakoff was brilliant in some ways, but a complete idiot in others. Not only had he kidnapped Robyn in some ass-cover scheme, but the stupidity in his execution of that scheme now endangered her life even more. Meeting out here, in the wide-open, in the middle of the night gave Polakoff no tactical advantage, either. If McDaniel had decided to run a risk, he could easily have officers ready to cut off Polakoff's exit as soon as the exchange happened and Robyn was safe.

The more he thought about it, the less he liked it, and the less he believed it had been Polakoff who chose this location. The other, McDaniel decided, the low voice in the background, Polakoff's partner, was the one calling the shots.

McDaniel turned the corner, from the dock to the boardwalk itself. He scanned the coastline, seeing only shadows. Below him, quiet ripples slid across black water. The handrail and its supports were heavy lumber, not great cover, but it was a start. There were also garbage cans every hundred feet or so. These were housed in decorative concrete boxes. McDaniel decided that would be his best cover if the guns came out.

As he neared what he guessed to be the middle of the board-walk, his cell buzzed. He retrieved it and saw a text message: *wait there*. He had not stopped walking to check the message. Rather than stopping now, he fiddled with the phone, pretending he was having trouble viewing the message. Someone had to be watching him. He intended to give them a good show. When he came up alongside one of the concrete trash boxes, he stopped suddenly and popped his head up, making a show of looking for whoever had sent him the message.

The sender had to be somewhere in the buildings overlooking the waterfront. McDaniel felt terribly vulnerable. This was a snip-er's dream, a target silhouetted against a uniform backdrop at a fixed range and lower elevation with minimal cover and nowhere to run. If there was a sniper up there, and McDaniel now felt sure there was, he could easily pick off all three of them in under half a minute.

He knew this, but had no idea what to do with the knowledge. Before he could think on it further, he heard footsteps. McDan-iel froze. He did not have the gun out, didn't guess it would be of much use to him now, but rubbed his palm against the small lump it made on the surface of his jacket.

As the footsteps drew nearer, he noticed something wrong with their cadence. He could track the right, left, right, left, tap, tap, tap of a walker in heels, which he hoped was Robyn, but the rhythm of the second walker's footfalls was all wrong. It had an uneven irregularity to it, more like a shuffle than a walk.

McDaniel saw them as shadows, first, but quickly they came into full view. Robyn still wore the thin band tee and ripped jeans she had been wearing when he saw her in the kitchen this morning. She walked with her head up and shoulders back. McDaniel felt grim admiration.

Then he saw the thing around her neck. Polakoff walked directly behind her, using her as a shield. McDaniel would not have risked taking a shot at him even if he had had his .40 H&K. With the ancient .38, it was completely out of the question.

McDaniel studied Polakoff and Robyn as they drew nearer. Polakoff limped and staggered. He used Robyn for support as much as for a shield. One hand clamped tightly over her shoulder, the loop of some sort of strap hanging from his wrist. The other hand dangled at his side, gripping a long-necked roofing hammer. The hammer swung like a pendulum as he hobbled forward.

The worst thing, the most terrifying thing, was the canister that hung around Robyn's neck. It looked like a piece of PVC pipe, about three inches long and one inch in diameter, secured by a black ribbon as if it were some sort of choker.

They had drawn within fifteen yards of McDaniel. Polakoff must have known what McDaniel was focused on. He said, "It's C-4," then coughed and gasped, doubling over. It took a moment for him to straighten. When he did, blood dribbled from his lip. He spoke again, softly to prevent another burst of coughing, "It's C-4. I do not know if it is a sufficient quantity to remove her head. I have never worked with it before, but it is certainly sufficient to remove her face, should you decide to make this difficult."

This was the darkness, the entropy incarnate. The black void stretched to infinity above. The black water below mirrored the emptiness, it's lapping waves carrying voices of the family he had lost. In all the intervening years, he had placed himself between the darkness and those he loved, the new family he had built. The rage he felt focused on Polakoff, but only as a representative of the greater darkness. Now he had a choice to make. If he was right about the sniper on the cliff side, as he certainly was, the only way to save Robyn was to protect Polakoff. His only chance to defeat the darkness was to embrace its agent.

"Mr. Polakoff," McDaniel said, "I have what you asked for. I will do whatever you ask. But I have to warn you, you've been set up by your partner. Did you choose this location, or did he tell you to meet me here?"

"Don't ask me anything," he said, gritting his teeth and shuddering. "*I* am not a criminal. I don't think this stuff up. I just do the books. You and your partner forced this, the blame is on you if anything goes badly tonight." He lifted his hand off Robyn's shoulder, grasping the strap and displaying it. "This is similar to one of those party poppers you buy for New Years. I pull the leash and...*POP!*" He grinned broadly, displaying bloody teeth. "You shoot me and I fall, same result. I found instructions on YouTube."

McDaniel slowly raised both hands, the iPad in one of them. "I have it right here. I will do whatever you ask."

Polakoff began to speak, but grunted, his face pinched, and almost doubled over again. He leaned heavily on Robyn. She half-turned and helped steady him. When he rose, he said, "You bastards gut-shot me. My associates gave me something to keep me going. They have a physician prepared to put me back together. But first, I have to 'clean up my mess,' as they put it. You, Detective, are my mess. The only reason I am not going to just shoot you where you stand is because I don't have a free hand in which to hold a gun."

He again displayed the leash in one hand and held up the hammer in the other. "Now, my associates are more forgiving than I would have been. All they ask is that you hand over the iPad. I will then smash it to powder and throw it into the sea. Having accomplished that, I will release your daughter and exit the dock at its north end. You two will exit to the south, and neither of us shall see the other again."

McDaniel focused on Robyn, looked into her eyes, hoping to convey reassurance or comfort. The unquestioning trust he saw there nearly broke him. He clenched his jaw, then turned his gaze on Polakoff. "Whatever you say, just tell me how you want to play it."

"Place the iPad on the rail and step away."

McDaniel set the iPad on the wooden railing but did not yet step away. "Polakoff, I am doing as you ask, but please listen to me. The second you destroy this iPad, you lose all your leverage. I am willing to bet my life that there is a sniper on that hill--"

"Move *away*!" Polakoff barked, then started coughing again.

"I'm moving," McDaniel again raised his hands and took a step backward. "But please think this through, Mr. Polakoff, from a business standpoint. You have been compromised. You were useful to them because you had a legitimate business. You could help them clean their money. But now…now everyone knows who you are. You are a liability. The only reasonable course of action is for them to liquidate you. The second you smash that, your buddy," McDaniel nodded to the hillside, "is going to shoot all three of us where we stand. Your only hope is to protect that iPad. Come in with me. We can protect you. We can get you out of--"

"Shut up! Shut the hell up. Unless you want to see what your daughter's face looks like with no skin on it. Just shut the hell up. And keep moving back." Polakoff pushed Robyn forward, hobbling worse than ever. "You are probably right about the sniper, you bastard. But they have men at *my* home, with guns on *my* mother, because of you, you son of a bitch. You have no idea what you've done. These people, they are horrid. You think *I'm* a monster? You have no idea. What I did, it was a mercy. I gave so much…and asked so little. And now…" he swayed, his eyes glazing. McDaniel prepared to lunge forward and catch him if he fell. But two heartbeats later, Polakoff revived, and said, "I hope he does shoot you. I hope he shoots your girl, too. I hope he shoots her first. You bastard."

Polakoff reached the iPad. He moved Robyn to the side but still appeared to be putting much of his weight on her shoulder. "You better hold real still, sugar," he coughed into her ear. "You don't want Uncle Anton falling over, now do you?"

The two now stood less than five yards from McDaniel. Robyn's eyes pleaded with him. She mouthed, *I love you, daddy.* The wind fluttered through her tee shirt and McDaniel could see her trembling. He felt infuriated anew at Polakoff. This time his anger centered on the fact that Polakoff had not provided something warm for her to wear. It was nonsensical under the circumstances, but he felt it none-the-less.

Polakoff hesitated, raising the hammer, but not yet bringing it down. He knew. McDaniel realized, Polakoff knew everything he had said was true. McDaniel started formulating another appeal, but before the words were out of his mouth, Polakoff slammed the hammer down on the iPad. Glass and bits of plastic flew. He raised and dropped the hammer again, staggering as he did. Robyn caught him as he started to fall. The accountant stood and slammed the iPad again and again until the powder and shards had all fallen to the saltwater below. Then he panted and sagged against the rail.

McDaniel had been inching forward as Polakoff's attention had been consumed with the iPad's destruction and maintaining his own balance. But now, Polakoff turned to him, grinning through bloody teeth, and held up the loop end of the leash. "One more step, detective, and pop goes the weasel."

"Let her go, Polakoff. You got what you came for." He let his fingers curl around the .38's grip. Polakoff was no longer directly behind Robyn. McDaniel could make this shot, easily. Maybe if he could warn Robyn, maybe she could fall with him to prevent his fall from triggering the bomb.

"Don't try it, Detective…" Polakoff started. But as the words left his lips, a shot rang out from the hillside. The little man's head snapped to the left, a pancake-sized piece of scalp flapping seaward. Robyn screamed. McDaniel lunged toward her, trying to tackle her on top of Polakoff to prevent his dead hand from pulling the leash as he dropped. The shot's echo rolled back to them from across the bay as they fell in a heap.

Then the bomb went off.

CHAPTER 45

T WAS A pop and a burst of light like an old-time flash photograph. Robyn screamed again, this time in pain. McDaniel
felt his own scream inside his head, and an icy wave of help-
less horror rising above him, preparing to crash over him as it
had done the last time his family died as he watched. But through
the chaos of the moment and the terror of his expectations and
fears, reality called.

Robyn was screaming. That meant she was breathing. That
meant that she was alive. That thought led to the realization that
the bomb could not have been C-4. Neither of them would have
survived if it had been.

His eyes desperately searched her face. Terror and disbelief
and confusion bulged her eyes. Her nostrils flared and her mouth
hung open as if trying to know whether to scream again. The PVC

pipe was gone. Her hands wrapped around the place where it had been, but no blood seeped from beneath them.

McDaniel wanted to move her hands to examine what wound may be there, but then he remembered the sniper.

He wrapped himself around Robyn, shielding her to the best of his ability and yelled. "Move! Now! You're still alive. You're going to be fine but you have to move!" He dragged her until she was moving with him, covering the distance to the concrete garbage can in a matter of seconds.

He pulled her in tight, ensuring she was completely concealed behind the can. He moved into cover with her, wrapping her in his arms. She cried against his shoulder, but it was the terror coming out, the relief flooding in that caused the tears, rather than pain. He thought she might be alright, if he could get them off this dock.

He reached into his pocket for his cell phone, but before he could call for backup, it rang in his hand. He answered, "McDaniel."

"I can see your whole right side. That can isn't big enough for the both of you." The voice was gruff but jovial, an older man who had once been cocky but was now just confident. "It was cute the way you threw your body over her. But, I gotta tell you, Darren McDaniel, I'm shooting an M-1 Grand. Your body, hell even your body *armor*, wouldn't slow that bullet down any more than that cute little tee shirt she's got on."

McDaniel took a slow, deep breath, centering himself. "You could have shot us but you didn't."

"I could have but I didn't. That's an astute deduction. You'd make a good detective."

McDaniel waited. He realized this call could be a diversion or a ploy to prevent him from calling for backup, but his mind was too frazzled at the moment to do anything other than continue the conversation.

"I want you to remember that, Detective McDaniel. I could have shot you, but I didn't. I could have given that little weasel real C-4 instead of gray modeling clay and a mini blasting cap, but I didn't. The people I work for are not in the habit of harming police officers, or their families. They find it to be very bad for business. Of course, debacles like this also tend to be bad for business. Taking the girl was an extreme measure, one they hope to never have to repeat. Do you understand what I am saying, Detective McDaniel?"

"I think I do," McDaniel said.

"You can walk off this dock any time you like. You can stop cowering behind that trash bin. No one will harm you. All we ask in exchange, just forget about all this. Drop it. Just walk away. We'll call it an unfortunate misunderstanding."

"I'm off the case already," McDaniel said. "The State has taken it."

"I understand that. We have it well in hand. The problem is, some cops get this weird, narcissistic, self-deluded idea that they are some sort of mythic hero, standing as a barrier between good and evil – and I just wanted to make sure that didn't happen to you. Because, although we don't make a *habit* of harming cops or their families, we will do so if the cop in question loses his sense of perspective."

McDaniel said nothing. Over the phone, he heard a metallic clink he associated with a Zippo being struck. Then he heard the long, slow inhalation as the sniper took his first drag. When he spoke again, he did so with a conciliatory tone.

"Hey, look, you caught CDK. It's a high profile bust, got the scary monster off the street. The good people can rest easy now, knowing their communities are safe. In fact, they'll probably love you even more than they did before this whole CDK thing, because now their safety and security are not taken for granted. They got a little peek at what life could be like without good guys like you around to protect them.

"In fact, I gotta tell you, *we* need you as much as the regular folks do. I mean, think about it, these guys I work for, what is it they really do?"

"They sell children to pedophiles," McDaniel said.

"Well, that's a bit crass. Let's say, they provide sexual partners for those with special needs. But here's where you come in. If providing for those needs was legal, well, what would anyone need us for? There'd be absolutely no profit in it. There'd be no way the people I work for could afford my fee. So, you see, Detective McDaniel, I really appreciate what you do for your community, and I really appreciate what you do for me, personally. I have a great deal of sympathy for the hardships you've been through in your life. I would really hate to see you endure any additional losses. Do you understand what I am telling you?"

"You are threatening my family if I--" McDaniel started.

"Let's not use inflammatory language, Detective McDaniel. I don't think…"

The sniper's voice trailed off. In the background, another voice came across the phone. McDaniel couldn't make out the words, but it sounded very familiar.

"Hey, buddy, you don't want to be doing that," the sniper said, his voice muted slightly as if his head was turned away from the phone.

McDaniel heard the other voice again but still could not make it out.

"You're making a mistake you're not going to live long enough to regret," the sniper said, anger coloring his voice now for the first time.

McDaniel heard the response clearly this time because it was shouted. "Drop the fucking gun you piece of shit!"

McDaniel heard the shouted command through the phone, but he also heard the live version, in his other ear, coming from the hillside above them. Griggs.

The sniper whispered, "Fuck," into the phone. Then gunfire cut through the night. Two different weapons fired, but neither was the M-1 that had killed Polakoff, and none of the rounds struck the boardwalk. McDaniel dropped the phone and again shielded Robyn, none-the-less. Six shots rang out, followed by their echoes. Then silence.

Time stretched out in the quiet dark. McDaniel measured it not in seconds but in heartbeats, his own and his daughter's. He cherished every one of them. Above them, lights blinked on inside the condos and hotel rooms. Voices called, waves lapped, a sea bird squawked.

He whispered, "How you holding up, pumpkin?"

"I'm scared," she said. It wasn't a whisper, but her voice was very quiet.

"I know, pumpkin," he said, "We're almost done here. We'll go home real soon. Are you hurt?"

"A little. It feels like a bee sting. Or a burn," she said, then, "I know where they took me."

"You're a brave girl," McDaniel said, bemused. "But I don't care about that right now. Right now, we're just going to focus on getting you home, okay?"

She looked up at him with huge dark eyes and nodded.

McDaniel's cell beeped. It lay on the boardwalk beside him. The display showed an incoming call from Griggs. McDaniel realized his phone was still on an open call to the sniper and he was suddenly terrified that the sniper had heard what Robyn had said.

The phone beeped again, asking him if he wanted to drop the other call to answer Griggs. He did.

Griggs's voice filled his ear "Listen to me, you little son of a bitch, you ever call me a dirty cop again, I'll leave your ass hanging in the wind."

"Griggs? Griggs, what are you doing?"

"I found your note, asshole. That got me here. Then I just followed the sound of gunfire. I know how to be a detective when I'm properly motivated."

"I heard shots up there, are you okay?"

"'Course I'm okay. This dipshit was a hell of a lot braver at 300 yards than he was up close," Griggs scoffed. "Now he's just dead."

McDaniel breathed a sigh of relief, but also felt fear nibbling around the edges of that relief. This might invite retaliation, or at least a visit from a second messenger telling him to stay away.

He asked Griggs, "You call backup and paramedics?"

Griggs whistled into the phone. "Now you're gonna start telling me how to be a cop? Boy, you need to remember something. It was me and Spivey that brought you into this business. We taught you the ropes. You don't know nothing except what you learned from us. And the one, most important rule I taught you was you never turn, no matter what. Don't you ever call me a dirty cop again." The line went dead.

Up the hill, McDaniel heard Griggs shouting orders at civilian spectators who had ventured out of their homes. Farther away, the sirens started up, wailing and warbling through the chill night air. McDaniel wrapped his overcoat around Robyn and helped her to her feet. A patch of soot darkened the right side of her throat, but she showed no other signs of injury. He wrapped his arm around her and together they walked off the dock.

CHAPTER 46

VANDERWYK WAS RELEASED from the hospital the following afternoon with plenty of pain meds and orders to take it easy. Both he and McDaniel had been placed on administrative leave while the department investigated their actions at the G Street house and McDaniel's actions regarding the theft of the iPad from the evidence locker. Rourke assured him that there would be minimal fallout from either event and that they would face no significant discipline. McDaniel assured Rourke that if anyone tried to tell him he shouldn't have traded the iPad for his daughter, he'd probably kick that man in the balls.

The following week, Rourke called McDaniel to advise him that the state had turned the case over to the FBI but he didn't have much information as to why this decision was made. McDaniel was not surprised. When he passed the news to his partner, Vanderwyk called Agent Hostetler, his FBI contact, and she agreed to meet with the two of them. In her notes, she logged this as an interview with the detectives that initiated the case.

They met at GGBG, at 9:00 a.m. Noreen unlocked the upstairs tattoo parlor for them so they could meet in private. Agent Hostetler had a video she wanted to show them and it wasn't something that would have gone over well if a random passerby happened to be shoulder surfing.

"Have they found Griggs, yet?" Hostetler asked, grinning and shaking her head.

"Oh, we know where he is," Vanderwyk said, "just can't do anything about it. He's got a lawyer negotiating with the DA and the brass at the station."

"I can't believe he just killed that professional and then flew off to Mexico like nothing happened," Hostetler said, still bemused.

"He claims he doesn't remember anything," McDaniel said. "He had so much whiskey in him, I almost believe it. And he already had the ticket in hand. He'd been planning that vacation all year. Says he remembers crashing out in Osen's office, remembers arguing with me about something, though he claims not to remember what we argued about. The next thing he claims to remember is having a cab drop him at the airport so he could catch his flight. It's a story so ridiculous you could only buy it from a guy like Griggs."

"That's just insane," Hostetler said. "You think he was Polakoff's inside man?"

"Not a chance," McDaniel said.

"It just doesn't work for it to be him," Vanderwyk agreed. "He's got a thing for McDaniel, here. Even if he was dirty, there's no way he'd let them mess with Darren's daughter."

"He's your buddy?" Hostetler asked, eyebrows raised. "I don't think I'd be claiming that friendship just now."

"We go way back. He and Spivey busted me once when I was a teen. He was just a rookie then, but those two helped me and my sister stay on our feet and out of the system after we lost our parents," McDaniel said.

She raised her eyebrows again. They were beautifully arched, but when she raised them like that, it reminded McDaniel of a seagull taking flight. He had mentioned this to Vanderwyk once, but Vanderwyk didn't find it funny. He liked her eyebrows.

McDaniel said, "I really think half the reason he kept his reservation with Cabo was to draw heat off me. Everyone is so spun up about his disappearing act that they haven't much energy left to fuck with me."

Vanderwyk chuckled, "And I bet he gets away with it, too. They'll give him a month suspension or something, then he'll be right back at it. I bet he's lining up a job down there as we speak. His suspension will just be another vacation."

"Back to your question, though," McDaniel said, "Griggs isn't the dirty cop. Which means someone else is. I'd sure like to find out who. Please tell me you guys are taking that part of the investigation seriously."

Hostetler looked at him long enough for him to understand she wasn't happy with the answer to that question. Finally, she said, "I cannot discuss any of that with you. There are some major players being sought in this investigation." The implication was, *your dirty cop isn't one of them*. "The FBI encourages your department to investigate that aspect of this case with all diligence."

McDaniel nodded.

She gave him a small smile by way of apology.

Vanderwyk cleared his throat, then smiled brightly. "Well, then, Patti, let's...um, let's focus on what you *can* tell us. You said you had news?"

McDaniel realized Vanderwyk was attempting to raise his eyebrows, as Hostetler had done. The problem was, his eyebrows and most of his hair had been singed off when the fireball came through the door at the G Street house. They had not yet regrown.

Hostetler noticed, as well. She cocked her head slightly, then smiled and looked at her laptop. "Well, ah, yes. Let's see. We identified one of the fingerprints found at Polakoff's kill house. It matched a print from a preteen girl who went missing from a foster home in Indiana about six years ago."

"I'm surprised you have prints on file for a preteen," McDaniel said. "I thought fourteen was the youngest you'd print a kid."

"It is very uncommon. This was part of a local initiative to keep track of at-risk youth," Hostetler said. "It was billed as a way to help protect these children, but the real reason for the program is 'at-risk' kids tend to grow up to be criminals and this gives the cops a head start on nabbing them."

"I'm from the government. I'm here to help," Vanderwyk said, sarcasm dripping from his words like the syrup from his pancake.

Hostetler frowned at him. "Well, it worked out this time. That print ties this case to others we have been working for years. This is another piece of the puzzle."

"That's why you guys took the case?" McDaniel asked, "Because it crossed state lines?"

"That," she said, "and other things. What we know about this organization, they'll pick up children anywhere they can, but they mainly traffic in children taken from third-world Asia. These children are brought in through ports on the Canadian west coast, due to Canada's lax immigration controls. From there, it is fairly easy to cross the land border into the U.S.

"Polakoff, it seems, laundered money for the organization. His partner is being very cooperative, helping us find money that Polakoff had hidden in various accounts he managed. It's going to be into eight figures by the time we scoop it all up."

"So, Schechter was completely clear?" McDaniel asked. "Didn't even know what his partner was up to?"

"He knew something was going on. He claims he confronted Polakoff about irregularities in several accounts, but the organization had someone visit Schechter and suggest he mind his own business. After that, he didn't say anything more to Polakoff, but he did keep meticulous records of the irregularities, which are proving to be very helpful."

"That'll set them back a bit, I guess," Vanderwyk said, grinning.

"A bit," Hostetler acknowledged, "but *only* a bit. Sex trafficking is a billion-dollar industry. Annually, these organizations bring in more revenue than Microsoft and Amazon combined. And, this is going to set us back as well," Hostetler sighed.

"These people are very careful. If this were your typical serial pedophile, he'd have to strike again, sooner than later. Their psychopathy compels them, despite the danger of being caught. But these guys are businessmen, not psychopaths. They make rational decisions. When they take a hit like this, they might disappear completely, for years. Their clientele will be forced to make stupid decisions, and we'll catch some of them, but the men at the top…" Hostetler shook her head. "We may never see them again."

McDaniel thought about this. This organization, whoever they were, had just lost tens of millions of dollars, as well as a valuable money laundering agent, but Hostetler was telling him it was a drop in the bucket, maybe even just the cost of doing business. He remembered how it felt to hold his daughter, cowering behind a concrete trash barrel, waiting to see who would die first. He suddenly felt like a child who had just poked a bear. Hostetler was telling him the bear would get away and he'd never see it again. He wondered if he should be disappointed or relieved.

"We do have this, however," Hostetler said, placing her laptop on the table. "This is the video from one of the cameras in Polakoff's kill house. I'm not authorized to let you hear the audio. He says three names, toward the beginning of this clip. We know he was talking to his L.A. connection, and we know where he went in L.A. the day after this video was captured. Between that and the information Schechter is providing, there is still hope that we might catch these guys. You two were instrumental in making that happen."

She pushed *play* on the video. They watched the images on the screen. Polakoff had spared no expense in his recording system. The picture was in full color and much sharper than McDaniel wished for. He could see all too clearly the vacant emptiness in Seong's eyes as she sat across the pink plastic table from Polakoff. He had the comic smile and huge eyes of an adult trying to engage a reluctant two-year-old in play.

He poured liquid from a plastic teapot into Seong's cup and coaxed her to take a sip. She did so, slowly and without expression, as if in a dream. Polakoff responded with clapping, laughing and general exuberance. He talked rapidly, with exaggerated facial expressions and wild hand gestures. McDaniel was glad the video was muted so he didn't have to hear Polakoff's voice. Just imagining how it might sound and what he might be saying were disturbing enough.

Then Polakoff's demeanor suddenly changed. He stood and pulled a phone from his pocket. It looked identical to the one he had used to trigger the bomb at the kill house. He quickly lost the sickly-sweet smile and began yelling into the phone. He held the phone away from his ear, looking at it, held it up near the ceiling, then brought it back to his ear, yelling some more.

"This call is the key to everything. Here he drops the names, as well as a few other details, that are keeping this case alive, moving it forward, even," Hostetler said. "This call causes him to leave in a hurry and it upsets him to the point that he forgets his umbrella when he leaves. That one mistake brought his whole fantasy crashing down around his ears. Check it out."

They watched as Seong struggled to reach the umbrella, as she used it to loosen the eye-bolt from the wall. McDaniel felt her triumph when the chain finally pulled loose. He saw her face show expression for the first time in the video. Her eyes brightened, her cheeks dimpled with a smile of genuine excitement.

They watched her joy turn to frustration as she tried, time and again, to open the door. McDaniel experienced with her the final thrill of success when she threw the table and it punched through the drywall. Watched her thrill to discover that the wall would easily crumble under a barrage of umbrella strikes. Vanderwyk even let out a giddy laugh, watching her bash open the wall.

Then they all sobered as she began to step through. McDaniel's entire body prickled with gooseflesh. Seong stood halfway through the hole in the wall, peering down at the dirt floor. McDaniel understood that she knew about the others, knew that the girls who had been there before her were now buried in that dirt. He felt a second chill course through him when he realized her lips were moving. She was talking to the dead ones.

Then she was through the hole and gone from view. In a few hours, she would find a bus stop booth and lie down. McDaniel wanted to reach through the screen and pull her back. He brushed at his eye, wiping away the moisture there. He felt self-conscious about the tear but noticed Vanderwyk doing the same thing, then decided he wasn't interested in the opinions of anyone who could watch that and not shed a tear.

CHAPTER 47

THREE WEEKS LATER, McDaniel shed another tear for Seong, as he stood at her graveside under a slate-gray sky. Wind flipped the hem of his overcoat and riffled through the papers in his hand. Robyn stood to his left, her arm around him, her ear on his shoulder. Katheryn stood to his right, also with her arm around him, but standing straight. The restless air tossed strands of her hair this way and that.

A crowd of dark-clad people had gathered, some to gawk, some to report, most to pay their respects to the girl who had been the beginning of the end for Polakoff. McDaniel would have spoken the words even if he had been the only one there, but he felt gratified to see that so many others would hear them. He looked at the papers in his hands and did his best to say the words clearly and without too much awkwardness.

"Thank you for being here today. Your presence honors the short life of this young girl, Seong. You, no doubt, have heard countless news broadcasts about the man they call CDK, the man who was responsible for Seong's death, but you have heard very little about Seong, herself. This is partly because we know so little about her. We don't know where she was born. We don't know when or how she came to our corner of the world. We don't know what her favorite color was, or her favorite food."

He glanced back at his notes, sniffed, then folded the papers and returned his eyes to the crowd.

"I felt compelled to speak here today because I know something about Seong. Anton Polakoff and his associates sought to deprive her of her humanity, told her in no uncertain terms that she had no value as a person. But Seong did not accept that message. On the night of November 17th, Seong found a way to escape. She walked a mile and a half through dense forest and freezing rain before succumbing to the elements. Before she died, Seong left a message. Her own name, and the number of other girls who Polakoff had killed.

"She valued her own life, and she valued the lives of those other girls. She recognized and acknowledged the humanity of her fellow captives. As she lay dying, her last thoughts were not only for herself but also for the others who had suffered her same fate. Her courage, to resist the darkness, her selflessness, to remember those it had already taken, these are what I want you to think of when you remember Seong. Her name, Seong, means 'Victory.' I want us to remember that, too, because it was her courage and her selflessness that alerted us to Polakoff, and ultimately led to his demise. This little girl ended his atrocities."

He heard Katheryn sniffle, felt her arm tighten around his waist. He had to pause a moment before he was able to finish.

"The darkness and evil in this world sometimes seem insurmountable. When it feels that way to you, please remember Seong. Acknowledge the humanity of the people around you. Value the humanity of the people in your life, whether you know them, whether you like them, whether they know or like you. This is how we keep the darkness out. This is how we sustain the light. Thank you for being here. Thank you for honoring this brave and noble young girl."

When they left, hand in hand, McDaniel felt the weight of sorrow settle over him. No matter how courageous she had been, in the end, the darkness had taken her. No matter how hard he had worked to shield his family from the darkness, it had found them, too. He worried that when they returned home, it would be to a house that was a shade darker than it had been a month before, and perhaps a shade colder. He could only hope that the words he spoke over Seong's grave were true, that humble courage and selfless compassion were enough to hold back the night.

Sooner or later, McDaniel knew, he would find out.

ABOUT THE AUTHOR

AXEL BLACKWELL LIVES aboard an old trawler in a misty bay on the northwest edge of America. He has written two paranormal thrillers, *The Timeweaver's Wager* and *Sisters of Sorrow,* and is the co-author (with Dawn Lee McKenna) of the *Stillwater Suspense* Series.

You can find all of Axel's books on his Amazon Author's Page
WWW.AMAZON.COM/AXEL-BLACKWELL/E/
B00W0I2UO4/

You can find Axel, himself, on his Facebook page,
WWW.FACEBOOK.COM/AUTHORAXELBLACKWELL/

To make sure you don't miss out on any new releases, giveaways, or live events, sign up for Axel's newsletter
WWW.AXELBLACKWELL.COM.COM

Made in the USA
Monee, IL
26 October 2021